'25

TIME TO DIE

She couldn't understand why he was so determined to get her into her apartment. They would
be alone there, yes. But how could he kill her
there and get away with it?

She didn't know, couldn't think. What was water
in her bones was fire and brimstone in her head.
If only somebody from one of the other apartments would come along.

Gasping, panting, thinking she would keel over
and die from exhaustion before he had a chance
to kill her, she wanted to ask him why. Why.
Why. She wanted to say never mind why, please
stop, please don't do anything to me. She wanted
to beg him for mercy. How could he do whatever
it was he was planning to do to her...

STALKED

FRANCES RICKETT

AVON
PUBLISHERS OF BARD, CAMELOT, DISCUS AND FLARE BOOKS

STALKED is an original publication of Avon Books. This work has never before appeared in book form.

AVON BOOKS
A division of
The Hearst Corporation
959 Eighth Avenue
New York, New York 10019

Copyright © 1983 by Frances Rickett
Published by arrangement with the author
Library of Congress Catalog Card Number: 82-90489
ISBN: 0-380-81463-3

First Avon Printing, January, 1983

AVON TRADEMARK REG. U. S. PAT. OFF. AND IN OTHER COUNTRIES, MARCA REGISTRADA, HECHO EN U. S. A.

Printed in the U. S. A.

WFH 10 9 8 7 6 5 4 3 2 1

For
ROBERT CENEDELLA
and
ROBERTA REARDON

One

As she stepped off the elevator Susannah heard the telephone ringing in her apartment. Hurrying down the short hallway, fumbling with her keys, perfectly well aware it could be a wrong number, somebody selling perpetual-life lightbulbs, or her former mother-in-law, she nevertheless willed the caller to hang on, stay with it, give her another few seconds.

Flinging the door open, she reached into the kitchen at her left and pulled the red wall phone off the hook, kicking the door shut behind her. "Hello?"

"Susannah? This is your service calling."

It was the creep, the kid who imitated Carlton the Doorman on *Rhoda*. Dropping her shoulder tote, shrugging out of her heavy wool coat, Susannah swallowed her distaste. Creep or not, he wasn't calling to tell her she had no messages. Nor was it likely he was calling with some low-priority item like "Friday's dance class has been canceled." Any time the service called to give you a message instead of waiting for you to check in with them, they charged you a quarter. It had to be Weingarten's office. It had to be.

It was.

Her spirits soared. That meant either a callback or she had the part. Nobody ever called to say better luck next time.

"They want you at the theater tonight. Seven-thirty at the latest. Seven, if you can make it by then."

"Did they say why?"

"Some bigwig is flying in from L.A. for twenty minutes or so before he has to fly back out again. While he's here he wants to get a look at everybody they're considering."

A callback, then. One of the men from TransFilm, the company putting up the money for the show. "Okay. Thanks."

She was ready to hang up when he said in a normal tone of voice, "Good luck, Susannah. I know how much this means to you."

Astonished, touched, suddenly sorry she'd never asked him his name, she thanked him as warmly as she could, exchanged goodbyes, and replaced the phone. She thought how quick she was to label and condemn. If she were stuck in whatever hole in the wall housed her answering service, taking phone calls all day long day after day for a flock of actors—most of the calls from the actors themselves—she might start imitating Carlton the Doorman, too.

She hung her coat in the closet off the postage-stamp foyer and checked the kitchen clock to see if she had time to wash her hair. Almost four-thirty. Time enough if she did it now.

Thank God it was Wednesday. Monday and Wednesday were her only free nights during the week. She would check her appointment book to make sure she hadn't scheduled anything, but at least she didn't have to call the café or Dr. Dubinsky to beg off work.

Checking the clock again—why, she didn't know— she rummaged in her shoulder tote for the little black appointment book. She fingered lipsticks, comb, pen, billfold, eye shadow, change purse, an old audition script for a commercial she'd waited in vain to get a callback on, crumpled Kleenex. Honestly. She ought to start practicing what she preached to Jill.

Jill. Now she knew why. If it was almost four-thirty, Jill should be home from school.

Maybe she was in her room doing her homework. With her headset on—one of the terms of surrender in the Long Rock War—she wouldn't hear the coming of Judgment Day. Still rummaging in the tote, Susannah walked through the living room, switched on a lamp against the gathering dusk, and continued into the back hallway. She knocked on Jill's door. "Jill? Are you in there?"

Getting no answer, she opened the door and walked in.

Her first thought—not thought, gut reaction—was that the room had been burglarized. She stared at the chaos. Bureau drawers pulled out, their contents spilling over onto the floor. The desk a litter of papers and books. Junk jewelry strewn all over the bed.

But it didn't make sense. The front door had been double-locked when she came home. And what would an eleven-year-old kid have in her bedroom that a burglar—

Susannah hastened to her own bedroom. Nothing. And nothing was disturbed in the living room.

Not a burglar. The knot in her stomach eased.

But what, then? What could have made Jill—because it had to have been Jill, and granted she was messy, her room never picked up, but this was— From the foot of the bed hung a thin wool red-plaid shirt, one of Jill's favorites, old and worn. It had been ripped to shreds.

Susannah went back to the kitchen to look at the school calendar, taped to the side of the refrigerator. The middle school at Shipley had Assembly every Wednesday, with parents welcome to drop in, but Jill hadn't said anything about today's—

Wednesday, January 25. Folk dancing.

That told her next to nothing.

Nor did she know where Jill might have gone.

Turning to the red wall phone as if it might come up with a suggestion, she realized she was still clutching the tote. She started rummaging again, her fingers finally closing on the appointment book.

Checking the date, seeing the entry, she said aloud, "Oh, damn." She had promised the guy at Horlick's she would take part tonight in a reading of a play he had written. Susannah made a face. Another creep. But he was always doing favors for her—appreciated if unasked—and anyhow, a promise was a promise. Only now, with the callback, it would have to be broken. She was sorry, but if he couldn't find a substitute for her, he would have to reschedule the reading.

She heard Jill's key in the lock and called out, "I'll get it," then reached into the foyer to open the door for her.

Jill made no move to come in, but stood at the doorsill looking at her. The small round face under the peaked stocking cap was set like stone and streaked with dirt—from using the sleeve of her nylon jacket to wipe away tears. Susannah called the jacket the quilted blue sausage-casing. Privately. The long blond hair was streaked, too. The summer sun did that. Jill was the image of her father, a dark-complexioned, brown-eyed blonde, with the same straight nose, the same small round mouth, the cleft in her chin. But that was something else best left unspoken.

"Well," Susannah said, trying for lightness, "are you going to stand there, or are you going to come in?"

Jill came in and stood in the foyer taking off the sausage-casing.

"Where have you been?"

"Nowhere."

Susannah considered a moment. "Let's start over, okay? Hi, Jill."

The stocking cap joined the sausage-casing on the foyer floor. "Hello."

"Would you mind hanging your things in the closet?"

Compliance, no answer. Jill's thin shoulders were rigid. Then, unexpectedly, "Mr. Schlosser said to remind you about tonight."

Susannah frowned. "Mr. Who?"

"You know. Mr. Schlosser. Herb Schlosser. Herb. At Horlick's."

"Oh. Herb. I didn't know that was his last name. How did you know?"

A shrug of the rigid shoulders. "I asked him. Isn't it on the copy of his play he gave you?"

"I suppose it is. I didn't pay that much attention. And that's—I have to go tell him I can't do the reading of his play tonight." Her first impulse had been to call him, but Horlick's was only a block and a half away, and it would be kinder to tell him in person, let him see she wasn't brushing him off. "But first I—come in and sit down a minute." She beckoned Jill into the living room, where she turned on another lamp. It was almost pitch-dark outside. The short days of winter. She had given up on washing her hair. "Jill," she began again, sitting opposite her, keeping her voice matter-of-fact, "was your father supposed to come to Assembly today?"

"You don't have to cancel tonight because of me."

"I'm not canceling because of you. The service called a few minutes ago." It seemed like half a year ago. "I have another callback tonight for *The Glory Road*."

"Oh." Jill's set face gave way to a frown, and she began fingering the hem of her gray wool winter uniform. A couple of callbacks ago—and that really was half a year ago—she and Jill had celebrated prematurely. Never again. Especially not this one. An off-Broadway production, *The Glory Road* was the most important thing that had happened—or almost happened—in her progress so far as an actress.

"Was your father supposed to come today and didn't?"

"I guess I had it wrong."

"There's no need to run yourself down to make excuses for your father."

They had had this conversation, or a variant, many times before. Susannah congratulated herself on how well she was handling her end of it. Voice still calm and matter-of-fact, attitude toward father neither harsh nor soft. Realistic. She wished she could read sometime for the part of a custodial parent trying to help her daughter develop a good self-image. She was typecast for it.

Jill was silent so long Susannah began to believe she had missed something.

"We went on a field trip last Friday."

This was familiar, too. Ducking away, some expert had dubbed it. Time needed to digest realistic but still unpleasant truth about father, who was quick to make promises he seldom kept.

"Oh? Where to?"

"Grand Central Station. It's a landmark." Jill frowned. "Or maybe they're still trying to get it made one."

"I don't remember either."

"Anyhow..." Another lengthy silence while Jill looked down at something—lap, fingers, shoes.

"Yes?"

"We went through this building to get there."

Susannah had been trying to think what Jill might be getting to, why this particular topic for the ducking away. Now she knew. The Graybar Building. Jill's middle name was Graybar. At eleven she hadn't yet outgrown the pleasure of seeing her name on various possessions. What fun to see it on a building. Susannah smiled. "You mean the Graybar Building? I've been meaning to take you there."

Jill wasn't smiling back. She looked ready to cry again. "Diana Grosvenor asked me if I was named for it."

Susannah stared at her. So much for the great job she was doing with her daughter's self-image. And so much for her snotty-smug assumption that Jill had been ducking away from an unpleasant truth. "Named for it? For the Graybar Building? Jill, you know better than that. You were named for your great-grandmother Fitzhugh. Your grandmother Whitney's mother. She set up the trust fund for your education. Her maiden name was Graybar."

"Oh."

"Well, I should say, oh." Susannah was aware her voice had risen. "You mean to tell me you believed Diana Grosvenor?"

Jill nodded.

"Well, why on earth, why, when you knew better?"

Another long silence. "I don't know."

Susannah was silent herself. Something was going on here that had to be gone into. Something more than her father not showing up today for Assembly. "Look, Jill. We have time to talk before I go to the theater. But first I have to let Herb know I can't make it tonight. I have to give him time to try to find somebody to replace me. Or at least let the other actors know. Okay?"

Jill nodded.

"Do you want to come with me?"

"No."

"Will you be okay here?"

"Yes."

"I won't be long. Ten or fifteen minutes at the most."

Jill frowned, her voice turning petulant. "I said I'm okay."

"All right. Fine. And while I'm gone, suppose you get a start on straightening up your room."

Jill gave her a look more challenge than fear.

"Yes, I've seen it. Start on your desk, Jill, so you'll be able to do your homework after dinner." Susannah went to the foyer closet for her coat. "When I get back I'll help you with it."

Jill didn't answer but got up from her chair and headed back to her bedroom, not even staying to double-lock the door after Susannah went out. Double-locking it herself, Susannah headed for the elevator, then decided to walk down the four flights. Exercise, exercise. Reach for your mate instead of your plate. Only she was out of mates at the moment.

So that couldn't be what was bothering Jill.

Something at school, maybe. Some quarrel with Diana Grosvenor, who had to be stage-center no matter what it took to get there.

Coming out of the renovated cold-water tenement—renovated about fifty-eight years ago—Susannah shivered in the raw night air. Rain had been threatening all day. If it would just hold off until she got to the theater. One drop of rain in New York City and traffic tied itself up in knots. And she wasn't about to take the subway. Not after dark.

She set off for Columbus Avenue and Eighty-sixth Street, wishing now she had acted on her first impulse

and called Herb, wishing she had never agreed to do
the reading in the first place.

He was a nice enough person, what little she knew
of him. Well-meaning. Friendly. Shy. A bit self-effac-
ing. A bit obsequious?

It was hard finding adjectives to try to describe him.
Like the business of seeing his name on the play, she'd
never paid that much attention to him.

She probably should have. He had talent. No question about it. His play was good. It was more than good.
It was weird in places, but it was also brilliant. And
her role, the central one, was so right for her it was as
if he had written it with her in mind.

But there was something about Herb that put her
off. He was so intense. Single-minded. Especially lately.
And so—well, all bound up with it somehow. Susannah
frowned, trying to think. Like something was hovering
inside him trying to break out.

She shook her head at herself. A would-be playwright was hovering inside him. Herb was only trying
to make it in the theater like everybody else, herself
included. And no wonder he'd gotten so intense. Tonight's reading was important to him. Very important.

She didn't know how he'd take the news she was
about to hand him. He'd be disappointed. For sure.
Which was one reason she wished she didn't have to
hand it to him.

But mostly she wished she didn't have to have the
talk with Jill afterward. She had stopped kidding herself. She knew what was bothering Jill. Somehow or
other Jill had found out.

Rounding the corner onto Columbus, Susannah
hunched her shoulders against the blast of wind that
whipped up the avenue, rattling the tinned-up windows
of abandoned buildings, kiting whirlwinds of paper and
other debris.

Maybe it was just as well. Jill probably had to find
out sometime.

Two

Horlick's was on the west side of Manhattan at Eighty-sixth and Columbus Avenue. In the days when New York had maybe a dozen daily papers, it had started out as a newsstand with a roof over its head. Over the years, as the number of papers dwindled, other merchandise was added. Magazines. Candy. Cigars, cigarettes, tobacco. A soda vending machine. Paperbacks. Sometimes now you could even get a container of coffee, depending on the day of the week or the prevailing mood of whoever happened to be in charge.

Because of the heavy concentration of actors living in the neighborhood, Horlick's carried the theatrical trade papers. It also carried the *Village Voice*. Liberal, aware, the *Voice* covered and critiqued every form of art and aided the artist's struggle to survive by featuring shopping bargains and want ads for part-time and temporary jobs. The theatrical trades, *Back Stage* and *Show Business*, had a narrower, more intense appeal. Both papers included casting calls—on average about eighty a week—and on Thursdays, when the two papers came out, actors and would-be actors streamed in and out of Horlick's all day long.

Walter Zekiel, who owned the place—nobody remembered any longer who Horlick was—treated the
actors the same as he did everybody else. A big, even-
tempered man in his early sixties, he was friendly without being pushy, interested without being involved—
a man who let other people's gripes and opinions roll
off him and seldom mentioned his own.

Sometimes Walter's wife filled in for him, but mainly
he relied for help on Herb Schlosser. In his mid-thirties,
Herb was as stocky as his employer but much shorter,
a dumpy-looking fellow with dark-blond hair that stood
out from his head in a tangle of curls, and with a stubble
of streaky beard on his face. Like most of the Thursday
clientele, Herb wore jeans and sneakers and T-shirts
or turtlenecks, usually dirty and in disrepair.

He was like them in manner as well as dress—ded-
icated, serious, diligent in pursuit of something so dif-
ficult to achieve, the odds stacked so heavily against
you, it could almost be said not to be there at all. Success
in the theater.

Of course, as Herb saw it, they were actors, while he
was a playwright, but the odds were about the same.
Or they had been up to now. If an actor got a good part
in a successful play and did well in it, the odds began
to change. Just like the odds were about to change for
him. And not only for him. For her as well. For both
of them.

There had never been a play like his new one, *Possessed.*

Queer how fate played a hand in things. Whenever
he wrote a play, he reduced his medication because it
affected his vision and made it hard for him to concentrate. In writing *Possessed*, a play about diabolical pos-
session, having to put himself into the role of the one
possessed, the drug became a hindrance, and he stopped
taking it altogether.

He had told himself he'd go back on the medication
once the play was finished, but he hadn't done so. Being
off the drug had done more than enable him to create
a believable character in a terrifying situation. It had
proved what he had long suspected—that the doctors,
with his mother's connivance, were up to the same old

game of protecting his father's name and reputation, not interested in him as a person or playwright, seeing him only as a potential troublemaker.

Well, he would show them, all of them. Not only that he could keep control of himself, but that, starting to-night, he was on his way to becoming a major new talent in the American theater.

The bell over the door jangled as a customer came in. Herb looked up from the entry he was making in his diary about tonight's reading and saw it was Cervantes, the film photographer who lived upstairs over the store. Sweat broke out on the palms of his hands. This morning when Cervantes had come in for the *Times,* he claimed that the dollar bill he had handed Herb was a five-dollar bill. When Herb refused to give in, Cervantes threatened to speak to Zekiel about it. Now here he was.

"Hello, Herb," he said, smiling.

The smile didn't fool Herb. "You want Mr. Zekiel? He's in the back room."

The smile faded into a puzzled look. That didn't fool him either. Before switching to photography Cervantes had tried acting for a while. "No. I don't want Mr. Zekiel. I want a pack of Larks." He handed him a dollar.

So. He was going to try the same trick again. Herb laid the dollar bill down on the counter. There wouldn't be any accusation this time. He rang up the sale, handed over the cigarettes and change, and waited, his hands sweating profusely, his heart starting to pound.

"Thanks," Cervantes said. "See you around, Herb."

The bell jangled again as he went out.

Herb stared after him, his heart still pounding. The photographer must be going to wait until he could see Zekiel alone.

Zekiel came out of the back room with a box of Her-shey bars and a new Tic Tac display rack.

"Cervantes was just in here," Herb said. "I told him you were here, but he didn't want to talk to you with me around."

Zekiel looked up from the candy counter. "Talk to me about what?"

"About that four bucks he says I cheated him out of this morning."

"What four bucks? He didn't say anything to me about it."

Herb started sweating again. He wiped his face with the sleeve of his turtleneck. "I just now told you," he said irritably. "He wants to wait till he can get you alone."

Zekiel was filling up the Tic Tac rack. "I don't know what you're talking about. Cervantes was in here two or three times this afternoon. He didn't say anything to me about any four bucks. Or anything else."

"Well, all I know is he said he was going to." Herb was sorry he'd opened his mouth about it. Either Cervantes had decided he was wrong, or he was going to try to get back at him some other way.

The bell jangled again, and three neighborhood boys came in asking for change for the soda vending machine. Insolent young toughs, they were always looking to rip somebody off. You had to keep a constant watch on them. But for once Herb was glad to see them. They would take Zekiel's mind off Cervantes.

He wished Cervantes had carried out his threat. He'd been prepared for that. This way he didn't know what to expect. Or what he could do about it.

The toughs hung out in the store drinking their soda, turning cool stares on the other customers who came in, their jiving larded with "Yeah, man," "Shit, man," "Fuck, man." Finally they took off, crushing the empty cans, throwing them into the gutter outside.

In a lull between customers Zekiel said from behind the candy counter, "About your wanting to get off early tonight..."

Herb spun around to him. "What do you mean, wanting to? We had it all worked out."

Zekiel frowned. "Take it easy, Herb. I didn't—"

Herb cut him off. "You take it easy. You can't do this to me. I told you about tonight at least two weeks ago. I told you I had everything lined up—the room at the Esplanade, the actors, everything." His words sprayed the room like an Uzi machine gun. "And Mel Goodrich, who has an inside track at the Manhattan

Theater Club. He said he'd come tonight." Sweat poured off him. It glistened at the corners of his eyes, putting a halo around Zekiel. "And now you're going to blow the whole thing out of the water by telling me I can't get off?"

Zekiel stared at him. "My God. What's got into you? All I wanted to know was what time you said you wanted to leave."

Herb didn't believe him. "You're in this with Cervantes, aren't you?"

"In what? What are you talking about? Herb, you're not making sense. What's the matter with you?"

"Nothing's the matter with me." He had gone too far. He had to get hold of himself. What made him think Zekiel was in with Cervantes? Or that there was anything to be in with him about? "I didn't mean that about Cervantes," he said, backtracking, forcing himself to concentrate on finding a way out, shutting the core of himself away from the sudden barrage of ghosts and specters clamoring to get at him. "I just don't like him, that's all. Throwing his weight around every time he comes in here, like he owns the place. Trying to put things over on me. He thinks he's so goddamned smart."

Zekiel frowned. "What was all that about you cheating him out of four dollars?"

"Nothing."

"After the way you went on about it, now you say it's nothing?"

"I didn't mean to go on about it." He was going to throw up if he wasn't careful. He was lightheaded with nausea. "It upset me, that's all." What could he possibly say about Cervantes? Damn the man anyhow. "It was a misunderstanding. He thought he gave me a five-dollar bill when it was only a dollar. I showed him I didn't have any fives in the cash register." What had made him come up with that? No fives in the cash register? Zekiel would never go for that.

"Well," Zekiel said with a shrug, "that should have settled it then."

"It did settle it," Herb said. "I told you it did." The nausea subsided. Zekiel had gone for it. And no reason he shouldn't, when it had happened that way. Now maybe they'd be finished with Cervantes.

They *were* finished with him. Zekiel was no longer staring at him through that halo. He was bent over the counter replenishing the supply of chewing gum, the mist around him melting away as Herb wiped his face again with the sleeve of his turtleneck.

If he had any of his medication here at the store with him, he'd take some to settle himself down. Only he didn't have any. He'd have to settle himself down without it.

He could do it if he concentrated. The way his mother had taught him long ago.

Concentrate.

Keep the ghosts and specters out of your head. Don't give them room. Or credence.

He didn't hear the bell over the door. The bell couldn't have rung. Yet there she was, standing in front of him, that little half-smile on her face.

Susannah.

Sometimes he thought she couldn't have any idea how beautiful she was. Tall, full-bodied, regal, she came from a mostly Irish heritage and looked it, with curly dark hair and blue eyes and a fair, fair skin, and a smile that, at its fullest, set her blue eyes dancing and transformed her face with light.

Other times, times like now, he was sure she had to know. The little half-smile, the silvery-blue eye shadow, the gray man's cap she wore, its saucy little bill tilted over her forehead. Advertisements of self. Invitations. Challenges.

Susannah.

He flexed and unflexed his fingers, sweating again.

The smile widened a little, became merely polite. The beginning of a frown appeared. Another wave of nausea washed over him. She was going to tell him she couldn't make it tonight.

She was telling him.

He couldn't believe it. He had written the play for her. She was the central character, the one possessed. It was a part an actress might wait a lifetime for. He had given it to her. She was giving it back.

"If you can't find anybody else..."

He didn't believe it. He hadn't heard the bell ring. He only thought she was standing there. He had been so afraid she would say what she was saying, he was putting the words in her mouth.

"Like I said, Herb. If you can't find anybody else— and I realize it's terribly last-minute. I'm really sorry. But if you can't find anybody to take my place, then maybe you could set it up for some other night. Maybe one night next week."

Did she have any idea what she was saying? The room at the Esplanade cost sixty-five dollars. Cash in advance. And trying to find one night when all the actors were available...Susannah herself was only available two nights a week. And Mel Goodrich, his contact with the Manhattan Theater Club, one of the best showcase houses in the city, one of the few the *Times* critics took any notice of. After going to the trouble Mel must have gone to free himself up for tonight, was it likely he'd be willing to do that again? Especially when Herb didn't know him all that well.

And what made him think next week would be any different from this week? She'd find some other excuse. Or she'd get the part in that play she had the callback on tonight, and then she'd go into rehearsal, and she wouldn't have any time for him and his play.

She was apologizing again. About something else. There were so many things inside his head competing for his attention it was hard to separate her out.

"I'd offer to stick around and help you call people to set up another date, but I can't."

He must have told her he couldn't find anybody to take her place, that it was out of the question. Had he told her why?

Had she said she was flattered? She would at least have said that, maybe more, like nobody else had ever written a part for her, let alone a play. Had she said anything like that? He didn't know. He couldn't think.

"Something's upsetting Jill. My daughter. You know. Jill."

He knew who Jill was. She didn't need to explain. Did he look like she needed to?

"I promised we'd talk as soon as I got back from telling you about tonight."

Had she been talking with Cervantes? Was that it?

He gripped the edge of the counter. No. Fool. Cervantes had nothing to do with her. Or anything else. All that business about Cervantes, he'd made that up. It was all inside his head. Wasn't that what the shrink at the clinic said last time?

He had to get hold of himself. He had to. Did he want her to guess what he worked so hard to keep anybody from finding out?

"I'm sorry," she said. She smiled. "But let me know when you've got it worked out, and I'll be happy to do it for you." Her smile widened to its fullest, setting her blue eyes dancing. "For sure."

She was always saying "for sure." She said it the way other people said "yeah" or "right" or "you said it, jocko." It didn't mean a thing.

He didn't hear the bell when she left either, but that was because the jangling was drowned in a crack of thunder. What in the hell was it doing thundering in January? The weather was as crazy as he was.

He hated thunderstorms. They made him nervous, and he was already too near the edge.

He had to call the other actors. And Mel Goodrich. But first he had to call the Hotel Esplanade and try to get his money back. They had said no refunds, but if he explained he wasn't canceling, only postponing...

Had he handled his end of it with her all right? He must have or she would have looked at him funny instead of smiling and saying she'd be happy to do it for him.

Assuming she'd said that, that he hadn't made it up. Or made her up.

There was too much going on inside his head.

Another crack of thunder. The storm was about to break.

"Listen, Mr. Zekiel..."

Zekiel looked around a customer he was waiting on. "Yes, Herb. What?"

He had to organize what he wanted to say, and then he couldn't get the words out. He struggled with them.

The customer turned around to look, and Zekiel frowned. "What is it?"

"You heard what Susannah—Mrs. Whitney. You heard what she said."

"I wasn't paying particular attention. Just a minute, Herb, until I finish with this customer. Then I'll be with you."

He hadn't made her up, then. She had been here. He hadn't put the words in her mouth. She had said them.

He cracked a knuckle. How could she have turned him down when so much was riding on tonight?

Had been riding. Not any more.

How could she have done it when it was for her sake as well as his? Her future as well as his. Didn't she understand? Had he never explained it to her?

He cracked another knuckle. What good were explanations? What good had they ever been? Hadn't his mother explained things over and over?

He hated his mother.

Rain burst against the plate-glass windows.

"Now, Herb. What was it you wanted?"

He stared at Zekiel. What had he wanted?

Zekiel frowned again. "Are you all right, Herb?"

He rubbed his sleeve across his face. He had to get out of here before the forces inside him thundered up out of him like a shout to heaven.

Zekiel let him go. Zekiel said he was crazy to go out in this downpour when he could phone the Esplanade to ask for his money back, but go ahead and go.

He put on a slicker and a pair of galoshes he kept in the store. He wished he had the nerve not to wear the galoshes. Get his shoes wet. Ruin them.

He didn't have the nerve. He hated his mother as much as he hated the galoshes, but he didn't have the nerve.

He'd found a way to get back at her, though. He dragged his feet when he wore them. He started dragging them now. *Scrape, scrape* along the sidewalk. *Scrape, scrape.* Out of the corner of his eye he would watch first for the frown, then for the tightening of her lips until finally, exasperated, she would say, "Pick up your feet."

He threw his head back to laugh. The wind drove the rain against his face like somebody throwing a bucket of water into it.

At least his mother was still here to get back at. The thought of his father filled him with rage. He could never get back at his father. Never.

Facing into the wind-driven rain, lowering his head against it, he set off for the Hotel Esplanade on Broadway, his galoshes going *scrape, scrape* along the sidewalk.

Three

Leaving Horlick's at the first peal of thunder, Susannah peered up into the murky darkness above the coral haze of the sodium street lights, then raced home to beat the rain. She had hung her coat in the foyer closet and was on her way back to Jill's room when the storm broke. Crossing the living room, she glanced out into the airshaft that separated her building from the next one. Even in this protected area the rain beat against the windows, while at the back of the room, the French doors that opened onto the fire escape rattled and shook. With a shake of her head she continued on her way. At the rate it was coming down, maybe it would be over by the time she had to leave for the theater.

Jill was sitting at her desk frowning at the untouched litter of paper. She didn't look up.

"I'll tackle the bureau," Susannah said. She put out a hand in passing to ruffle her daughter's hair. Jill flinched.

Shocked to a standstill by the reaction, Susannah stood for a moment rubbing the offending hand, then with another shake of her head she crossed to the bureau with its tumble of clothing. She picked up a sweater, folded it, laid it on the foot of the bed. "Do you want to talk about it?"

"Talk about what?"

"What's bothering you. What made you trash your bedroom."

"No."

Another sweater joined the first one. "No, you don't want to talk about it?"

"Yes."

"I'm afraid we have to, Jill."

"Then why did you ask me if I wanted to?"

A third and fourth sweater. She ought to go through Jill's things and weed out what she no longer wore. "Because sometimes I'm not as clever as I am other times." She picked up a white ruffled petticoat. It, too, had been ripped. Maybe another approach. "Herb asked me to give you his regards."

Jill turned to look at her. She still hadn't touched a paper on the desk. "Why should he do that? I saw him myself a little while ago. Just before I came home."

Susannah shrugged. "Maybe he forgot. He was upset about the reading having to be postponed. Upset and trying not to show it."

"Well, it wasn't just the reading," Jill said. "He's been more and more that way since his father died last month."

Susannah stared at her. She hadn't known Herb had a father. She didn't know anything about him beyond the fact that he worked at Horlick's and considered himself a playwright. "How did you know that?"

Jill scowled. "What's wrong with my knowing it?"

"Nothing." The top bureau drawer, pulled out to a precarious angle, was jammed. Susannah jockeyed it back and forth to release it. "I was surprised, that's all. You know more about him than I do."

"That's because you can't be bothered with him."

She had heard that charge before, but not from her eleven-year-old daughter. She yanked at the drawer, it gave, and she snapped it shut. "That's right. He's not anybody I need to be bothered with. Or care to." She tackled the second drawer. "And it's not Herb Whatever-his-name-is we need to talk about either. It's you and me."

Jill turned to the litter on her desk and began to poke around in it. "Don't you have to study your script for tonight?"

"I don't have one to study. They didn't give any scripts out."

"Well, don't you have to think about the character?" She always tried to do at least that much. "If you had an exam coming up at school, and you came home and found my bedroom looking like this one, what would you be thinking about?"

"I didn't know you had a callback tonight." Small, sullen voice. Small shuffling of paper.

Susannah closed the second drawer and moved on to the third. "I didn't mean to imply you did. I was trying—in my usual clumsy way—to talk about priorities." Maybe tomorrow night, after the last group-therapy session, she should talk to Dr. Dubinsky. She wasn't doing something right, or she and Jill wouldn't be at each other like this.

"His parents farmed him out when he was a kid."

Susannah looked up, frowning. Jill had turned around to her again. "Whose parents?"

"Mr. Schlosser's. Herb's."

"What do you mean, farmed him out?"

"They only had him weekends. He lived with somebody else during the week. At the other people's house. Miles away from where his parents lived. He lived there and went to school there. He hated it."

Susannah straightened up from the bureau drawer. "How do you know all that? Did Herb tell you?"

Jill shrugged. "He didn't tell me he hated it. He didn't have to."

"How much time do you spend in Horlick's?"

"What does that have to do with anything?"

"I don't like the idea of your hanging around there. Any free time you have you should be spending with your friends, not somebody like Herb."

"Just because you can't be bothered with him doesn't mean he isn't interesting."

Susannah bent to the drawer again. Like the top

one, it was jammed. As before, she yanked at it. This time the drawer not only gave, it came out altogether and fell to the floor, banging her shins in the process. "Damn," she said. She picked up the drawer, inserted it onto its tracks, and closed it. Then she came over and sat on the side of the bed, pushing away a yellow plastic bracelet and a strand of pink glass beads. "Jill, I haven't got all evening. What time I do have I'd like to spend on something other than your friend Herb."

"He's not my friend."

"Then why are we going on and on about him?"

Her voice had risen, and now Jill's rose to match it. "Well, who would you like to go on and on about? My father? Assuming he *is* my father."

Susannah gasped, and Jill shrank back against the desk. "What made you say a thing like that? Who have you been talking to?"

"Nobody."

"I asked you a question, Jill."

"I answered it."

"As much as she dislikes me, I can't believe your grandmother Whitney would say a thing like that."

"She didn't."

"Well, who did, then?"

Silence.

"Jill, I'm not going to leave this subject until you tell me. And I mean if we have to spend the rest of the winter on it."

After another few moments of the same stony silence, Jill stood up. "I have to get something," she said, and walked out of the bedroom.

Despite the unexpectedness of the crack about Joe not being her father, Susannah wasn't surprised when Jill came back bearing the brown manila folder that contained, among other documents, the marriage license she had guessed was behind all this.

When Jill handed it to her, she handed it back. "I don't need to see it. I know what it says."

Jill put the license back in the folder. Since coming back into the bedroom she had not once looked directly at her. "Why didn't you tell me?"

"What would have been the point?"

"He isn't my father, then, is he? He only married you so you'd have somebody to be married to."

"Oh, yes," Susannah said, only barely aware of the savagery in her voice, "by all means. Because, of course, your real father was even more of a shitheel than Joe Whitney is. Is that what you want me to say, Jill? Or no. Wait. We can do better than that. Why not make me into a slut by saying I don't know who your father is? I was so busy going from bed to bed I can't possibly say. There. Is that what you were hoping to hear?"

Jill was looking at her now.

Aghast at what had come pouring out of her, Susannah fought back tears, then gave way to them when she saw that Jill was crying, too. "Darling," she said, "I'm sorry. That was mean and cruel and vicious. And I'm sorry about Joe and how he hurts you. He doesn't mean to do it. He is your father, Jill, and he does love you. Honest he does. But he has problems in all of his relationships. Not just with you. With everybody. Even his own mother. You know how much they care about each other and always have. Well, he treats her the same way he does you."

Susannah wiped her eyes with the back of her hands. What this was accomplishing, she didn't know. Not what she had hoped. Jill's crying hadn't brought release. She was as stony-faced as before. And she was no longer looking at her.

"Jill, what is it? What do you want me to say?"

"Nothing."

"Darling, I want to help you. But how can I, if I don't know what's bothering you?"

"You call everybody darling."

"As an act. Not the way I'm calling you darling. And that can't be what's bothering you. A little thing like that."

"No."

"Then what?"

Jill looked at her, struggling to say something.

"Go ahead," Susannah encouraged her. "Get it out. Whatever it is, say it."

"Why did you have me?"

Susannah frowned. "Why did I have you?"

"You couldn't have wanted me. Why did you have me?"

"Jill—"

Jill shook her head, a fierce look on her face. "No. You're going to make something up."

Another silence.

"All right," Susannah said. "I had you because—because it didn't seem to me I had any choice."

"You could have had an abortion, couldn't you?"

Susannah stared at her daughter. At Jill's age had she even known where babies came from? Well, yes, probably. But not what you could do about having them or not having them. "I didn't want to have an abortion. I didn't think it was right. Morally right. My father and mother—" She fingered the pink glass beads. "Abortions were illegal then. They were done mostly by quacks in dirty back rooms. I was afraid to have an abortion."

"And that's why you had me."

"Jill—" What could she say to her? "Jill, I could have had you and given you up for adoption, but I didn't."

"Because my father wouldn't let you."

Jill was going to cling to her illusion of Joe no matter how many times reality slapped her in the face. "No. Because I didn't want to. Not your father. Me. It was my decision." Susannah frowned. "Not that I mean Joe wanted me to give you up." Christ, whatever she said, it only opened other wounds. "We both wanted to keep you."

"How could you want to keep me if you didn't want to have me?"

"Jill, it wasn't *you* I didn't want to have. What I didn't want was to be pregnant. Can you understand the difference? I was young. I was scared. Joe and I weren't married. We were a couple of college students who wanted to be part of the now generation, who thought it would be super chic to live together." She frowned again. "Not that I mean we didn't love each other." God. Every time she tried to explain one thing, she had to explain something else. "We did love each other. That's why we got married. That's why we went ahead and had you. That's why we wanted to keep you. And why we did."

Wasn't that at least partly the truth? Hadn't she married Joe at least partly because she loved him, not entirely because she didn't know how else she could face her parents or his mother?

She didn't know.

Jill was crying again. "If you loved each other, then why didn't he stay here with us? What did you do to him to make him go away? What do you keep doing to him that he doesn't want to see me?"

"Jill, I don't do anything to him. I didn't do anything to him to make him go away. I just explained it to you—or tried to. Your father is a very confused person. He's confused about himself, and that makes it hard for him to have a straightforward relationship with other people. Especially the people who mean the most to him. Especially you. Darling, he does love you. If he didn't, he wouldn't want you to be proud of him, and he wants that in the worst way. Because he's your father, and fathers are supposed to be people their kids can look up to. People to model themselves on. But what has he got—I mean visibly, not inside—what has he got for you to be proud of? How does he compare—in his own eyes, not yours—to the fathers of your friends at school?"

"Then why do I have to go to that school? Why can't I go to an ordinary school, so he wouldn't have to compare himself to all the fathers at Shipley?"

She shouldn't have tried to explain Joe to Jill. Jill wasn't old enough yet to understand. "Do you think it would be any different with the fathers at P.S. 28? Do you?" She waited, but Jill didn't answer. "It wouldn't. Darling, believe me, it wouldn't. Because don't you see? What's wrong isn't what other people are or aren't. What's wrong is what's inside your father's head."

Jill still didn't answer, but what was there to say? What was there ever to say about Joe except to try to excuse what she couldn't explain?

Susannah glanced at her watch. She had to get dinner on. And there hadn't been any letup in the storm. What a rotten evening this day had turned into. To cap

it, the Hollywood bigwig would probably turn thumbs
down on her.

She got up from her perch on the bed. Careful this
time not to touch Jill, she said, "Try to get your desk
cleared while I scrounge up a meal. Do you have homework tonight?"

Jill nodded.

"How much?"

"I guess an hour."

"Okay. You can do it while I'm at the callback, and
then when I get home we can talk some more if you
want to."

"I don't want to."

"All right. That's all right, too." She must speak to
Dr. Dubinsky tomorrow night. Maybe he would agree
to see Jill, though how she would pay for that, she didn't
know. She was barely making ends meet as it was.

In the kitchen she surveyed the contents of the refrigerator and decided on scrambled eggs and a tossed
green salad. Plus frozen french fries for Jill. Anything
heavy before an audition was out for her.

If Joe would start coming across with his twenty-
five-dollars-a-week child support.

If rain would start falling from the ground to the
sky.

She rinsed the Boston-lettuce leaves, shook them,
and wrapped them in a towel. She could add Saturday
night to her schedule at the café. That would bring in
another thirty or thirty-five dollars a week and still
leave all day Saturday and Sunday to spend with Jill.
They seldom did anything Saturday night anyhow except stay home and watch TV. Jill could as easily do
that by herself.

She turned on the oven to heat the french fries. Almost a week had gone by since she'd sent in a picture
to the agency that had announced in *Back Stage* they
were looking for soap-opera people. Why, they hadn't
said. Maybe a new soap or maybe only a new agency
trying to get into the existing market. But she'd done
enough bit parts to qualify as experienced, and she
worked well in the medium. Photographed well, too.

She'd stop by there on rounds tomorrow to see what
was up.

If she could get even a small running part on a soap
opera.

If every raindrop were a silver dollar.

She set the table in the living room and listened to
the rain lash against the windows and the French doors.
What she ought to do was forget about acting. She
would be thirty-one in August. Time to stop frittering
away her life. Admit she wasn't getting anywhere in
the theater and probably never would. There were too
many actors for too few jobs. Yesterday she had audi-
tioned for a showcase production, a crummy little off-
off-Broadway play with five parts. Eight hundred sixty-
four people had turned up for it.

A play that would rehearse for a month and run for
three four-day weekends in a shabby little theater in
some God-forsaken corner of the city. A play that would
pay nothing for rehearsal and only round-trip bus fare
for the twelve performances that a handful of critics
and/or agents might or might not come to, and eight
hundred sixty-four people had turned up for it.

Insanity.

Granted that some of those eight hundred sixty-four
were fringe people who had no talent, no looks, nothing.
Granted as many as half of them were. That still left
four hundred thirty-two people for five jobs.

Dr. Dubinsky had offered her full-time work as a
psychodramatist. Why not take it? She wouldn't have
to waitress any more. She could move out of this rotten
apartment in this rotten neighborhood. Go to the suburbs. Put Jill in public school there and save great-
grandmother Fitzhugh's trust-fund money for college
and graduate school. That would give Joe's mother one
less thing to be affronted by.

She poured a glass of skimmed milk for each of
them—if she had drunk skimmed milk at Jill's age,
she might not be fighting a weight battle now—and
cracked the eggs into the skillet. If nothing came of
tonight's callback, maybe she would quit. Maybe she
owed it to Jill as well as herself. What was Jill doing
at Shipley anyway? The posh private girls' school

provided Jill with a first-class education impossible to approach, let alone duplicate, in the city's rundown public-school system. It also enabled the two of them to live in Manhattan, so Jill's mother could pursue her will-o'-the-wisp acting career.

And have an occasional live-in friend. Try doing that in the suburbs. Try finding somebody in the suburbs to do it with.

She called back to the bedroom, "Jill, wash your face and hands and come to dinner!"

She took the french fries out of the oven and sprinkled salt on them. Had she ever talked to Jill about Shipley? Really talked to her? Or couldn't she be bothered with that either?

Jill wasn't the only student at Shipley who couldn't afford to go there without outside help. There were the scholarship kids, paying little or nothing for their costly schooling. Proud of its outreach to the less fortunate, Shipley took pains to protect their identity, to keep anybody from knowing who they were.

But *they* knew. When Diana Grosvenor brought her seashell collection from her family's summer home in Southampton to science class, when Wendy Chapin talked about her family's latest trip to Europe in geography, when Patsy Holliday climbed into her father's chauffeur-driven limousine, *they* knew who they were. Poor kids in a rich kids' school.

Jill picked at her food. Susannah would have chided her, but she wasn't doing any better herself.

A couple of times Jill looked up from her plate, frowning, struggling to say something, but nothing came of it.

"Jill," Susannah said at last, "what would you think about living in the suburbs?"

She asked the question almost on impulse, thinking back more than ahead, unprepared for the terror that flashed across her daughter's small round face before the brown eyes shuttered it into sullenness.

"Jill," she said, aghast, "what is it? What made you look at me like that?"

By this time Jill had on her face what Susannah

called her closed-in airport look. The voice was closed-in, too. "Like what?"

"Like you were scared to death."

"I don't know what you mean."

"You must know. When I asked you about living in the suburbs. What's so frightening about that?"

But the airport wasn't opening. Not tonight. And finally Susannah had to leave to get to the theater by seven.

She had double-locked the door and was halfway down the stairs to the third floor when she heard the phone ring. She stopped, ready to turn and go back, then decided against it. It wouldn't be Weingarten's office changing the callback. Not this late. And she didn't have time to go back for anybody else. In this weather she had to allow an extra twenty minutes getting to the theater. For sure.

On the stoop outside the building she raised her umbrella, feeling the wind tug against it, wondering if it would blow inside out. Bending into the wind and the rain, she set off for the bus stop on Columbus Avenue.

She was waiting for the light to change so she could cross Columbus to the other side when it dawned on her what had frightened Jill. What must have. She couldn't think of anything else.

Joe's mother lived in the suburbs. In Syosset, Long Island. Jill must have thought she meant to send her out there to live with her grandmother, to—what was the expression she had used talking about Herb? To farm her out.

Dear God. First the shotgun wedding, and now this.

Susannah crossed the avenue, fishing in her shoulder tote for her change purse, looking up Columbus to see if a bus was coming. There was a phone booth on the corner. She would call Jill and reassure her.

The phone was out of order. Naturally. Why would a block of boarded-up, abandoned buildings need a pay phone that worked?

She walked up to the bus stop in the middle of the block. She would call Jill from the theater.

A gust of wind tore at the umbrella. She twisted it

around into the wind. A new umbrella was one expense she didn't need.

The gust subsiding, she turned again to see if a bus was coming. In spite of being pitch-black out, it was only about six-fifteen. Still rush hour. But the traffic was rushing up Amsterdam, not down Columbus. Here the traffic was sparse. Not even many pedestrians. Not on a block like this one.

Susannah shivered and looked again to see if a bus was coming. One advantage of a night like this, the muggers tended to stay home too.

Maybe the theater didn't have a phone. Or maybe she wouldn't have an opportunity to use it. She could walk over to Broadway and take the bus from there. She hated for Jill to think she would farm her out. To her grandmother Whitney, of all people.

After one last look to see if a bus was coming, she walked up to the corner of Eighty-eighth Street and turned west toward Amsterdam and Broadway. This wasn't the greatest block in the world either, but she wouldn't be in it long. Bending into the storm again, she picked up her pace. Ahead of her, coming toward her, she could make out a faint *scrape, scrape.*

Four

The Esplanade wouldn't refund his sixty-five dollars. Or let him use it to rent the meeting room one night next week instead of tonight. The girl at the desk spoke to him like she'd been programmed. The hotel's policy was spelled out in the contract he'd signed. No refunds. No exceptions. He could see the manager if he cared to wait until such time as the manager was available, but the manager didn't set policy either.

She went back to filing her nails.

Picking a chair in a far corner of the cavernous, once ornate lobby, he sat down to wait. Not because he expected anything from the manager. Because he needed time to sort everything out.

Everything was all mixed up in his head. Susannah. Cervantes. The three neighborhood toughs with their insolent stares and their "Yeah, man," "Shit, man," "Fuck, man." He wanted to yell at them to shut up, get out.

He cracked a knuckle and frowned down at his feet. Beads of water rolled off his galoshes to make little puddles on the ancient, worn marble floor. His mother was saying something to him, too.

He frowned harder. He wasn't sure any longer how to behave. His mother would tell him.

Shit, man.

Will you shut up? My mother's trying to talk to me.

I told you you were throw·*ng your money away, Herbert, renting that room. I told you if you had to have a place, bring your friends here.*

Shit, man. Listen to her.

She wasn't telling him anything he didn't already know. What good was that to him?

I said I'm sure my living room is as clean and presentable as anything the Hotel Esplanade can come up with.

You gotta be kidding, lady. That chickenshit place?

But, no. You had to play Mister Big Shot. Mister Important. The world's most famous unproduced playwright. And now look at you. No reading, no room, and no money either. Tell me, Herbert. How long will it be before you can put together another sixty-five dollars to throw away?

It depends, ma'am, on how many customers he can cheat out of four dollars the way he cheated me this morning when I came in to buy the Times.

No. Fool. Get a grip on yourself. You didn't cheat Cervantes out of four dollars.

He was making everything up.

Except his mother *had* said that to him about the hotel. And the gibes. She'd made them, too. Mister Big Shot. Mister Important. The world's most famous unproduced playwright.

Bitch.

Shit, man. If your mama's a bitch, that makes you a son of a bitch, don't it?

Peals of laughter reverberated around the cavernous lobby, bouncing off the dark wood, echoing back from the worn marble floor. People sitting on the peeling fake-leather chairs and sofas put down their papers and looked around to see where it was coming from. He pretended not to have heard it, to know nothing about it.

Abruptly the laughter stopped.

Hey, man. Son of a bitch. Now there's a mama for you. But what's she doing with that dude?

He stared at the couple coming toward him, not believing what he saw. Susannah and Cervantes. Susannah shaking the rain out of her curly dark hair, beaming up at Cervantes, putting her hand on his wrist, bending him to her so she could whisper in his ear. Cervantes laughing. Both of them laughing.

Peals of laughter, the same as before. Only this time nobody looked up, nobody heard. He couldn't believe it.

He waited for Susannah and Cervantes to catch sight of him. That would put a stop to their laughing at him.

He cracked a knuckle, and they turned to look.

Fool.

Not Susannah and Cervantes. Two strangers. No resemblance even. What was happening to him?

Shit, man. Ain'tcha gettin' any?

Get out. Finish your soda and get out.

Cervantes been puttin' it to you again? Or maybe he's been puttin' it to her. That more like it?

Cackles of laughter.

Get out, I said. Get out!

Somebody else was speaking to him.

Somebody real. Outside his head.

The manager of the Esplanade.

Herb frowned up at him, trying to keep the others quiet. Cervantes, Susannah, the neighborhood toughs, his mother, all talking to him, competing for his attention. Couldn't they leave him alone long enough to—

Keep quiet, will you? I can't hear what he's saying. Listen. What have I ever done to you that you should treat me this way?

"—have to have a fixed—"

Shit, man. Why do you need to listen to this shit? What the honk is saying is you ain't gonna get your money back. No way.

"—sorry for the—"

Yeah, man. U-total. Can you lend me a hank, honk? I got this need to cry, see?

Shrieks of laughter.

"—hope to be able to do business with—"

Do business with? Fuck, man, you were given the business.

The manager was walking away from him.

He didn't have anything sorted out, but he couldn't sit here any longer. He had to get back to Horlick's.

They all went with him. Every one of them.

Susannah and Cervantes, arm in arm, laughing at the rain, laughing at each other, laughing at him.

The neighborhood toughs, challenging the rain, challenging the traffic, dodging cars, foul-mouthing the drivers, tossing their crumpled soda cans back and forth to each other, their sneakers squishing through swollen gutters.

His mother walking beside him, frowning, tight-lipped.

Sixty-five dollars. You might as well have thrown it in the furnace.

Scrape, scrape.

And throwing your life away as well on this grandiose idea you have about yourself.

Scrape, scrape.

A playwright, is it?

Scrape, scrape.

Spending sixty-five dollars to rent a room so half a dozen down-and-outs like yourself can sit around reading this masterpiece you've written called Possessed. *Sixty-five dollars. If you ask me, you're possessed.*

Scrape, scrape.

Herbert, for the last time. Will you pick up your feet?

You tell him, bitch lady. What this fuckin' town needs is more fuckin' playwrights who pick up they feet. Ain't that right, man?

Screams of laughter, piercing the night sky in jagged streaks of light, bouncing off buildings, flattened by a thunderclap.

Holy Jesus, man. That was some piece of shit.

Scrape, scrape.

God, Cervantes. I mean, you should have seen the look on his face when I told him I couldn't read his play.

Yeah, I can imagine. What excuse did you give him?

The one we agreed on. I said I had a callback for an off-Broadway play. Can you imagine? An off-Broadway play. You know how many of those there are bouncing around. But he bought it.

Shrieks, screams, cascades of laughter.

You know, Cervantes, I felt kind of sorry for him. I mean, he's told me over and over how much tonight meant to him. Careerwise, I mean.

Yeah, I know.

And he did put out all that money for that room. And he said that guy—you know—the one with the in at the Manhattan Theater Club—he said he was coming, though I find that hard to believe. I mean, of all the plays Herb has written, he's never had a single one produced or optioned or anything.

Yeah. I know that, too.

Well, then, can you see somebody with any connection in the theater going out of his way for a nobody like Herb?

Yeah. To avoid him.

Stings of laughter.

Oh, Cervantes. Oh, God, I'm glad you called me tonight.

Yeah. Me, too, Susannah. It's been a hell of a long time. Too long.

For sure.

What do you think Herb would do, Susannah, if he knew the real reason you backed out of his reading?

I don't know. Not that I give a fuck. Speaking of which . . .

Buckets, gusts, whirlwinds of laughter.

God, this is good, Susannah. I'd forgotten how good. Mmm.

Shit, man. Look at him puttin' it to her.

Shut up. Drink your soda and get out of here. All of you. Get out! Get out!

It was all in his head. All of it. None of it was true. Not Susannah, not Cervantes, not any of it. Susannah didn't even know Cervantes. He had made it all up.

If only they'd leave him alone.

Instead of going back to Horlick's he'd go to the clinic. Go see the shrink. Ask for a shot. That would get rid of them right now, all of them. The shrink wouldn't like it that he'd stopped taking the drug, but he could explain it.

Couldn't he?

If he could only think.

Wasn't it because of the play?

Yes. The play.

And his father. Damn his father. It had something to do with him.

Shit, man, you gonna be like everybody else and lay everything off on your daddy?

Don't listen to them. Don't answer them. Don't pay attention. They're not real. They're only inside your head. Keep walking. Go to the clinic. Turn east on Eighty-eighth and head over to Central Park West.

Scrape, scrape.

The shrink would give him a shot, and that would calm him down, carry him through, until he could get everything sorted out.

The shrink would help him do that, too.

All he had to do was get to the clinic.

Shit, man. You think that's all there is to it?

Pitiful, man. That's what it is. Pitiful.

He wouldn't answer.

Maybe Susannah and Cervantes knew each other enough to say hello, but that was all. There was nothing more to it than that.

Scrape, scrape.

She hadn't made up the callback. Or the off-Broadway play. He read the trade papers. He talked to the actors. He knew what was going on.

Shit, man. You don't know nuthin'. The two of them been gettin' it off regular. At the Assplanade.

Howls, shrieks, blinding bursts of laughter.

He lashed out at them. Again and again. They dodged him the way they dodged the cars, foul-mouthing him, laughing at him.

He grabbed hold of a black iron gatepost and leaned against it panting for breath. He had to get to the clinic. He had to.

He peered through the rain at the brownstone in front of him. This *was* the clinic. He tugged at the gate, pulling it open, walked the few steps to the street-level door, searched for the bell, pounded on the door.

Nobody buzzed him in. Nobody came.

Rain streamed down his face. Tears, too, maybe. He wiped his face with the harsh sleeve of his yellow slicker, searching again for the bell.

The door was boarded up with a sheet of rusting tin.

Shit, man. You been given the business again. This ain't no clinic.

Hell, no, man. It ain't even the Assplanade.

Tinkles of laughter like breaking glass.

His mother beside him, the same as before. Frowning, tight-lipped. He thought he had left her somewhere behind.

You wouldn't need to go to the clinic if you'd listened to me, Herbert. How many times have I spoken to you about not taking your medicine?

Leave me alone. All of you. Leave me alone.

It's only another example of how you're throwing your life away.

Shit, man. Listen to her. Bitch, bitch, bitch.

Hey, son of a bitch. Can't you shut the old bag up?

And don't hand me that paltry excuse about it interfering with your writing. You know how you delude yourself, Herbert.

I don't think he does, ma'am.

That was Cervantes. And Susannah with him. Herb wiped his face again. He thought he'd left them behind, too.

Remember the four dollars I told you about? There wasn't any four dollars. What he wants to get from me is Susannah.

He had to get out of here before it happened again.

Darling, getting it from isn't his problem. It's getting it up.

Torrents, gusts, gales of laughter.

He lashed out at them, flailing his arms, punching with his fists, hitting, hitting.

The neighborhood toughs, his mother, Cervantes. All phantoms.

Susannah was real.

Five

He sat on the stoop of another abandoned brownstone, huddled there in the shadowy darkness under a broken street light, the rain dripping off his face—and the tears, his mind unable to accept what his eyes and hands told him was fact.

He was alone.

The others had fled.

From somewhere to his left, probably Broadway, came the piercing cry of a siren, its *bleat, bleat* climbing in pitch as it climbed in intensity. He turned to look. The siren belonged to an ambulance racing toward him, its blue light in a frantic spin. He jumped to his feet and ran to the curb, arms outstretched, wondering which of them had called for help—his mother probably, always anxious lest he get in trouble—but the ambulance raced by, headed for some other broken body.

He went back to the stoop, averting his eyes from where she lay sprawled on the sidewalk, one arm outflung, her dark-blue coat sodden with rain, her face white and still.

He hadn't meant to kill her. He didn't know what had come over him.

Or what would become of him.

The need to run, to hide in some far corner, rose up in his throat like bile, but when he stood up his legs trembled, scarcely supporting him, and he sank back down.

He needed somebody to tell him what to do.

He needed somebody to tell him what he'd done.

How he could have done it, when she was more precious to him than anything he'd ever known.

He wept for her, wept for himself, wept for both of them—abandoned together there in the rain—got to his feet again, fumbled his way down the steps and over to where she lay, knelt down, touched the still face, felt the small flutter under his fingers, the faint pulsing in her throat, and wept again, wanting to shout instead.

He hadn't killed her. She was alive.

He had hurt her, but he hadn't killed her. It could still come out all right, like a movie running backward.

"Susannah," he said, cradling her in his arms, rubbing her cold hands. "Susannah."

She didn't answer him or move.

He spoke louder, more urgently, cradling her closer, but there was no response. Fear stabbed at him. He might be hurting her more. She might be dying in his arms. He had to get help.

With utmost care he lowered her head to the sidewalk. He couldn't wait for his mother to call an ambulance. He would run over to Amsterdam for a cab, take her to the hospital himself, tell them—

Yeah, man. Tell 'em what?

A ripple of laughter.

He covered his face with his hands, forcing himself to concentrate. No. He could not let that start up again. He could not.

Uncovering his face, he looked around for the shoulder bag she always had with her. It lay in a corner at the foot of the steps. He picked it up and rummaged through it. They always grabbed the billfold, took the money and credit cards, then dumped the billfold in a trash can.

Her billfold had a Master Charge and twenty-two dollars cash in it. He thrust the money in his pants pocket, staring at the Master Charge, trying to think, wiping the rain off his face. If somebody found it and used it...She had no money.

With a shake of his head he pushed the card down into his right galosh, into his shoe. He would deal with it later. Putting the shoulder bag beside her, he ran to the corner for a cab, throwing the billfold into a vacant lot along the way.

He remembered so little of the ride to the hospital, he and Susannah might have been picked up by some giant hand and deposited there. He was trying so hard to shut out all the voices but his own, to concentrate on what he would say when they asked him what had happened. In the emergency room they had to pry his hands loose, so tight was his grip on her, then they wheeled her away through swinging doors, leaving him standing there, not asking him anything.

The waiting area was a zoo, every chair taken, people jammed against the walls. White faces and black ones, male and female, old, young, in between. Faces wide-eyed with fear, faces strained with waiting, faces that stared at him without taking him in, just something else in their line of vision.

The room was steamy with sweat and carbolic acid and the musty odor of decay. The feeling of standing at the edge of some unknown fate, waiting to be sucked in, passed from hand to hand, poked, pressed, looked at and into, defenseless, hurting, dehumanized.

He wanted to run, to slip out unnoticed into the night, but what if he couldn't manage it? What if they saw him and called him back? They'd never believe him then.

What if Susannah had regained consciousness and, right now, was telling them he had attacked her?

Did she know he had attacked her? Did she know he'd tried to kill her? Had he said anything to her? Had she seen his face?

He tried to think, but he couldn't. There was too much noise, too many voices outside his head as well as in. Phones jangling, papers rattling, heels clattering.

And his mother was at him again.

Haven't I told you, Herbert, that keeping your balance is what matters most? So the drug makes you impotent. So what? What do you want to do with girls? Haven't we talked about that, too? You're to stay away from girls, Herbert. Leave them alone. They're not for you.

Shit, man, you gonna sit there an' let that old lady go on at you like that?

He wanted to tell both of them to leave him alone, but at times like this he could never be certain whether his own voice was inside his head or out of it, and he was fearful of what he might say. The clerk behind the counter—the one who called out the names and told them where to go—was already giving him funny looks.

Maybe, the next time she had her eye on somebody else, he ought to try to slip away. Pretend he'd accomplished what he came for and go. He'd done all he could for Susannah. Anything more was up to the doctors.

And God.

Fear stabbed anew at him.

From the moment he realized what he had done, he had prayed to God she would be all right. Had tried to explain. Had begged for assurance as well as forgiveness.

What had he heard in response? Nothing.

He closed his eyes and concentrated as fiercely as he could, ignoring all the other voices, seeking out the one. God had spoken to him before. Why shouldn't He speak to him now?

Shit, man. You think that mother gives a shit for you?

He had to bite back the cry that welled up in him.

If you'd spoken to me, Herbert, instead of to God, if you'd listened to me, you wouldn't be in the trouble you're in now. How many times do I have to say it? Without your medication you can't maintain your balance. You fill your head with crazy notions.

His mother was right.

Crazy to think the clerk was giving him funny looks, when she had hardly more than glanced at him. Crazy to think Cervantes tried to cheat him every time he thought he could get away with it. Crazy to think Susannah would ever take any notice of him, even after writing a play for her.

His play.

Tonight he had thought he was heading for a future in the theater. He had been certain of it.

What would become of his play now?

What would become of him?

Why was it always his father who had to be protected?

Why couldn't he do something to protect himself?

His father was dead. Dead.

Damn his father.

He seethed with rage. He had better get out of this zoo before he let everybody see how crazy he was.

Let them catch him going and call him back. What difference did it make? What difference did anything make now?

He stood up, and the clerk beckoned to him. He couldn't believe his eyes. He turned to see if she might be signaling somebody else. No. Him. Nausea roiled up along with the rage. He would have to talk to her. There was no way out.

He could do it if he had to. Put a clamp on the voices. Act normal, the same as everybody else. Concentrate. Work at it.

He walked over to the counter she sat behind.

"I need some information," she said, her pen poised on the form in front of her. "Name?"

Name. Whose name? His?

She looked up from the form. "The name of the young woman you brought in. The accident victim."

Accident? How could she know that when they hadn't asked him anything? Had they asked him, and he didn't remember?

She frowned. "Don't you know her name? I thought you said you knew her."

His heart contracted. What had he told them? "Her name is Susannah. Whitney. Mrs. Whitney."

"Mrs.? There's a husband, then?"

"No. I mean, yes, but they're divorced."

"Can he be contacted?"

"No. I don't know. I mean, he lives somewhere here in New York, I think, but I don't know where."

"Do you know his first name?"

"Joe." He wiped the sweat off his face with the sleeve of his shirt. "But he doesn't have a phone. I mean, I don't think he has a phone. Not listed under his name anyhow."

"Does Mrs. Whitney live with anybody?"

"She has a daughter. Jill."

"Age?"

"I don't know. No. Yes, I do. Eleven. I think eleven."

"Anybody else?"

He frowned at the clerk. "Anybody else what?"

She gave him an exasperated look. "Does Mrs. Whitney live with anybody else?"

"Oh. No. I don't think so. I mean, yes, I said I know her, but I don't know her very well. I mean, she comes into the store where I work. Horlick's. At Eighty-sixth Street and Columbus Avenue. She—" He broke off, frowning. "What did— Her address? I don't know. I— yes, I do. On Eighty-seventh Street. Between Columbus and Central Park West. I don't know the number. I know the building, but—yes, in the phone book."

Sweat was pouring off him.

Money? Was she asking about money? Should he offer to pay for Susannah?

He reached into his pants pocket for his billfold and came upon the twenty-two dollars he had taken from her. He jerked his hand out. "I don't know about money. I told you I don't know her very well. I happened to come along and find her lying there on the sidewalk after somebody must have mugged her. Would you rather I'd left her there instead of bringing her here?"

The clerk was staring at him.

Shit, man, that's puttin' it to her.

Yeah, man, that's gettin' it off.

Fuck, man, that's gettin' you off. Gettin' you off into the slammer.

Another ripple of laughter.

He thought he would faint. He grabbed hold of the counter. Underneath. Where the clerk couldn't see.

"She's trying to make it as an actress. She works as

a waitress. And for a shrink. She doesn't have any—I mean, I don't think she has any money. Who? I don't know." If he had his medication. He tightened his hold. "She has a mother-in-law. Ex-mother-in-law. I don't know. Somewhere on Long Island. The kid would know. The kid—Jill—she can tell you more than I can. I told you, I don't know her all that well. She comes into the store where I work. Horlick's. At—"

He broke off. He was repeating himself.

"Name?"

He frowned at the clerk. She was repeating herself, too.

The clerk frowned back at him. "Your name?"

He had a harder time getting his own name out than Susannah's. He didn't want to give it to her, to have it written down. He wanted to give her a made-up name, but he couldn't think of one.

She took his address, too, and his phone number. So they would know where to reach him, she said, not specifying who they were. She picked up the phone, and his heart contracted again. Was she calling the police?

No. Fool. A three-digit number. Inside the hospital. Somebody named Barbara. About the kid. Jill.

She gave him a look that said she was finished with him. He expected to feel relieved, but he only felt more frightened. He turned and walked back to where he'd been sitting, the Master Charge he'd taken from Susannah riding up in his shoe. Somebody had taken his seat.

He stood against a wall, wedged between an old white man and a young black one. Both of them smelled.

Why didn't he go? Walk out into the night. The clerk was finished with him. What was he waiting for?

The old man turned and made a face at him like he smelled too. Maybe he did.

His legs started trembling.

What did you do, Herbert, to get yourself in trouble this time? And what's it going to take to get you out of it? Or haven't you thought that far ahead? You haven't, have you? In spite of all my warnings to you that you

*must consider the consequences. In spite of everything
I've told you.*

Shit, man. Tell that old lady to piss in her own pants.

His mother was right again. He had to think.

If Susannah recovered...

She had to recover. God had never let him down
before. He wouldn't now.

If Susannah recovered, and she didn't know what
had happened to her—how it happened—everything
would be the way it was before. Everything would be
all right.

If she did know...

No. He would not think that. He couldn't bear to.
Susannah was the last person in the world he wanted
to hurt. Unless—

Maybe she was already recovering. Already telling
them what had happened to her.

His legs still trembling, he went back to the clerk
at the counter.

The clerk shook her head. No, she hadn't heard anything. She didn't know when she would. When the doctors got around to telling her. When they had time.
When there was a letup, whenever that might be. Why
not go home and call the hospital in the morning? Somebody ought to know something by then.

He was afraid to go. As afraid to go as to stay. But
he couldn't go on standing there. She was giving him
funny looks again.

She had said to go. He would have to wait until later
to see what he might have to do.

He gathered up his slicker and his galoshes, put
them on, went out.

It was still raining. He walked over to Columbus
Avenue and headed north, dragging his feet, daring his
mother to say something.

Scrape, scrape.

Scrape, scrape.

Scrape, scrape.

His mother was no longer there.

Six

Barbara Caitlin was putting on her coat, going over in her mind the probable conversation she would have with her husband when she got home, about working late again tonight, when her phone rang. With a sigh she picked it up, thinking the conversation was about to start. "Social Services. Mrs. Caitlin."

"Barbara? This is Connie, in Emergency."

"Oh. Yes, Connie. What can I do for you?"

"We have a young woman in coma—a mugging victim apparently—with an unattended eleven-year-old child at home."

Barbara frowned. "Who gave you the information?"

"The man who found the woman and brought her in. A neighbor. Just a minute." In a fainter voice Connie said, "That will be all, Mr.—uh—Schlosser. Thank you." A longish pause. "Assuming we can go by what he said. He's kind of out of it, if you know what I mean. Shock, I suppose."

"Did he give you any names we can call?"

"No. He mentioned a former mother-in-law on Long Island and the ex-husband here in the city, but no address or phone number for either one."

"And the child is alone, you say."

"According to him. Like I said, he's a little spooked. Plus he says he doesn't know her all that well. Which makes it odd he's spooked, doesn't it? But maybe he's that kind. Faints at the sight of blood. We get them often enough. Anyhow, he's still here if you want to talk to him."

"Did you get the victim's home phone and address? What's her name, by the way? And the child's." As the information was read off to her, Barbara jotted it down. "Thanks. If he says that's all he knows, it probably is, so there's no point in my talking to him. Not now anyhow. Unless—he didn't offer to take care of the child, I suppose."

"No. And if it were my child I'd be glad he didn't."

"Is Mrs. Whitney still in Emergency?"

"Hold on while I check." After a long wait, Connie came back. "Sorry to be so long, but this place is a madhouse. No, she's not still here. She's up on seven. In Neurosurgery."

A call to Neurosurgery produced the information that Mrs. Whitney was still in coma. Barbara sat frowning at the phone, then picked it up and dialed the number she'd been given. The child answered the phone.

She had the light, thin voice one would expect of an eleven-year-old. It said nothing about her character or personality or maturity of mind or emotion.

"Hello, Jill?"

"Yes."

"Jill, my name is Barbara Caitlin. Your mother asked me to call you."

An intake of breath. "To say she got the part?"

Taken aback, not understanding what the child was talking about, Barbara struggled for an answer, then settled for "No."

"Oh." Letdown.

Was the mother an actress? Why hadn't she thought to ask Connie what other information there was, if any? Why hadn't Connie thought to tell her? Why, her husband would have interjected, don't you try working a normal eight-hour day? It would do wonders for your thinking ability as well as your marriage.

"What your mother asked me to call you about, Jill,
was to say she can't come home tonight."

"Oh."

More letdown? Resignation? Was the child accustomed to getting this kind of phone call? One-word answers weren't easy to analyze.

As if to extend a helping hand, the child went on to
say, the words running together, "Are you at the theater? Are you from Mr. Weingarten's office?"

Not accustomed to getting this kind of phone call,
then, or no questions would be asked.

Questions that had to be answered.

Choose the smallest lie. "No. I'm a friend of your
mother's."

"Oh."

All right, friend of her mother's. You should know
who fills in for mother when she does stay out overnight, which surely she must do once in a while unless
she's given up sex for motherhood.

"The thing is, I forgot to ask your mother who usually
stays with you when she doesn't come home, and she's
not available right now for me to ask."

"Oh." Pause. "Well, the lady in the building who
used to trade off with my mom—they moved to Yonkers
right after Christmas, and we don't really have anybody
any more."

Terrific.

"Is it because of the play that my mother can't come
home? Will she be there all night trying out for it?"

Okay, Barbara. You suspected from the start it
would come to this. "Look, Jill. Your mother also asked
me to pick something up for her. So why don't I come
over now, and then I can explain everything to you.
Okay?"

"Okay."

Before leaving the office, Barbara called home to
explain her further delay in getting there. George's only
comment was, "What about your own children?"

"Look, George," she said, keeping her voice even,
"we'll talk about it when I get home." Though what
that would accomplish, she didn't know. They had
talked about it several times already.

On her way out of the hospital she stopped in the emergency room. The man who had brought Mrs. Whitney in was no longer there, and aside from what she had written down on the form, Connie remembered little of what he had said about her.

"Look at how they're jammed in here," she said, waving a hand. "And it's been like this since I came on at four. No letup, storm or no storm. Oh. Yeah. He said she worked as a waitress." Connie frowned. "And for a doctor, I think he said. She's trying to make it as an actress. Or was before this happened to her."

Outside, it was still raining, the hospital parking lot full of puddles. Stepping around them, Barbara wondered what the parking situation on Eighty-seventh Street would be. No good, probably.

Wrong. There was a spot in front of the address she was looking for. A small building. Maybe there were other tenants Mrs. Whitney was on friendly terms with, somebody to take the child tonight, until a family member could be contacted. Identifying herself on the intercom, she pushed open the lobby door when Jill pressed the release.

An old building, run-down. Ancient elevator that creaked to the fourth floor, whining all the way.

Identifying herself a second time, she waited for Jill to unlock the apartment door.

The child was smaller than she had expected, making her seem even more vulnerable to what would be devastating news, and the fierce look on her round face indicated she already suspected something was wrong and was trying to brace herself for it. As soon as they were settled in the living room Barbara said, "Jill, your mother has been hurt. She's in the hospital."

The child gasped and stared at her, wide-eyed, frightened.

"I didn't want to tell you on the phone. I don't like telling you now, because I don't want to upset you, but—"

"How is my mother? Is she going to be all right? What happened to her?" The questions tumbled out like dice from a shaker.

"We think she was mugged. A neighbor found her

and brought her to Oldenham Hospital. A Mr. Schlosser."

Jill's eyes widened again. "You mean Mr. Schlosser from Horlick's? Herb Schlosser?"

"Yes."

The frightened look came back. "You didn't say how she is."

"Because I don't know exactly. She was knocked unconscious, and she hasn't come to yet. The doctors are with her now, taking tests and seeing what they can do for her."

Jill was sitting in an armchair that looked as if it had been brought in from the sidewalk. She jumped up and came over to Barbara. "Can I go see her?" She was near tears. "Please?"

"Not tonight, Jill."

"But what if—" The fragment of sentence hung in the air.

"That's not going to happen." Hadn't the resident said Mrs. Whitney's vital signs were good? Barbara gave the child a reassuring smile. "You can see her tomorrow. Maybe by then she'll be conscious."

Jill searched her face. "You're not making things up like you did on the phone?"

"No."

After a moment she went back on reluctant feet to the shabby armchair. "How do you know about my mother?"

"I'm a social worker at the hospital. The clerk in the emergency room called me to say you were here alone. It's my job to find somebody to stay with you."

"I don't need anybody to stay with me. I'll be all right staying by myself."

"I'm not just talking about tonight, Jill. I'm talking about however long your mother is in the hospital and unable to take care of you. Now. Mr. Schlosser said you have a grandmother here. What about her?"

"You mean my grandmother Whitney? She doesn't live here. She lives out in Syosset."

"That's not so far away. Couldn't she come in and stay here with you? Or maybe you could go out there."

Panic flooded the child's face, and she gripped the

arms of the chair so hard her knuckles turned white. "No."

Barbara frowned. "What is it, Jill? Don't you like your grandmother Whitney?"

"No. I mean yes. I mean it isn't not liking her." The tears that had been so near spilled out. She wiped her eyes with the back of her hands. "Why can't I stay here by myself? If I don't mind doing it, why should you care?"

"Jill, this isn't something between you and me. The city has laws about children. If I can't find a friend or neighbor or a member of your family to take care of you, then I'll have to call the Child Welfare people, and they'll put you in a foster home."

The panic flooded back. "No!"

"Let me call your grandmother."

A pause. A sigh. A closed-in look. "Okay."

There was no answer at the grandmother's home.

"She's probably out playing bridge somewhere," Jill said, sounding relieved. "She plays bridge a lot."

Barbara glanced at her watch. Almost eight o'clock. She wouldn't get home in time to put the children to bed. The second time this week, and it was only Wednesday. "Is there anybody in the building, Jill, who could stay with you tonight? Or let you stay with them. Then I could talk to your grandmother tomorrow about making some more permanent arrangement."

Jill considered. "There's Mrs. Babcock in 4A, but I don't know if she's home either."

She wasn't.

"What about your father?" Why hadn't she thought of him before? Whatever his relationship with his former wife, whatever the custody agreement, he would surely take responsibility for his child.

His child was a study in conflicting emotions. Something was going on here that Barbara didn't understand.

"Could I speak to him myself?" Jill asked. "Instead of you?"

"I don't see why not. You know what to say to him."

Jill headed for the back of the apartment.

Barbara frowned. "Where are you going?"

She turned. "To use the phone in my mother's bed-room."

"Why?" They had called the grandmother on the kitchen phone.

Jill looked at her, her expression unreadable, then she shrugged and headed for the kitchen.

The call was brief and so matter-of-fact the person lying in the coma might have been some stranger, and Jill looked flushed—and flustered—when she came back into the living room. "He said he would come stay with me. He said you don't have to wait."

She had intended to ask him about Mrs. Whitney's parents and other family members. She asked Jill instead. The parents were a Methodist minister and his wife named Burke living in Northpoint, Indiana, the wife housebound with arthritis. There were two older brothers, both with families, one in California, one in Chicago.

Jill rattled off the information, obviously anxious to have her gone. Only as she was leaving did she get the impression the child wanted her to stay, wanted it desperately. "Are you sure you don't want me to wait until your father gets here?"

Jill shook her head, the fierce look back on her face. "No. No, I'll be fine."

"But you do want me to call the school for you to-morrow?"

"Yes, will you, please?"

"And you'll call me in my office at the hospital?"

"Yes."

Jill held the door for her. Heading down the hall, Barbara listened for the door to close, the double lock to click into place, but when she reached the elevator and turned to look back, Jill was still standing in the open doorway, looking as if she couldn't bear to see her leave. Barbara half turned, and Jill ducked inside and closed the door, the double lock clicking into place.

The next morning when Barbara arrived at her office a little before nine, Jill was in the corridor outside hud-dled on a chair, looking lost and frightened. For a moment Barbara thought the mother had died, but how could the child have learned about it? Unless the husband—

"Jill, have you heard anything?"

Jill shook her head. "I was waiting to ask you."

"Come into my office, then, and we'll call."

The mother's condition was unchanged.

"What does that mean?" Jill asked, her brown eyes shimmering with tears.

"It means she's still unconscious, Jill. Sometimes it takes more than a few hours to come around. Sometimes it takes a few days."

"Can I go see her?"

"As soon as somebody else gets here, I'll take you up to see your mother. Okay?"

She nodded, the tears receding.

Barbara took off her coat and hung it up. "Did your father get there all right last night?"

"Yes." Sitting by her desk, Jill fingered the pencil cup Barbara's son had made in kindergarten. "He said he'd stay with me as long as I want him to. So you don't have to call my grandmother."

Barbara looked at her in surprise. "Your father didn't call her last night?"

A pause. "Yes. But she still wasn't home. And then we went to bed. You see, my father has to get up early. So he didn't call her this morning either. Because it was too early." More fingering of the pencil cup. "Actually my father isn't very good about calling people. Especially people he's close to. Like my grandmother. He's very close to her. But—" Another pause, and then she sighed. "When my mother wakes up and you talk to her, she'll explain it to you. She can explain it better than I can."

Barbara sat down at her desk. "What does your father do, Jill?"

Jill shook her head. "I don't know exactly. Different things, I think." She shook her head again. "Nobody ever wants to talk about it."

"Did he bring you to the hospital this morning?"

"Yes. Well, I mean he dropped me off. He didn't come in." She struggled to say something else, then didn't.

"He's not very good at calling about your mother either? Is that what you were trying to say?"

"Well—sort of."

Barbara's secretary came in.

The child's mother was in a four-bed ward in Neurosurgery. Her head bandaged, her face bruised and swollen, she was not a pretty sight. Jill gasped as she had the night before and squeezed Barbara's hand so hard she winced.

A house staffer—Bob Aaronson—was with the patient in the next bed. Noting the child's reaction, he came over to reassure her, explaining what all the various tubes were for and how the swelling would go away and what he and the others were doing to try to bring her mother around.

"I talk to her," he said, smiling at Jill. "I think she hears me." He leaned over the still figure in the bed. "Susannah? Can you hear me, Susannah?" He turned back to Jill. "Did you see your mother's eyelids flutter?"

Jill shook her head.

"Well, they did."

Back at her desk, Jill on her way to school, Barbara telephoned the grandmother and explained what had happened. "Could you come into New York and stay with Jill at least for a few days until we can work something out?"

The grandmother agreed to come, somewhat grudgingly, Barbara thought. She debated mentioning Jill's father, the lady's son, then decided against it. She was almost certain now that Jill's phone call to him the night before had been one-sided, that the child had spent the night alone.

Off and on during the day, as swamped as she was with other problems, that thought came back to haunt her. That and the image of Jill leaning over her mother's still form as Bob Aaronson had done, saying in that thin, light voice stretched tight with anxiety, "Mom? Mother? Mama, can you hear me?"

Seven

Somebody seemed to be speaking to her. Susannah opened her eyes, trying to get the sound into focus. No, that couldn't be right. She was—what was she trying to do? She closed her eyes. She couldn't remember.

The person went on speaking to her. Or maybe it was somebody else some other time. She opened her eyes again. Everything was blurry. Her head hurt. Keeping her eyes open hurt. The durbingler hurt, whatever a durbingler was.

They wouldn't let her be. They kept at her. She was at one end of a rope and they were at the other, tugging, pulling, not caring how much they hurt her.

"Susannah? Susannah? Do you hear me?"

I hear you. Go away. And take the shower curl with you.

They wouldn't go away and take it with them. They stayed, it stayed, everybody stayed. Thank you. Next?

What a wonderful singer you are, Susannah! What a beautiful voice! So light, so clear.

Only the light hurt, and nothing was clear.

"Susannah? Do you hear me?"

That was yesterday.

Somebody turned her onto her side. Tapped her foot. Sat her up.

Somebody was talking to somebody else. About rain snappers.

About rain.

She felt herself jerk. What about rain? What was rain? She moved her head from side to side. She couldn't remember.

"Susannah? Wake up, Susannah. Come now. Wake up. Your cadgerman is here to see you. Don't you want to see your cadgerman?"

What is a cadgerman?

She looked, frowning. It was small and had long blond weaverwills. She lay back, exhausted, and closed her eyes.

"Susannah? Can you see me? Look at me, Susannah."

Somebody was standing over her. She was in a bed somewhere, and somebody was standing over her. A man. Did she know him?

"I'm Dr. Aaronson, Susannah. Do you know where you are?"

She hardly knew *who* she was, and by the time she had considered that, she had forgotten why she was doing it.

"Good morning, Susannah. It's Dr. Aaronson. Do you remember me?"

She opened her eyes. Her head hurt. A man she had never seen before was standing by her bed. Her bed? Not her bed. Some bed.

Bed. What was she doing in bed when she had to call Jill to tell her—what? Something important. Something that couldn't wait till she got to the theater. She had to get up, get out of here.

She tried to take hold of the bedrail with her right hand, but her hand wouldn't move. She stared at it, panic-stricken. Why couldn't she move it? What had happened? What was the matter with her? What was she doing here?

Where was here?

She tried to think, but she couldn't. It hurt too much.

She was crying. She could feel the tears. On one side of her face.

The man was still standing there. In a long white coat. Doctor. Had he said doctor?

"You've been hurt, Susannah. You're in the hedgerow."

She frowned at him, the part of her that could frown. In the what? Where?

She tried again to move her right hand, tried as hard as she could. Never mind the sledgehammer in her head, she had to move her hand, lift it, move a finger. Nothing.

She lay back so exhausted she couldn't move any other part of herself either, couldn't think, couldn't feel.

"How do you feel, Susannah?"

She opened her mouth to say something, but nothing came out. Somebody had taken her voice out and put it in a glass of water for the night. She must remember to ask for it back in the morning when she finished whatever it was she was trying to finish.

"Susannah? Wake up, Susannah."

She opened her eyes to see a man looming over her. She started trembling.

He smiled at her. "Dr. Aaronson, Susannah. Do you remember?"

No.

She looked at her right hand, remembering that. She couldn't move it. She could move her left hand. Why not the right one?

She tried again. She still couldn't move it. Couldn't feel anything in it. If she couldn't move her hand, she couldn't get out of here. Couldn't do anything. Couldn't protect herself.

The trembling became panic, and she was crying again.

He put out a hand to her, and she flinched, the same as—the same as what? Who? When? Why couldn't she think?

"Don't be frightened, Susannah. There's nothing to be frightened of. You've been hurt, but you're pedaling crossbears every day. Can you tell me how you fly?"

He was crazy.

He was also waiting for an answer, standing there
smiling at her, looking like a doctor in his long white
coat. Doctor. Had he said he was a doctor?

She frowned, though it hurt to frown. She couldn't
remember anything. Couldn't think. Didn't know where
she was or what she was doing here. What he was doing
here either.

Maybe he was a doctor, come to see about her hand.
Ask him about it. What was the matter with it? Why
couldn't she move it?

She struggled to get the words out. Why wouldn't
they come? She tried harder.

"Y-y-y-yem say?"

He nodded.

She wanted to scream. She was as crazy as he was.

"You've been hurt," he said.

She already knew that. Hurt how? With her left hand
she pointed to the right one, struggling to speak. "Y-y-
y-yem say?"

It was no use. She lay back, exhausted. Why couldn't
she say what she wanted to? Why wouldn't words come?
What was the matter with her?

She was almost asleep when he spoke to her, rousing
her. "Your right review is penciled."

What the hell did that mean? She hadn't been given
the part yet, let alone opened in the show.

She wasn't going to make the seven o'clock audition
time either, the way things were going. And she had
to call Jill. She had to tell her—tell her not to—not to
something.

Maybe if she rested for a few minutes, closed her
eyes long enough to...

"Susannah? Are you awake, Susannah?"

She opened her eyes. A man stood over her, his face
close to hers. She cowered against the bedclothes, trembling so violently her body shook.

He straightened up, looking distressed. "What's the
matter, Susannah? What are you frightened of?"

She stared at him, waiting for the answer to come,
then shook her head. She couldn't tell him even if she
knew.

"I'm Dr. Aaronson. Do you remember?"

The man in the white coat. The crazy man.

"Do you know where you are?"

He didn't sound crazy any more.

"I-i-i-icehouse." He didn't, but she did. She wasn't in an icehouse. She was in a hospital. If she could say icehouse, why couldn't she say hospital?

"You're in the hospital."

All right. Yes. But what was she doing here? And why did she feel she had to get out before—before what?

Why was she trembling again?

She didn't know. She couldn't think any better than before.

And she still couldn't move her right hand. It had no feeling in it. Like it belonged to somebody else. She could feel it, but it didn't feel back. The same with the right side of her face. Her right foot. Her right leg. Her right side.

She was paralyzed.

Oh, my God. What had happened to her?

If she couldn't talk straight, she could get through to him some other way, couldn't she? With her left hand she grabbed hold of his arm and pointed to her right hand.

He nodded. "Your right side is paralyzed."

She wanted to scream. Why was he always telling her what she already knew? Why didn't he tell her how? Why was he keeping it from her? Why couldn't she know?

She formed her lips into as much of a circle as she could with her lopsided mouth and tried to get the single word out. How? How?

"O-o-o-oay."

Not what she wanted to say. Nothing like it. Frustrated, she started to cry again. That seemed to be the only familiar thing she could do.

He sat down at her bedside and took her left hand in both of his. "You were attacked on the street. Mugged. You were knocked unconscious."

She stared at him, barely able to understand, not certain she did.

"The head injuries you sustained have caused the right-side paralysis. They've also caused a loss of language—an inability to say what you want to, even though you know what you want to say."

She struggled to ask him something. Tried so hard she forgot what she wanted to ask. Oh, God, what was going to become of her?

He patted the good hand. "Don't be upset, Susannah. Don't be frightened. We're going to help you get better. We're going to fix you up as good as new. It will take time, that's all. Time and work."

Time. That was it. What she wanted to ask him. Would they fix her up in time for the audition?

She had to ask him, had to know, but if she couldn't say the single word how, how could she manage a question as complicated as in time for the audition?

How could she remember it long enough to ask it?

Hold on to it. Concentrate. In time for the audition?

She could write it. No. Her hand. Yes. Her other hand. She could print with her left hand. She could manage that.

Did she have anything to print with?

In time for the audition? Remember. Concentrate.

She pantomimed writing to him. He took a ballpoint pen from the breast pocket of his white coat, then opened the top drawer of the white metal stand next to her bed and took a pad of paper out of it, handing them both to her. She sat up straighter.

Her head hurt fearfully, but she had to know. In time for the audition?

Laboriously, awkwardly, repeating the question over and over to herself, she printed it, then looked at it.

IN TRUMFER SHOE

She went cold with fear and, not knowing why and unable to ask, started crying again.

Dr. Aaronson tried to console her, tried to explain that her inability to express herself in writing was merely another aspect of her inability to speak properly, but—as much to her surprise as his, since a few minutes earlier she had cowered from him—she clung to him with such ferocity, half paralyzed or not, he had to peel himself from her. And when he did, she whim-

pered so piteously he gave her an injection that lulled
her to sleep.

She heard her name called and opened her eyes to
see a woman she didn't know. Or didn't recognize. She
wasn't sure which.

She could no longer be sure of anything. That was
why she had to be doubly careful.

She frowned, trying to think. Why why? Careful of
what?

It was no use. She didn't know.

The woman was speaking. Introducing herself. Barbara Something. Social worker. Explaining how—
something about Jill.

Susannah listened as hard as she could, trying to
understand everything the woman said. Unable to.

Too many voices in the room. Three other beds with
three other patients, one of them an old lady who kept
exclaiming "Isn't that interesting!" over and over. To
nobody in particular.

Visitors at the other two beds talking in voices too
low for her to understand what they were saying, but
loud enough to join the clamor in her head.

The Barbara person smiled.

When in doubt smile.

Commas, Use of. When in doubt don't.

Don't, Susannah. Don't drift away. Hang on. You
have to hang on. Your life depends on it.

She frowned again, trying to think. Why did her life
depend on it? What was it?

Oh, yes. Hanging on. That was it. She had to hang
on. That was what her life depended on. Hanging on.

Why? Hanging on what?

What difference did it make? She couldn't hang onto
anything. Her right side paralyzed, unable to speak
straight or write straight or think straight.

She was holding onto the Barbara person's hand so
hard with her left hand it hurt. And no recollection of
reaching out to take the hand. Oh, God, oh, God, what
would become of her?

She started trembling.

"Don't be frightened, Susannah. There's nothing to

be frightened of. We're all your friends here. We're here to help you. Do you understand that?"

She understood nothing, only that she was all mixed up inside, that she needed to be taken apart and put back together again.

"Susannah? Wake up, Susannah. Somebody's here to see you."

"Mother?"

Jill stood at her bedside looking anxious.

Susannah put her left hand out. Hello, baby. She hadn't called Jill that in a long time. She didn't dare. Jill hated it. Now it didn't matter. She was only saying it to herself. Hello, baby.

"Mother, are you okay?"

Jill. Hadn't called.

Oh, my God. She had forgotten. She hadn't called Jill, hadn't told her not to—not to worry. Yes. That was it. Not to worry, she wasn't going to—she wasn't going to—

"Mother, what's the matter?"

"B-b-bayside."

Jill looked scared. "What's bayside? What do you mean?"

Try again. Try harder. Never mind that you can't remember what you were going to tell her. It doesn't matter. Say you love her. That's what matters. I love you, baby. I love you.

"I-I-Idlewild."

Jill looked more scared and backed away.

It was then she saw her. Not until then. Saw her reach out and take Jill by the arm. Put her arm around her to shelter her, shield her.

Shield her from her mother. Also known as Unfit Person.

The self-righteous Mrs. Whitney, senior. She would take Jill away from her if she could.

Susannah started trembling.

Maybe she already had.

Something clicked. That was what she was going to tell Jill. She wasn't going to farm her out to her grandmother Whitney.

Why had she needed to tell her that?

She didn't know. She couldn't think.

It made no difference. Her grandmother had her.

Mrs. Superior Person smiled. What a routine she put herself through. For the Child's Sake. Bend over backward to be polite. Maintain neutrality. If at all possible try not to show what you think of that idea, that job, that apartment, that neighborhood. Do not even consider who is trooping in and out of that bedroom now that my son has been shown the door. "The doctors say you're better today, Susannah. You look better."

How did she know? Had she been here before?

She must have been, to say that.

Susannah sighed. What must be going on that she knew nothing of.

She was trembling again.

"Mother." Jill stepped forward from the sheltering arm. "Mr. Schlosser—you know—Herb—he asks about you every time I see him."

Every time? How much time? How long had she been here?

She struggled to ask, then gave up. It would come out jabberwocky and frighten Jill again. She nodded and smiled her lopsided smile to show she understood.

"He always says to give you his regards."

She nodded again.

Mrs. Superior Person was looking pained.

What a joke. As if Herb was anybody in her life.

She frowned. She had something to tell Herb, too. Something she couldn't do for him. What? She didn't know.

Something about rain?

What did rain have to do with anything?

Was it raining out? She turned her head to look. In the next bed the old lady smiled at her and said, "Isn't that interesting!"

You said it, lady. About a hundred times a day.

Her ex-mother-in-law was speaking to her again. She turned her head back. She couldn't think about the rain and listen, too. She couldn't think about anything and listen, too. One thing at a time. In or out.

"...in the apartment."

Whatever that meant.

"Your father called last night, Susannah. And your mother, too, of course."

That one she got. A hundred percent. Instead of being critical, she ought to thank God for her ex-mother-in-law. In a world of breaking prisms and shifting sand, her ex-mother-in-law was immutable. *And your mother, too, of course.* Mrs. Whitney, Sr., who barely tolerated men, had no use at all for their wives.

"Your father wants to come see you, but I've persuaded him to wait until you're better—until at least you would know he had been here."

Susannah frowned again. What was that supposed to mean? Did her ex-mother-in-law think she had lost her mind as well as her power of speech?

Was she going to use that to take Jill away from her?

Had she lost her mind? Parts of it anyhow?

Wouldn't they come back? Restrung on a necklace like pink beads scattered in rage?

Susannah sighed. She wasn't making sense again. Too tired to.

"Susannah? Are you awake, Susannah?"

The Barbara person.

Stop calling her that. Stop thinking like a crazy. Her name is Barbara. Never mind the last name. Barbara.

She held out her good hand to say hello.

"You're looking better, Susannah. The swelling has gone down quite a bit. How do you feel? Are you feeling better?"

She nodded.

"There's somebody here to see you. The friend who found you the night you were mugged and brought you to the hospital. Do you remember my telling you that?"

No. She didn't remember. She shook her head. What friend?

"He found you lying on the street. Well. Not literally the street. A sidewalk."

"Isn't that interesting!"

The old lady again. Please be quiet, old lady.

"Your friend Herb. Herb Schlosser."

Herb? Herb from Horlick's? Herb had found her lying on a sidewalk?

"He's been so anxious about you. He comes by every day. I thought if you were up to seeing him for just a few minutes..."

She nodded.

"I've already explained to him that you're not able to speak yet, but he wants to see you anyhow." She smiled. "I think he needs to see with his own eyes that you're all in one piece, and I guess we owe him that. If it hadn't been for Herb—" Instead of finishing the sentence, Barbara smiled again.

She didn't need to finish it to get the message through. If it hadn't been for Herb, God knows what would have become of you. Instead of lying here half dead, you'd be all the way dead.

She owed him for more now than the trade papers he never charged her for and the oversize tips he left when he ate at the café. She owed him her life.

She tried to hold her head up, to look alert, to make him feel it had been worth whatever effort he had gone to.

Barbara was right. He must be anxious about her. He looked it. Like he was searching for something. The answer to something.

Join the club.

She was searching for so many answers she couldn't remember from one to the next.

She smiled her lopsided smile, and a look of horror flashed across his face.

"It's the paralysis," Barbara said. "Remember? I explained it."

He nodded, and the look on his face changed to— what?

Something unreadable.

She would never have thought she couldn't read an expression, but then there were a lot of things she could no longer do.

And for all she'd seen of Herb in Horlick's and the café and sometimes in the supermarket or on the street, she'd never paid enough attention to him to really get to know him.

He was a loner. She knew that much.

Kept to himself.

Never had much to say.

Did something besides work in Horlick's. Something that had something to do with her.

Could that be right?

Herb?

Yes, Herb.

Standing by the bedside, he shifted position, and she remembered she had something to tell him. Something she couldn't do for him. What was it?

She tried to think, then gave up, exhausted.

What difference did it make when she wouldn't have been able to tell him even if she knew?

He had something to tell her. No. Not tell her. Ask her.

"Are you—will you be all right?"

She didn't know. She hadn't asked. Maybe she hadn't thought about it.

Barbara answered for her. "She's making good progress. Dr. Aaronson told me she starts therapy tomorrow. Physical therapy. Speech therapy. Occupational therapy. It will take time, that's all. Time and hard work."

Something about time. Time for the audition.

Something to do with Herb, with what she had to tell him.

He was speaking to her again. "Do you know what happened to you?"

Barbara said, "Do you mean does she remember anything about it?"

He nodded.

"No." Barbara shook her head. "She doesn't remember anything."

"Isn't that interesting!"

Herb started, then turned to stare at the old lady.

"She isn't talking to you, Mr. Schlosser," Barbara said. "She's had a stroke and has lost her ability to speak, the same as Susannah has. What she just said— what she says over and over all day long—is called automatic speech. She has no control over it. It just comes out."

"Oh," he said.

The old lady smiled at them. "Isn't that interesting!"

Turning back to her, the unreadable expression on

his face again, Herb said, "You don't—you don't remember anything?"

Susannah shook her head.

"No," Barbara said again, "she doesn't. She doesn't remember anything—or much of anything—that happened to her that entire day. And her thinking is still fragmented." She smiled. "But that's something else time will do—time and the healing process. They'll straighten out her thinking and bring her memory back. A few weeks, a few months. Eventually she'll remember."

For some reason she couldn't understand, Susannah wanted to hear what Herb had to say to that. He said nothing.

And before she could figure out why she had wanted to hear what he had to say, she had forgotten what it was she was trying to figure out.

Eight

The day after it happened he had called Mr. Zekiel to say he was sick and couldn't come to work. He said the doctor had diagnosed it as walking pneumonia.

"And you going out in that terrible downpour last night," Zekiel said, buying the fiction. "It's a wonder you didn't catch your death."

A tremor shot through Herb at the mention of that word. He'd been to the clinic for a shot, but he wasn't stabilized yet. Maybe wouldn't be, even with the drug. Not with all he had to worry about.

"I didn't know what I was doing," he said, hoping Zekiel would buy that, too. "I had a high fever. I was delirious."

"Well, that explains it," Zekiel said. "Some of the things you said to me last night. I wondered at the time what was wrong with you. I even said something to you. But maybe you don't remember."

Not remembering was the safest refuge. "Not too well."

"Well," Zekiel said, "it's nothing to worry about as long as you're okay now. You are okay?"

"I will be," Herb said. "But I have to stay in bed a couple of days."

"Take all the time you need. The wife can help out until you're back on your feet."

He was ready to hang up when it occurred to him he hadn't mentioned Susannah.

Another tremor shot through him.

He'd never been in this kind of trouble before. He wasn't skilled in knowing what to do, what to say, what not to say, how to cover his tracks.

"I—uh—on my way back from the Esplanade last night, I—uh—took part in a rescue."

"Oh?" A rise in voice and interest. "What happened?"

"Susannah. Mrs. Whitney. You know? She comes into the store."

"Yeah, I know. What about her? What happened?"

"Somebody mugged her. On Eighty-eighth Street. Knocked her out. Left her lying there. I found her and took her to Oldenham Hospital."

"No kidding. She all right?"

"She's still unconscious."

An intake of breath. "She going to be all right?"

"The lady I talked to—a social worker—she says the doctors are very hopeful."

"And all because of you," Zekiel said. "I mean, if you hadn't found her, she'd probably—in all that cold and rain..."

"Yeah."

"Thank God you happened along when you did."

"Yeah."

He was learning.

One thing he'd learned a long time ago was to stick to the same story with everyone he talked to. The actors he hadn't called last night to say the reading had been canceled. Mel Goodrich, his connection to the Manhattan Theater Club. His mother.

He put off calling his mother as long as he could without getting her worried to the point of calling him. And then, of course, he couldn't just call her. He had to go have dinner with her.

The minute she set eyes on him she said, "Something's happened."

He was prepared for that. But he was nerved up, too.
More than a week had gone by, and Susannah was still
mostly unconscious.

He told his mother the rescue part of the story.

She didn't ask how Susannah was or how she was
going to be. She wanted to know how he had happened
to be the one to find her. "What were you doing walking
along there at that time of night?" she asked. "In that
terrible storm."

He told her about the reading being canceled.

He expected her to grouse about throwing his money
away. Instead she said, "That still doesn't explain what
you were doing on Eighty-eighth Street."

She was too quick for him. He couldn't think what
to say. But if he didn't say something she'd be even
more suspicious.

Something else he'd learned early on. Insofar as possible, stick to the truth. It kept things from getting
unmanageable. "I was on my way to the clinic."

She eyed him a moment. "Because you haven't been
taking your medicine. You're in some kind of trouble
now, aren't you, Herbert?"

He was thirty-five years old, and she treated him
like he was ten. "Why do you always say that?"

"I say it when I know it's true."

"You don't know anything."

"Only because you haven't told me. What are you
hiding, Herbert? What have you done?"

The unremitting strain and worry of the past week,
the limelight he'd been thrust into at Horlick's, the
need to stay on his toes, to keep his stories straight,
had given him a headache that hammered in his skull
and outlined everything he saw in red. Or maybe it was
his medication. The doctors had him on a new main-
tenance drug. "I haven't done anything."

She eyed him again. "Are you in trouble with the
police?"

She shouldn't have said that.

All week long he'd expected to be arrested. Every
time somebody came into Horlick's, jangling the bell,
he was sure it was the police. On busy days the urge

to disconnect the bell, rip it out, was so strong his fingers shook.

They were shaking now.

"Damn you," he yelled at her, clenching his hands into fists, wanting to strike her, "will you stop?"

She gasped and stared at him, her face chalky, her eyes wide.

He stared back at her, the rage draining out of him. "I'm sorry," he said, not sorry at all. "I—it's been a—a bad week. At Horlick's, I mean. I—my head—I—I went to the clinic that night because the doctors have me on a new medication, and it gives me these terrible headaches. I—I'm sorry."

She said what she always said when she wanted to be through with something, whether by way of pronouncement or acceptance of apology. "We'll say no more about it."

Whether or not she believed him, he didn't know. If she called the doctors, and she probably would, she'd find out he'd stopped taking his medication and had to come in for a shot. She might even find out exactly when they'd started him on the new medication, that it had been after the night in question.

Let her find out.

He didn't care. He had learned something else in those couple of seconds he had lashed out at her.

She was afraid of him.

In spite of all the strain and worry, he felt a surge of joy. Of power. Nobody he knew had ever been afraid of him before. Least of all his own mother.

That realization, picturing again—savoring—how his mother had looked, enabled him to get through the rest of the evening with her and the few days that followed until Susannah regained full consciousness and he was allowed to see her, when Mrs. Caitlin had raised his hopes and dashed them.

The next morning he went to the library, where he found a book that both confirmed and denied what Mrs. Caitlin had said about Susannah's memory. The book said a person suffering traumatic brain injuries from a blow on the head often had an amnesia about the accident and events prior to it, that gradually the amnesia would shrink and the prior events return, but almost never would the person remember the accident itself.

Almost never.

That was what his future, maybe his life, depended on.

From the library he went to Horlick's.

Zekiel looked up from the cash register as he came in. "Somebody was in here asking for you this morning."

Herb's heart started pounding.

"I took his name down," Zekiel said. "I've got it here somewhere." He fumbled among some papers by the register. "Goodrich. Mel Goodrich. He wants you to call him."

Herb took the paper Zekiel handed him. Fool. Irrational to think anything could happen to him today. Even if by some miracle Susannah's memory had returned to her overnight, she wasn't able to communicate with anybody. Nevertheless he was trembling as he dialed the number written on the slip of paper.

To forestall a different kind of trembling he didn't allow himself to wonder what Mel Goodrich wanted.

He wanted *Possessed.*

"I was talking to my friend at the Manhattan Theater Club about your play. He wants to read it."

The same joy, the same sense of power surged through him again. He had never had the slightest doubt that once his play was brought to the attention of somebody in a position to produce it, it would be produced.

He was on his way.

Unless...

He steeled himself not to think about it until his dinner break, when he delivered the manuscript of his play to the doorman of the building on Central Park West where Mel Goodrich lived.

On the way back he thought about it.

First had been the fear Susannah would die.

Next had come the fear she would live and point a finger at him.

Now the worst fear of them all—that he would have to kill her to prevent that happening.

Nine

The speech therapist arranged some objects on the small white table positioned between them. "I want you to tell me what each object is as I point to it, Susannah. All right?"

Susannah nodded, forcing herself to follow the therapist's hands with her eyes, trying to clear her head of the random thoughts, the blurred images, the flotsam and jetsam of fear that floated around inside it. Speech therapy lasted half an hour. From the clock on the wall she hadn't been here more than ten minutes, but she yearned for the thirty minutes to be up, for the therapist to get a phone call, for the hospital to catch on fire, anything that she might escape this assault on her poor befuddled brain.

The therapist pointed to a key.

Susannah tried to name it. She concentrated every bit of strength she could summon into the task of saying key.

"Coy. No." No was the one word she never missed. "No."

The therapist smiled encouragement. "Try again."

"Cable. No. Car." Worse. Tears of frustration stung

83

at her eyes. She blinked them back. Crying didn't do any good. Nothing did any good.

The therapist pointed to a spoon. "Try this one."

The therapist's name was Dorothy. Except for the doctors, everybody at the hospital she had come across so far was an anonymous adrift-in-the-world first name only. Barbara. Dorothy. Inez. Shirley. Like Jill and her school friends.

Jill.

Something about Jill. What?

A telephone ringing.

"Susannah?" The therapist pointed to the spoon.

The telephone must be somewhere else. In her apartment.

With her good left hand Susannah clutched her head, trying to shut everything out. The voices. The cries. The stirrings. The fear. Always the fear, the terrible feeling of helplessness, like the useless right hand that dangled at her side when it wasn't pinned against her.

Spoon. Spoon. Concentrate. Think.

"S-sp-spo-spoo." She frowned. "Spoo?"

"Spoon. You were very close, Susannah. You're getting better every day. All this week you've made giant strides. Now. How about this one?"

Pencil.

Think it. Say it. You know what it is. Say so.

"P-p-pl-no-pel-no. No." She couldn't go on. It was unfair of them to make her try so hard when it hurt so much.

The therapist took the objects off the table and put a lined tablet in their place. She printed a word on it.

CANE

"Do you know what word that is, Susannah?"

She nodded. "Can you say it?"

"C-c-cay-cane."

Dorothy smiled. "Beautiful. Now. You might use a cane to help you do what?"

"W-wal-walk."

"Marvelous. You're making great strides. Now. Can you think of a word—any word—that rhymes with cane?"

She tried to think. Cane. Ane. No such word. Bane?

Was there such a word as bane? If there was, could she say it? "B-bane?"

"Yes. Excellent. Another word?"

Cane. Ane, bane, cane, dane. Dane? Deign?

She was too tired to think. It hurt too much.

"Look out the window," Dorothy said. "What do you see?"

She looked out the window. It was raining. Rain. A violent tremor shook her body.

"What is it, Susannah? What's the matter?"

"R-r-rai-rain. Rain."

"The rain frightens you?"

She was still shaking, her teeth chattering. She nodded.

"Why does rain frighten you?"

She tried to think. She couldn't. She didn't know, and that frightened her more.

"Do you know why?"

"No."

Something about Jill. Telephone. Ringing? No. Different telephone. Different place. Where? She didn't know.

The tremors increased in their intensity. She had to call Jill. That was it. She had to call her to warn her— No. That wasn't right.

"Shall we go on with the therapy, Susannah?"

"No." She couldn't. She had to— "J-J-Jill."

Dorothy nodded, sympathy on her face. "Your daughter Jill." She waited, then, "Do you want to tell me something about Jill?"

"No. Cam— No. Car. No." She was sweating, though her teeth still chattered. Nothing made any sense. "C-call." There. She pointed to herself with her good left hand. "Call."

"You want to call Jill?"

"H-have." What went with have? She couldn't think. She shook her head. How could she call Jill when she didn't know why she had to and couldn't put two words together anyhow? "H-have." It was no use.

"You have to call Jill? There's something you have to tell her?"

"Yes." Yes was almost as readily available to her as no.

"What do you have to tell her, Susannah?"

"I-I-I—" She shook her head again. She didn't know.

The sympathy on Dorothy's face had changed to pity. The therapist probably thought she was crazy. She probably was crazy. On top of everything else.

Dorothy patted her hand. "Why don't we go on with the therapy? If you stop straining for it, maybe it will come to you." She printed another word on the tablet. Key.

"Key." There. No trouble at all. Susannah sighed. Something else that didn't make any sense. Why could she say key seeing the word printed and not say it seeing a key?

"Can you tell me a word that goes with key?"

"Lock."

"Very good. Another word?"

"Door." Suddenly no more stammering.

"And where do you find a door?"

"H-h-hou-house." Like hell no more stammering.

"And where do you find a house?"

"Street." Another tremor shook her. She reached out to Dorothy with her good hand, clutching the therapist's wrist. "Dark. Dark. Aban—aban—" What was the rest of the word? What was it? "Dark. Rain. Aban—aban—"

The therapist tried to help. "A bandit? A thief?"

"No. Aban—abar—no." Give up. Forget it.

Why was she trembling so? What was she afraid of? She wanted to cry. What wasn't she afraid of?

Why had everyone forgotten her? Jill, her parents, her brothers, her friends. Why had nobody come to see her? Alone among strangers, trapped inside herself, unable to get out, unable to understand anything whole, or piece the parts of things together, unable to protect herself from whatever it was that threatened her, what would become of her? Why hadn't the rest of her died with the part that had?

This time she let the tears come, sobbed uncontrollably while Dorothy came around the table to put an arm about her, trying to comfort her.

The sobbing drained away what little energy remained to her. She fell asleep in the wheelchair on the way back to her room.

A prickling sensation woke her up. Somebody was sticking pins and needles into her.

Dr. Aaronson.

No. He was standing at the foot of her bed looking at her. Not touching her. He smiled. "Hello, Susannah. Can you tell me how you feel?"

"Pins." She frowned. She wasn't making sense.

He came around the foot of the bed toward her, looking interested. "You feel pinpricks? A tingling sensation? Where?"

She *was* making sense. She pointed with her left hand to her right hand. Her right side. Up and down. Her face. All of it tingled.

She tried moving her right hand. No. Yes. She moved her index finger. The middle one. The little one. Hardly enough to see, the merest fraction of an inch, but still...Inchworm, inchworm, two and two are four.

Dr. Aaronson took the hand in his and squeezed it, grinning at her. "Good girl, Susannah. Good."

She was crying again.

Whatever else she might not be able to do, nobody could top her at that.

The physical therapist was also pleased—and showed his pleasure the way the speech therapist did. Work harder than before. Push, pull, lift, tug, push, pull, lift, tug, until she was ready to scream with the need to be left alone, even if it meant to be left to die.

Die.

Somebody was screaming that word at her.

She was working on the parallel bars. Raising her drooping head, tightening her grip with her left hand— her right hand, too weak yet to be any good, was tied to the bar—she looked around. She wasn't alone with the therapist. There were at least half a dozen other patients in the exercise room. Which of them was screaming at her?

She rubbed her face on her sleeve to get the sweat out of her eyes and looked again. Which of them?

None.

It was all inside her head.

Why would she imagine something like that?

Why was she trembling?

What was she afraid of?

One thing she could do now was hold onto a thought long enough to consider it. She had come that far.

"Push, Susannah, push. That's better. Keep going, keep going. Push, push."

One thing about the parallel bars. While the muscles of her body worked on ambulation she and her mind could go elsewhere.

Think about it, then. What was she afraid of?

That Joe or his mother or both of them would try to get custody of Jill. Sometimes she could hardly get that thought out of her head, she was so convinced of it.

Why?

She didn't know. And something about it didn't make sense. Something about promises. But the fear was real. She was trembling again.

Was that all she was afraid of?

No.

What else? When she wasn't thinking about losing Jill, what did she think of?

That she was finished as an actress. Finished before she'd gotten started.

She knew the why to that. Because of what had happened to her. Instead of being street-smart, as she was always warning Jill, she had been so incredibly careless as to get herself mugged. Stupid. She ought to start practicing what she preached to Jill.

Susannah raised her head from the bars again.

Ought to start practicing?

That didn't have to do with getting mugged. That had to do with something else she'd preached to Jill. Something not long ago.

What? When?

She couldn't remember.

Do what the speech therapist said. Stop straining for it, and maybe it would come.

All right, but when? In time to save her?

Another violent tremor shook her body. Save her from what? What had made her think that?

"All right, Susannah, Bill, Wendy, class. We'll break now. Same time tomorrow."

Sitting in her wheelchair waiting for an orderly to take her back to her room, she tried to hold onto her fears, to stay alert to whatever danger she was in, but she was too exhausted, too drained, the need to give in to sleep too overpowering.

She awoke to see Jill standing by her bed. Her first reaction was a thrill of joy, a thrill that shot to dizzying heights when she put out her hand and said, "Jill, darling," as though nothing were wrong with her.

Maybe nothing was. Maybe she had had a nightmare, and it was over.

Jill's face lighted up, and she squeezed the proffered hand. "Hi, Mom. Are you okay?"

The next thing Susannah knew she was crying. "Oh, bayside, bayside, where be? Where be?"

Jill clutched the hand, her round face frightened. "Mama, what is it? What's the matter?"

"Where be? Where be?"

"Mother, I'm here. Can't you see me? I'm here."

"No, no, no. I say where be?"

She couldn't stop crying. She couldn't make herself understood. She wanted to crawl into a hole and die.

Dr. Aaronson came in. "What is it, Susannah? What's the matter?"

She tried to calm down, think, collect herself. "Jill, where be?" It was the best she could do.

He nodded and turned to Jill. "Your mother wants to know where you have been." He turned back. "Is that right, Susannah?"

"Yes." So heartfelt was her gratitude she would be his slave for life.

Jill was frowning. "You mean at school?"

Susannah shook her head. "No, no. Where be? Me here. Where be?"

"She means," Dr. Aaronson said, "or I think she means, why haven't you been here before to see her?"

"Ray, ray," Susannah said.

"But I have been," Jill said, looking perplexed. "I've been here every day. Grandma, too."

Jill's grandmother Whitney? Was she here? With Dr.

Aaronson's help Susannah propped herself up in bed.
Yes. Her ex-mother-in-law was there, sitting in a chair
at the foot of the bed, holding Jill's blue sausage-casing
in her lap. Susannah frowned. Why didn't the sight of
her ex-mother-in-law make her tremble when the
thought of her did?

She didn't know. She couldn't imagine.

And what did Jill mean, she and her grandmother
had been here every day? They hadn't been here once.

Jill tugged at Dr. Aaronson's hand. "You tell her."

He nodded. "It's true, Susannah. They've been here
every day to see you. You just don't remember, that's
all."

Susannah stared at him.

"Don't be frightened," he said. "It happens to everybody who's been in coma. A period of maybe several
days after coming to when the patient is alert, wide-
awake, but later has no memory of it. And never will."

The more he tried to reassure her, the more frightened she became. It wasn't possible that Jill had been
here and she didn't remember it. Or her ex-mother-in-
law either. When they were on her mind almost without
letup?

Was that why they were? Because she couldn't remember them any other way?

Was she so screwed up inside, it was always going
to be like this?

"Don't be frightened," Dr. Aaronson said again. "I
think you're out of that period now."

She shrank from his touch. Everything else she was
trying to remember, would she never be able to recall
that either? Never know why she was in danger or what
it was that threatened her? Forever trapped inside herself, Jill lost to her, the theater lost to her, life lost to
her?

From down the hall came the rumble and chink of
the drinking-water cart.

Some other sound, too.

Some new sound.

Listening, Susannah froze.

Rumble.

Chink.

Scrape, scrape.

The cart rumbled through the doorway, the ice in the pitchers *chink-chinking.* A man was pushing the cart, a man she had never seen before, a man who didn't pick up his feet when he walked.

Scrape, scrape.

Scrape, scrape.

Susannah screamed, clutched Dr. Aaronson, clung to him, and screamed again.

Ten

It seemed to him he lived for the sound of bells. First the one over the door at Horlick's that he had longed to still. Now the telephone he willed to ring.

The bell at Horlick's didn't bother him any more. Or not much anyhow. It was the third week of February. Almost a month since the night it had happened. If anybody had seen anything they'd have come forward by this time.

The only person he had to concern himself with was Susannah. As long as she didn't remember—and in all his visits to the hospital she had shown no sign of doing so—he was safe. He and Susannah were both safe.

That was how he wanted to keep it.

The bell over the door jangled as somebody came in. With a slight start Herb looked up from the magazine he was leafing through and saw it was Cervantes.

All right. Two persons he had to concern himself with.

For some reason he couldn't explain, despite everything he had come up with that argued against it, he couldn't get it out of his head that Cervantes had something to do with what had happened that night.

Herb had never liked Cervantes. He didn't like him now. But he took pains not to show it. If the photographer was onto anything, if that was his connection with what had happened, if Cervantes suspected something that by itself didn't add up to anything, and he was looking for something to go with it, Herb wasn't about to help him find it.

Cervantes eenie-meenied the candy display. "How you doing, Herb?"

"I'm okay."

That wasn't the truth. He had stopped having headaches, but the new medication had other side effects. He didn't feel right. He felt as if part of him was one place and part of him somewhere else. And sometimes he felt dizzy as well. Like if he didn't watch out, the floor or sidewalk would rise up and tumble him.

But nobody, Cervantes or otherwise, wanted to hear all that.

Choosing a Hershey bar, Cervantes fished in his jeans for change. "What's the latest on Susannah?"

"She's still about the same."

"Did you see her today?"

"Yeah. I did."

Cervantes unwrapped the Hershey and bit into it. "Her speech any better?"

"No. Well. Maybe a little."

Cervantes was tall. Over six feet. And skinny. The kind who could eat half a dozen Hershey bars and not show it. Herb's mouth watered. He couldn't allow himself one.

"Did I tell you I went to see her the other night?"

That one took Herb by surprise. "No."

The photographer shook his head. "It's not easy trying to carry on a conversation with her. They keep saying her speech will get better, but I'm damned if I see any improvement."

Improvement since when? How many times had Cervantes been to see her? Why had he never mentioned it before? What did he suspect? What was he getting at?

Herb's heart started pounding.

"I suppose this means the end of her acting career."

Herb stared at the photographer, his heartbeat slowing. Was that all he was getting at?

Not that Herb didn't feel bad that that might happen. He knew how much Susannah's acting meant to her. But Patricia Neal had been in far worse shape than Susannah, and she'd gone back to acting. Triumphantly.

Cervantes crumpled the Hershey wrappings and tossed them into the waste receptacle of the soda vending machine. "Well, maybe it's too soon to tell for sure. I'll see you, Herb."

The bell jangled as he went out.

Herb went into the toilet off the back room to relieve himself. For a minute there Cervantes had gotten him all nerved up, the way he had been all the time a few weeks ago.

And for what?

Cervantes didn't know anything. He couldn't. He hadn't been on the street that night. With Susannah or without her. Herb had only imagined him being there, the same as a few minutes ago he imagined him having suspicions.

The new medication must be making him do it.

He'd have to speak to the doctors. The drug was supposed to keep him from getting paranoid, not help him do it.

He looked at himself in the dingy little mirror over the washbasin.

Or maybe it was his mother.

Beyond asking him how Susannah was getting along whenever he saw her, his mother hadn't said any more to him about that night—about being in trouble or what had he done or hiding it from her.

Pointedly not said any more.

Or maybe he was imagining that, too.

Herb sighed as he washed and wiped his hands. He was still a long way from being home free.

Coming back into the store, he could hear Cervantes moving around overhead. Funny him visiting Susannah. They must be better friends than he'd thought. He didn't know they even knew each other except to say hello.

He straightened the newspapers on the rack.

That wasn't the truth either. And this time he was the one who didn't want to hear it.

Hadn't he heard Susannah moving around up there too, last summer and fall? Hadn't he turned Zekiel's transistor radio up loud to drown out the two of them?

And now the photographer was seeing her again.

Face it, Herb. Think straight for once. Susannah doesn't care shit for you. Never has, never will.

Picking up an empty soda can left on the counter, he crumpled it with one hand and slammed it into the waste receptacle. If only, instead of Susannah, it had been Cervantes on the street that night.

The telephone rang.

And stop thinking it could be Mel Goodrich, when it never was.

The Manhattan Theater Club wasn't going to produce his play. They had decided it wasn't good enough. An interesting idea, but...Sorry. No wonder Mel Goodrich hadn't called. Who'd want to call with news like that?

It would be Mrs. Zekiel or the Zekiels' daughter Sylvia or one of Sylvia's kids or some other relative or friend.

Or his mother. Checking up on him. Always checking up on him. Why hadn't he called? What was he doing?

When she called him here at Horlick's, what in the hell did she think he was doing? Playing the stock market?

By the time he picked up the phone he was so enraged he barked into the mouthpiece.

It was Mel Goodrich.

The Manhattan Theater Club liked his play. They more than liked it. They were enthusiastic about it. They thought it was brilliant, a major new work. They wanted to produce it.

Herb was ready to burst as he replaced the phone. He had never doubted it. Not really.

The waiting got on your nerves, that was all. Waiting. Not knowing. Trying to guess what they were thinking.

He couldn't believe it. He wanted to shout. His play was going to be produced. He really and truly was on his way.

Only what if—?

No!

She was going to be all right. She would feel bad about not being in his play, but she probably wouldn't have been in it anyhow. The showcase production would be aimed at Broadway, for what everybody associated with it hoped would be a long, money-making run. Susannah's role was a big, important one. The Manhattan Theater Club would want an established star. If not in their showcase production, then when it moved to Broadway.

Susannah would understand that. She'd been in the theater long enough to know.

And he would make it up to her.

If *Possessed* was the big hit it should be and had a long run, by that time she'd be fully recovered and he'd be important enough to have a say in the replacement casting. He could get her in as understudy.

If only she didn't—

No.

Don't say it. Don't think it.

It wasn't going to happen.

Almost never would the person remember the accident itself.

The next morning Mrs. Caitlin called to ask if he would stop by her office that afternoon. She had something she wanted to speak to him about.

He couldn't imagine what she wanted, but from her manner and tone of voice she regarded him as a confidant, and he liked that.

He liked Mrs. Caitlin. From the beginning she had deferred to him. She seemed to think that, as the person who had found Susannah and brought her to the hospital, he deserved special consideration.

A slight person, shorter by a head than he was, she was friendly and outgoing—qualities he envied—with a round, cheerful face and close-cropped brown hair. Brown eyes that sparkled. Almost as pretty as Susannah, and not much older.

When he arrived at her office she was on the phone to somebody, looking a bit harried. Nothing unusual about that. She was always on the run.

Smiling, she waved him to a chair, and he sat down to wait.

"Thank you for stopping by," she said, cradling the phone, smiling again. "I wanted to speak to you about reporting the crime."

He couldn't believe he had heard her right. For a fraction of a second she slipped out of focus, he stared at her so hard. "You mean Susannah has—does she know I—I mean, does she remember?" He thought he would throw up.

"No," she said, shaking her head.

He stared at her again, not understanding. If Susannah didn't remember, then how—? Cervantes?

The room ebbed and flowed.

Mrs. Caitlin was saying more. He strained to listen, to understand. Something about encouraging Susannah, when she was well enough, to report the attack on her to the police. Something about bringing her to the hospital in a cab instead of an ambulance. Mugging not a reportable crime. Hospital not required. Maybe Susannah wouldn't remember anything, but maybe she would.

Mrs. Caitlin was frowning at him. "Are you all right, Mr. Schlosser?"

She might as well have told him he was dying.

"I—it's—I'm on some medication. I—it's an ear problem. It affects my balance as well as my hearing." He swallowed. Maybe he could save himself. At least he must try. "The medication makes me dizzy. I get attacks of dizziness. Vertigo. I'm sorry."

She looked concerned. "There's nothing for you to apologize about. Let me get you a glass of water."

He swallowed again. Smiled. "Yes. Thanks."

The time she gave him, as much as the water, settled him down.

"There," she said. "Better?"

"Yes. Now. I'm sorry. You were saying..."

She smiled. "I was saying Susannah might not remember anything about the mugging, but then again she might. And you might remember something, too, that would help the police. Something that escaped your notice at the time."

Nothing had escaped his notice. Nothing.

"Or something you didn't think had any connection to the mugging. You'd be surprised at how careless criminals can be. Or maybe it's fear." Little gold loops dangled from Mrs. Caitlin's ears, jiggling when she bobbed her close-cropped head. "Whatever it is, they often leave things behind that point to them."

He had left nothing behind. He had been back to that tinned-up brownstone over and over to make sure. There was nothing there.

"Of course, even if she does remember, it will be some time before Susannah is able to talk to the police about it. You've seen for yourself that her ability to communicate is still very limited."

He nodded. "Yes."

"Her therapists tell me she's making good progress. Good enough, by the way, that she'll be leaving the hospital soon. And that's something else I wanted to speak to you about."

He braced himself for another shock, but what Mrs. Caitlin gave him was the way out of a quandary he'd been in. How to keep tabs on Susannah after she left the hospital.

"She's going to need help. Quite a lot of it. At least for a while. And I'm afraid the bulk of it is going to have to come from friends and neighbors like yourself. You did say you'd be willing to help in any way you could?"

He nodded again. "Yes. Of course. Anything."

"Good." She smiled. "Susannah's lucky to have such loyal friends."

He felt himself flush and hoped she wouldn't notice. Or would attribute it to his medication. He wanted to do more than keep tabs on Susannah. He wanted to help her, to make her well again. He cared about her. He wouldn't be in the jam he was in if he hadn't cared so much about her. But when it came to choosing between Susannah and his play, he had no choice. He meant nothing to Susannah. *Possessed* meant everything to him.

"As I'm sure you know," Mrs. Caitlin was saying, "Jill's grandmother Whitney has been staying with her. And I'm sure once Susannah is home again, the senior Mrs. Whitney will continue to do whatever she can to help. But she does have a home of her own to tend to—a home she's been away from for almost a month now. And she's not young. She must be somewhere in her sixties."

He hoped he wouldn't have to make the choice. He hoped that more than anything. But he had to put himself first.

"And with Susannah's own mother an invalid, and her father not able to leave the mother—or his pastorate—for any length of time, and with her two brothers not readily available either because of their own situations and where they live—well"—Mrs. Caitlin shrugged—"you can see where that leaves us."

There was no way he could keep tabs on her full-time. No way at all. But whatever she did remember—if she remembered anything—wasn't likely to come in one big flash. Not according to the book he'd read. It would be a bit here, a bit there. A gradual shrinking. If he could find a way to be with her on any kind of regular basis, he would have time to decide whether or not he had to do anything. And when. He already knew *how*.

"You see, until Susannah has the strength and agility—and the self-confidence—that's a very important part of it, self-confidence—until she's able to come here to the hospital on her own as an outpatient—to continue her therapy—she's going to need somebody to come with her. To come with her and take her home again."

For the second time that day he couldn't believe he had heard her right. She was handing him the solution he was looking for. Come with Susannah to the hospital and take her home again. The two of them alone together. Day after day, five days a week.

He would have to work his schedule at Horlick's around it, but he could do that. Mr. Zekiel would oblige him. And who else was there to compete with him for the job of escort? Not likely the grandmother. And Jill had school.

Cervantes? No. According to *Back Stage*, Cervantes had signed onto a movie that was to start shooting this week.

And Susannah's other actor friends couldn't tie themselves down to an everyday commitment like that.

He was the logical one for it.

And not only in his eyes.

Like Mrs. Caitlin, Susannah's friends all thought of him now as her rescuer. They came to him all the time to ask how she was getting along, what they could do to help.

"And that's another thing," Mrs. Caitlin was saying. "Her therapy. Helping her with that. Supplementing the exercises she gets here at the hospital. That could do a lot toward speeding her recovery, toward making a full recovery possible."

He would be serving Susannah as well as himself. And God knew, he wanted her well. He wanted that as much as anybody. Would work as hard as he could to get it. A full recovery in mind and body—except for remembering the accident itself. Then he could forget about his terrible alternative, because everything would be okay. Everything would be the way it was before.

Well. Not quite the way it was before. Not for him.

A major new work, the Manhattan Theater Club people had said.

A major new work.

"You have to understand, Mr. Schlosser, that everything Susannah does or tries to do right now, even the simplest things, like naming an object shown to her, or taking a single step along the parallel bars—everything she does is a tremendous drain on her. It's an effort sometimes for her to stay awake. Only by fighting her own instincts—going against the grain of her desires, as a patient once put it—can she hope to make any progress. That's why you and her other friends and family are so important. Because she can't do it alone. She has to have help."

Mrs. Caitlin smiled and bobbed her head, the gold

loops jiggling. "I'm drawing up a list. May I put your name on it?"

"Yes. Yes. Of course."

"Good. When the time comes we'll talk again. About specifics." She stood up, glancing at her watch. "I'm going up to the seventh floor to look in on Susannah, if you want to come along. If you feel up to it."

He stood up, too. For a moment the floor threatened to rise, but he steadied himself against the chair until the feeling passed. "Yes, I'm all right," he said.

"Good."

Good? How little she knew. He had been on the brink of self-destruction, and he had pulled himself back. He was going to be great.

"I have to speak to the senior Mrs. Whitney," Mrs. Caitlin said, leading the way out of her office. "She and Jill should be there by now. They come about the same time every day."

"Yes. Yes, I know."

He could do anything.

His own mother afraid of him.

He could have shouted with laughter.

Instead, he allowed himself the luxury of a sigh, leaning back against the wall of the elevator they were riding in.

"I know," Mrs. Caitlin said, giving him a rueful smile. "It's been that kind of day for me, too. They all are. Rush, rush, rush. Never enough time to get everything done." She sighed, too, as the elevator stopped at seven. "My husband says if I don't stop working so much overtime he's going to divorce me." She gave him another rueful smile as they stepped out. "The only problem is his mother thinks he means it. She can't understand what he's waiting for."

He walked down the hall with her to Susannah's room.

No. Not walked. Floated. He had everybody fooled.

Going into the four-bed ward, he couldn't see Susannah for all the people clustered around her bed. Jill. The grandmother. Dr. Aaronson. A nurse. But he could hear her. She was screaming.

Eleven

Burying her face against Dr. Aaronson's shoulder, clinging to him, Susannah listened to the babel of voices.

"...hush...all right."

"...what's wrong?"

"...don't...suddenly, Barbara..."

"...upset...offset..."

"...paresthesia...hand...leg."

"...twice now, Mr. Schlosser."

"Isn't that interesting!"

"...mama okay?"

"...obvious..."

"...remembers..."

"Isn't that interesting!"

People talking the way she talked, in bits and pieces, the old lady in the next bed chiming in.

Herself trembling, unable to stop. Unable to comprehend what she knew to be true, what the man with the drinking-water cart had ferreted out of the mush in her head.

She hadn't been mugged by some hit-or-miss stranger

103

roaming the streets. She hadn't been mugged, period. Somebody—somebody she knew—had tried to kill her.

Out of the babel Dr. Aaronson's voice close to her ear. "Susannah, what is it? What's the matter? Susannah?"

She was trembling harder.

"Susannah?"

"Go. Go. Go."

Why had she said that? What did she mean?

Dr. Aaronson interpreted it to mean she wanted everyone to go. Maybe she did.

Except Jill.

"Bayside. Bayside. H-hu-hug." She put both arms—the strong and the weak—around Jill and hugged her tight. "Take—take—"

Take what?

Why did she keep asking herself questions she couldn't answer?

Jill looking anxious, trying not to.

Baby, baby, you should be anxious. Please don't go. Please don't leave me.

"'Bye, Mom. We'll see you tomorrow."

Don't go. Don't go.

Her ex-mother-in-law holding the blue sausage-casing out to Jill. "Goodbye, Susannah. Try to get some rest now. I'm sure you'll feel better tomorrow."

Mrs. Superior Person. How do you know I'll still be here tomorrow?

No use. They were going, Barbara with them, saying something about having to speak to her, see you later.

Susannah waved her good hand. "'Bye."

Herb in their place at her bedside. Herb from Horlick's. Her rescuer and newfound friend. Trying to say something. Having to work at it.

I know how you feel, Herb. I know how, and then some.

"You okay, Susannah?"

No. Since you've gone to the trouble to ask, no, I'm not.

She started to say so. Say no, at least. Her best word, the one she could always count on.

Something held her back.

She nodded. "Yes. I—okay."

He didn't seem convinced. Not surprising. She couldn't have sounded convincing. He also didn't seem to know what to do. Stay. Go. Then, with a glance at Dr. Aaronson, he said, "I'll see you tomorrow. Goodbye, Susannah."

Watching him go, she knew what had held her back. She didn't know who had tried to kill her. She didn't know whom she could trust.

Dr. Aaronson bent over her. "I'll be back in a few minutes."

He was going, too? Leaving her all alone?

She grabbed his hand. "No!" She could trust Dr. Aaronson. She hadn't known him before the attack. "No! No!"

Dr. Aaronson frowned. "Susannah, what's upsetting you? What is it? Can you tell me?"

Not can. Must.

She swallowed. "Cake. No. Candle. No. Children. No. No!" Next thing she knew, she'd be crying again.

He sat on the side of her bed and folded her good left hand in his. "Take it easy. Try to relax. You're wound up tight as a drum."

She nodded. "Dark. Rain. Aban—aban—" She swallowed again. "House. House street?"

Beep, beep, beep, beep. His pocket page.

He turned it off and reached for the phone beside her bed. Somebody wanted him somewhere else. He had to go.

"I'll be back as soon as I can," he said.

"No, no!" She clung to him.

"Isn't that interesting!"

Everybody in the room was staring at her.

Until now, except for the old lady's parrotings, the other patients in 726 had been little more than noise levels to Susannah, something else to add to the clamor and confusion in her head. The same as she had probably been to them, all victims of stroke, the old lady and another one in her seventies or eighties, a third woman in her forties or fifties. Now they and their visitors turned to stare, as suddenly wary of her as she was of them.

Crazy, they were saying. Sick in the head.

Dr. Aaronson pried himself loose, patting her hand. "Susannah, I have to go check out another patient. You'll be all right. And I'll be back. I promise."

She watched him go, looked at the others watching him go, clenched her teeth to keep from crying out to him. She must be crazy. She had to be. Why would anybody try to kill her? For what?

Who?

It didn't make sense. Nothing made sense, and this the least of it.

Nevertheless, somebody had tried to kill her. The thought of it made her start trembling again.

Why?

Who?

If she could figure out one, she would know the other, wouldn't she?

Futile question. She had no idea why or who.

Why, for that matter, the somebody who had tried to kill her hadn't stayed around to make sure she was dead.

He would know now she wasn't.

He?

Yes.

A man.

A man screaming, "Die! Die! Die!"

She was shaking so violently the metal bedrail went *tck, tck, tck* against the metal nightstand next to the bed.

Somebody wanted her dead. Had tried to kill her. Now that he knew she wasn't dead, he would try again, wouldn't he?

Maybe was waiting to try again now. Right this minute.

She had to get out of here, get away, run.

Run where? How?

She could hardly walk.

She wasn't going anywhere.

The bedrail went *tck, tck, tck* faster than before.

"I'm sorry, Susannah. I had to speak to Mrs. Whitney about—Susannah, what is it? What's frightening you?"

Barbara was back.

"Dark. Rain. Aban—aban— No. Wait. Please."

The social worker sat down in a chair by the bed, drawing it close. "Take your time, Susannah. I'll wait. Take your time."

"Dark. Rain. Aban—aban— No. Please."

She wanted to cry.

Forget about the dark and the rain. Forget about the houses and the street. They're not important. Get to what you're trying to say.

Barbara squeezed her hand. "Try again, Susannah."

She nodded, concentrating as hard as she could. "Dark. Rain. Aban— No. No. No."

What was the matter with her? She was like a broken record, stuck in a groove.

"Don't try so hard," Barbara said. "Take it easy."

She nodded again. "M-ma-man. Man."

There. She wanted to shout.

Barbara smiled. "Yes, Susannah. A man. Right?"

"Yes."

"What man?"

Susannah shook her head. "No. No." She circled one hand with the other to say turn it around. "Other. Other."

Barbara looked puzzled. "Other? You mean the other way?"

"Yes. Yes."

"You mean not what man but man what?"

Excitement started building in her. "Yes! Yes!"

Barbara looked more puzzled than before. "Man what." She shook her head. "I don't know what you mean. Man what."

Susannah concentrated. "M-man. Dough. No. Do. Do. Man do."

"Man do what?"

"Yes! Yes!" She pointed to herself. "Me. Me."

"Man do what to you?" Barbara's face cleared. "What you're trying to say is some man did something to you?"

"Yes! Yes!"

"Right. Of course." Barbara nodded, looking pleased. "Your memory is starting to come back, Susannah. That's very good. Yes. A man certainly did do something to you. He attacked you on the street. Mugged you. Knocked you out."

Susannah stared at her. "No. No."

"I'm afraid so, yes. You probably don't remember that exact part of it. When you were knocked out." She squeezed Susannah's hand again. "Don't fret, Susannah. You probably never will remember that."

Susannah shook her head. "No. No. Man—man caw. No. Key. No." She made another try. "Dark. Rain. Aban—aban— No."

"Yes." Barbara nodded again. "You're on the right track, Susannah. Yes. Now I see what you were trying to say before. It was a dark, rainy night. I'd forgotten. But I remember now. Very rainy. We had a big storm that night. Thunder and lightning. Crazy for the end of January."

About to protest again, Susannah hesitated. Something flickered at the back of her mind. She put a hand out to Barbara. "Wait. Wait. Say—say again."

"Say what again? What I just said, you mean?"

"Yes."

"I said it was a dark, rainy night. We had a big storm. With thunder and lightning. It was still raining when I left the hospital to—"

"No. No."

"No what, Susannah?"

"No. Back. Back. More. Dark. Rain."

Barbara nodded again. "Yes. I was coming to that. The rest of what you were trying to say. The street you were attacked on—the block, I mean—it's full of boarded-up brownstones. Abandoned brownstones. That's what you were trying to say, isn't it? Dark. Rain. Abandoned."

Giving up, Susannah nodded. Whatever had been there so marginally was gone. Beyond retrieval.

She was nearly beyond retrieval herself. Her body ached with fatigue, her head throbbing from the strain of trying to pull out words that were locked away, inaccessible.

She would rest a while. Close her eyes for a bit. Come back to this later when she felt fresher. The words would come more easily then.

A man walked into the room, and fear shot through her like adrenaline. She couldn't rest, couldn't wait. She had to make Barbara understand. Her life depended on it.

She watched the man hesitate, looking around.

"Susannah, you're trembling again. What's the matter?"

From catercorner across the room another man waved. "She's over here, Jerry." He turned to the fortyish-fiftyish woman. "Here's Jerry come to see you, Lisa."

Susannah sighed and turned back to Barbara. "Maman. Man do. Man tear—no—tum—no—tree—no!" She could not find the word she wanted. She clenched both hands into fists and flailed at herself, trying to compensate with her strong left hand for the weakly dabbing right one.

Barbara nodded. "The man attacked you, beat you. Yes."

"More. More."

The social worker nodded again. "Attacked you, beat you, robbed you."

"No!"

"Yes, Susannah. My dear, we have proof. He took your wallet with whatever cash you had in it. And your Master Charge. We checked with Jill and looked through your papers to see about credit cards. That's how we know. But you're not to worry about it. We called the Master Charge people right away to put a hold on your account."

Susannah shook her head, then covered her face with her hands, trying to think. Maybe Barbara was right, and she was wrong. She was wrong about so many things, so mixed up inside. And if they had proof...

A stranger might try to kill her for whatever money she had on her, but not somebody she knew.

She must be wrong.

Hearing somebody approach, she uncovered her face to see a man coming toward her. Barbara turned to look, then smiled. "It's your friend, Mr. Schlosser, come back for something."

Herb patted the pockets of his jacket. The jacket

looked new. "My glasses," he said. "I thought maybe I—"

"Your glasses?" Barbara said. "You think you left them here?" She looked around, moving things aside on the nightstand. "No, I don't think so. At least I don't see any. Are you sure you had them with you when you came to the hospital?"

"No, I'm not sure. But usually I have them with me. They're my reading glasses."

Reading.

She was supposed to take part in a reading of his play, *Possessed,* but for some reason she couldn't. And she had to tell him. No. Had told him.

"Reading," she said, getting it on the first try. "Play. Reading." She pointed to Herb. "Your play."

Barbara smiled encouragement and turned to Herb. "Her memory is beginning to come back to her. Isn't that wonderful?"

He nodded, looking from Barbara to her.

"She remembers your play, and the reading you were supposed to have. Right, Susannah?"

Susannah nodded.

"Do you remember why the reading was put off?"

"No." Hadn't she remembered once? "No."

"Don't worry about it," Barbara said. "You will."

Something about a telephone.

"Call. Call."

"You had to call somebody? Or maybe somebody was calling you."

She shook her head. She didn't know. Couldn't think. Too tired to think.

"Maybe," Barbara said, "you called Mr. Schlosser here to tell him you couldn't take part in the reading of his play."

"No."

She turned to him. He was looking at her—how? Like he was making up his mind? No. Having made it up.

Whatever that meant.

Susannah sighed. She could have a yard sale of all the junk that filled her mind.

What was it about a telephone?

A telephone ringing.

No.

A telephone not ringing?

Not something.

A telephone not—

She shook her head. Whether she was tired or not, it either came or it didn't. There was no way she could make it come.

"Dark. Rain. Aban—aban—"

Why did she keep coming back to that? What good did that do?

"Abandoned," Barbara said. "Remember? The abandoned brownstones on the dark, rainy street." She turned to Herb. "She's beginning to remember the mugging, too. We were talking about it just before you got here. She knows somebody—some man—attacked her. Beat her."

Susannah sat up straight. "Do. No. Day. No. Dog. No. No. Die. Yes! Die. Die. Die. Man—man say—man yellow. No. Yell. Man yell. 'Die! Die! Die!'" She sank back against the pillow, drained.

Barbara stared at her, a perplexed frown on her face. "You're saying the man who attacked you yelled 'die' at you?"

Susannah nodded, trying to find the strength to speak. "'Die. Die. Die.'"

"Three times, you mean?"

She nodded again.

The perplexed frown gave way to skepticism. "Well," Barbara said, "I don't know. I can't imagine. I suppose it could be one of those cult things. Devil worship. You know. That's what it sounds like. Though I must say I never heard of any of them mugging anybody. Of course, New York is full of kooks, but—" She shook her head. "I think it's more likely you're mixed up, Susannah."

"No. No."

"Yes, I think so. It could be a kind of juxtaposition. You may have been watching television earlier that evening. Or the night before. Saw a scene like the one you're describing, and it stuck in your mind. That's what it sounds like to me."

"No."

"Well, let's not argue about it now. You're worn down to a frazzle as it is. Mr. Schlosser, I wonder if you'd mind just this once—I've got to get back to my office, and Dr. Aaronson told me he'd be along as soon as he could, but Susannah doesn't want to be left alone, so I wonder—would you mind staying with her until he gets here?"

He shook his head. "No. Not at all."

"Good. Susannah is probably too tired to talk. Under the best of circumstances it's an effort for her. As you know. And she's had a very trying time of it this afternoon. She may even doze off. She probably will. But if you'll just sit with her. Keep her company." Barbara turned from Herb to her. "All right, Susannah?"

Susannah nodded. She could probably trust Herb. He couldn't have wanted her dead. If he had, he wouldn't have saved her life.

And maybe Barbara was right. Maybe it was only her imagination all screwed up with *The Late, Late Show*.

Twelve

Leaving the hospital with her grandmother, Jill walked with her in silence to the bus stop over on Central Park West. They usually made the walk in silence. The question uppermost in Jill's mind each day at this time—was her mother going to be all right—she could never bring herself to ask, partly because her grandmother might not know the answer, partly because she might.

She didn't know what her grandmother was thinking to make her so quiet, too. She couldn't bring herself to ask that either.

Today there was another question—what was her mother so afraid of?—but nobody, not even the doctors, seemed to know the answer to that.

Mr. Schlosser—Herb—he kept telling Jill to call him Herb—Herb had started to leave the hospital with them, but then he said he'd left something behind in her mother's room and had to go back for it.

Her grandmother didn't think Herb was much in the way of company, and she was right. He wasn't.

He never had been. What little Jill knew about him—his farmed-out childhood, his feelings about his mother and father—had spilled out of him in fierce

113

little outbursts around about Christmas. Since then—
well, not exactly since then, but some time after that—
he had gone back to being the way he usually was.
Keeping himself to himself.

With a difference.

Jill lengthened her stride to keep pace with her
grandmother, who didn't believe in lollygagging, as she
put it.

What the difference was, Jill hadn't been able to put
her finger on, partly because it meant being critical,
and it was hard to be critical about somebody your
mother owed her life to.

But he was—well, sterner somehow. Harder maybe.
She frowned.

Like he was standing up for something. Or to somebody.

His mother, maybe.

Maybe that was it.

Like, I've had enough of you, old lady. Stand aside.
Move. Get out of my way, or I'll put you out of my way.
No matter what it takes.

Jill shivered. Her imagination was running away
with her.

The bus stop had a new glass shelter. The shelters
were one of the few positive things her grandmother
had to say about the city. She had nothing at all to say
about the apartment or the neighborhood or the café
where her mother worked two nights and one day a
week, even though the owner, Mr. Capistrano, had said
they should come in any time for some nice *gnocchi* on
him.

Dr. Dubinsky was something else again.

Although Jill's grandmother didn't have much use
for psychiatry—her grandmother didn't seem to have
much use for anything or anybody not of her own choosing—working for a doctor was one thing she could say
to her friends about Jill's mother without looking
pained.

Dr. Dubinsky had explained to her grandmother
what kind of work her mother did for him, but what
really interested her was his saying he had offered her
mother a full-time job.

After he left the apartment her grandmother said, "I don't know why she didn't take it."

"Because she wants to be an actress," Jill said.

"Well, it amounts to the same thing, doesn't it?" Her grandmother frowned. "What does the doctor call what he does?"

"Psychodrama."

"And what does he call what your mother does?"

"It's called a professional alternate ego, Grandma. Mom plays all kinds of different roles, depending on who the patient is and who he—or she—is having trouble with. You know. Like a man's boss or his mother or a woman's husband or her mother."

"Well," her grandmother said, "that's acting, isn't it?"

"Well, yes," Jill admitted, "but it's not the same."

She looked down Central Park West to see if a bus was coming. They had just missed one.

She remembered a time three or four years ago when her grandmother had taken her and a cousin shopping on Fifth Avenue, and whenever she'd been able to manage it she had walked a few steps behind them, hoping people would think she wasn't with them, not wanting people to think her grandmother was her mother.

She didn't know how she could have been so mean. Or how she could be so mean about her now.

Her grandmother tried very hard to keep her opinions to herself, even when it meant clamping her mouth shut. And for all she seemed so forbidding—she was tall and big-boned and heavy in the chest—she got wounded the same as everybody else.

Jill had seen more of her father in the nearly six weeks her grandmother had been staying with her than she had in the six months before that, but her father wasn't very nice to his mother, grumbling when she asked where he'd been or what he'd been doing or why he couldn't have called the other night to say he couldn't make it when he knew she was keeping dinner for him.

Jill didn't blame her father for grumbling at anybody leaning on his case like that, but she felt sorry for her grandmother, who had once been in and now was out and didn't understand why, since she hadn't done anything she was aware of to change things between her son and her.

Jill didn't understand it either. She only knew the feeling. Like the few months before and the time ever since Diana Grosvenor first came home from school with her.

A bus rumbled up, hissing as the driver lowered the front end to make the first step easier to get to.

Rush hour was starting and the bus was full, but it was only about a ten-minute ride.

When they got off at Eighty-seventh Street and headed for the apartment, Jill said, "What did Mrs. Caitlin want?"

"She gave me a list of things your mother will have to take with her when she goes to apply for welfare."

Jill stared at her grandmother. "Welfare? Mom has to go on welfare?"

"It's nothing to be ashamed of," her grandmother said, a stiff look on her face. "It's not like your mother was a no-account or a cheat, like so many of them are. And it's going to be a long time before she's back on her feet and able to work again."

Jill waited for her grandmother to add, "If she ever is."

She didn't. What she said was, "I don't know where else the money would come from for the two of you to live on all that time. I can't support two households indefinitely, even with the help your grandfather Burke has been giving me. And he certainly can't do it alone. And you heard what the doctor said."

Dr. Dubinsky had given her grandmother a check for three hundred dollars, saying he knew it wasn't much, but he didn't carry the kind of insurance that would have paid her mother's salary while she was recuperating. Mr. Capistrano at the café was sorry, too. All he had was Workers' Compensation, and that only applied when the accident was job-related.

"Anyhow, as Mrs. Caitlin pointed out, your mother is entitled to welfare. There's no need for her to be beholden to other people when the city will provide for her. And should, considering she's the victim of a crime on the city streets."

Welfare.

Jill wondered if she would be the first student at Shipley whose mother was on welfare. Probably.

Instantly she felt ashamed. What a time to be thinking about herself when she should be thinking about her mother and how her mother would feel about having to go on welfare.

On top of everything else that had happened to her.

Jill sighed. Especially when it was her fault her mother had been mugged. If she hadn't gotten her all upset that night, she would have been paying attention to where she was and what she was doing, and it wouldn't have happened. Any of it.

"Do you have homework tonight?" her grandmother asked as they turned in from the sidewalk to the building's entrance.

"No, Grandma. I finished what I had in study period."

"Maybe you'll play me a couple of hands of gin, then."

"Oh." Shoot. "Sure."

Jill tried to sound enthusiastic, but she didn't play well and didn't care enough to want to, something her grandmother, who was dead earnest about cards, couldn't understand.

She was saved both from the game and the sighs that went with it by Cervantes. He came out of the building as she and her grandmother started up the steps.

"I just rang your bell," he said to Jill. "How are you, Mrs. Whitney?"

"Very well, thank you."

Cervantes was not one of her grandmother's favorite people. She couldn't understand, for one thing, why he only had one name.

"But he doesn't, Grandma," Jill had told her. "He has two more, the same as anybody else. His name is Timothy Ward Cervantes."

"Then why doesn't he use his other names?"

Jill shook her head. "I don't know."

The conversation had taken place back when her mother was still unconscious, when her grandmother hadn't been with her very long and was still trying to find out where things were kept and how things were done and who was who and what was what.

"You're going to wear that sentence out," her grandmother had said. "Do you have any idea how many times you've said it to me in the last week?"

Jill shook her head again. "I don't know." Glancing at her grandmother, she started to giggle, had a fit of the giggles, harder and harder, and then, unable to control herself at all, had an even harder fit of sobs, winding up in her grandmother's arms.

"I thought," Cervantes said, going back into the building with them, "maybe Jill would like to go ice-skating with me in the park and then have a hamburger somewhere."

"Oh, super," Jill said with a clap of her hands. "Can I, Grandma? Please?"

"Well, I suppose—if you really want to."

Her grandmother, though she tried to be polite, didn't take to any of her mother's friends, most of them actors or trying to be. She thought their clothes were tacky and their hair a mess, and when were they going to give up this nonsense and settle down and start living like civilized people?

Jill didn't have the answer to that one either.

Three of them, Cervantes and Eugenia Eckardt and Polly Berkmyer, had come over one night—the night her mother first opened her eyes—to see what they could do to help. Her grandmother thanked them, saying there wasn't anything right now, maybe after her mother came home from the hospital.

Instead of taking that as an invitation to leave, they took it as an invitation to stay, dropping their ponchos and shoulder bags in a corner of the living room, sitting crosslegged on the rug, speculating about the attack on her mother, going over and over it, like maybe that would make it go away.

The same as she had tried.

Eugenia Eckardt, along with her mother and four other actors, had been going to take part in the reading of Herb Schlosser's play *Possessed*.

"We didn't know what was going on," she said. "We came out in all that downpour and sat around in that lobby for nothing. Herb never called any of us to cancel. Not until the next day."

"He was probably too upset," Polly said. "After finding Susannah."

"Well, at first, sure. Okay. But after he got her to the hospital, and she was out of his hands. He still had time to call."

"It isn't a question of time," Polly said. "You don't understand. Listen. My father's a doctor. A general surgeon. You can imagine what he's had to look at in and out of the operating room all these years. Well. Last week he and my mom were driving home after being out for dinner, and there was this accident on the Long Island Expressway. Some crazy person tried to cross the expressway on foot, if you can believe that, and she got killed. Well. Since my father's a doctor, and since he was there, he was asked to pronounce her. Pronounce her dead. Which he did. And Mom said it took him hours to get to sleep that night. I mean, he was shook."

"I think Polly's right," Cervantes put in. "Think how you'd have felt if you'd been the one to find her."

"I suppose so," Eugenia said. "You know," she added, "Herb's play isn't bad at all. I mean, I thought it would be a piece of shit, but—oh. Excuse me, ma'am. I wasn't—well, anyhow. I thought it would be terrible, like most of the new stuff you're asked to read these days. But it's not at all. It's a little weird in places, but parts of it are brilliant. I mean brilliant. And Susannah's part—wow. It is really something."

"Do you suppose," Polly said, almost in a whisper, "Susannah will ever—"

She hadn't finished. Cervantes had cut her off with a look.

Cervantes had his skates with him in a green canvas bag. "There's room for yours in here too," he said as they rode up in the elevator.

"I'm always afraid this elevator is going to get stuck between floors," her grandmother said.

"If it does, give it a kick right here," Cervantes said, demonstrating.

Cervantes was joking. He had to be. Jill had never heard from him or anybody else what to do if the ele-

vator got stuck, which it sometimes did, except yell
your head off and hope somebody heard you. But her
grandmother thought he was serious, and you could
almost see the wheels turn in her head. That meant
he'd ridden this elevator often enough to know, and
that meant he'd spent a lot of time with Jill's mother,
and that meant—

Glancing up at Cervantes, seeing him wink at her,
Jill clapped a hand over her mouth to keep from gig-
gling, afraid of ending up like last time. She was almost
as nerved up today as then.

She supposed that was the real reason her grandmother didn't like Cervantes, who had almost moved
in with them last fall, but then, to Jill's disappointment,
hadn't.

It didn't make sense. Her grandmother oughtn't to
care who her mother spent time with. Her grandmother
didn't like her mother, and she hadn't liked her being
married to her son, but then her grandmother also
hadn't liked it that her mother had divorced him.

Something else her grandmother didn't like was Cervantes taking her skating. Her grandmother thought
her father should be the one doing that. Jill thought so
too, but, as much as she loved going out with her father,
she was glad it was Cervantes who had come around
today. When Cervantes said he would do something, he
did it.

She held off asking him until they were on the rink
and had finished their second waltz, which she ended
in a spiral, her best yet. One thing about Shipley, you
could learn some really neat things on school time.

"Before we go get the hamburger," she said, catching
her breath, "could we go see my mother?"

"I thought you just came from seeing her."

"We did, but—well, I'd like to go see her again. This
afternoon when Grandma and I were there, Mom didn't
remember us being there before. Not once. Can you
believe that? Every day all those weeks, and she didn't
remember it at all. She got very upset that we hadn't
come to see her."

The music started up again, and Jill and Cervantes
skated around the rink side by side, arms linked.

"You think it will be the same tonight?" he said. "She won't remember you were there this afternoon?"

"Dr. Aaronson said not. He said she was through all that, but—I don't know. Can we please go, Cervantes? Just for a little bit?"

"I don't see why not. Here. Let's try a few crossovers."

On the walk to the hospital, Cervantes said, "Did you hear what Dr. Dubinsky wants to do for your mother?"

"No. What?"

"Have a psychodrama for her."

Jill frowned up at him. "A psychodrama? What for?"

"To help her work out whatever problems she has. Because of the mugging. Polly Berkmyer was telling me."

Polly was in group therapy with Dr. Dubinsky, one of the groups where her mother worked as the professional alternate ego.

Jill frowned up at Cervantes again. "You mean with Polly's group?"

He shook his head. "No. With a group made up for the occasion. You'd be in it, I expect. And your grandmother. And some of your mother's friends. Maybe your father, too. I don't know. Whoever your mother is involved with emotionally. And some other people, too, I guess. I suppose, now that I think about it, Dr. Dubinsky might ask us to play other roles besides our own. Somebody might play the mugger, for instance. And Herb. Herb could play himself, I guess, as the rescuer. And maybe Dr. Aaronson and Mrs. Caitlin would join the group. It could be quite a gathering."

"Will it help my mother?"

"I should think so."

Jill shivered. "It sounds scary."

He looked down at her. "Why scary?"

"I don't know. It just does."

They walked in silence for a bit.

"Cervantes?"

"Yeah. What?"

"How can Dr. Dubinsky put on a psychodrama for my mother when she can hardly talk?"

"He'll wait until she can talk better."

Another stretch of silence.

"Cervantes?"

"Yeah?"

"Will my mother get so she—will she?"

"Will your mother get so she what? Talks better?"

"Yes."

"I don't know, kid. But I think everybody thinks so."

"Cervantes?"

"What?"

"I don't know. If only..."

"If only what?" he asked when she didn't go on.

"I don't know." She was filled with a sudden sense of urgency. Grabbing Cervantes' hand, she started walking faster.

"Take it easy, kid," he said, but he picked up his pace, too.

Thirteen

He had never believed it would happen this soon. He had hoped against hope it wouldn't happen at all.

The book had been wrong.

Dr. Aaronson, too.

Dr. Aaronson had said he didn't know what Susannah was afraid of. He didn't think she knew herself.

She knew.

Herb looked at her lying back against the pillow, her eyes closed, maybe asleep, maybe not.

Any moment now she would open her eyes, point a finger at him, and say, "You were the one who screamed 'die' at me. You tried to kill me. You."

Any moment.

She wouldn't be able to say it that smoothly, with all the connectives, but she'd get the message across. And she could point.

It was God's wonder she hadn't already done so.

He hadn't known he'd screamed anything at her. What else would she remember about him he didn't know?

What difference did it make? He wasn't going to know, and neither was anybody else.

He stood up to draw the curtain around her bed to screen her from the other people in the room. She opened her eyes and looked at him.

His heart strained against his chest.

She said nothing, pointed no finger, looked away.

Not yet that moment.

As quietly as he could, with as little motion as possible, he sat back down.

"Reading," she said in a faraway voice, her eyelids drooping. "Play. Your play."

He nodded. If he didn't speak to her, didn't stimulate her, maybe she'd drift off. What he had to do would be easier if she were asleep.

"Telephone. Telephone not—not—" Her head rolled weakly from side to side on the pillow. "Telephone not—"

He didn't know what she was trying to say. Had no idea. What did a telephone have to do with what had happened that night?

A flash of white in the doorway filled him with nausea.

No.

Not Dr. Aaronson. A male nurse with a medications cart. Going to one of the other patients.

Enough to remind him he didn't have time to waste on nonessentials like wondering about a telephone. Think instead of what he had to do, exactly how he had to do it.

Her eyes closed.

He sat motionless, watching her. He had to wait until the nurse finished his rounds.

He willed the two men visiting the middle-aged woman to say their goodbyes and leave. As if on cue, they did. He looked around. He was the only visitor remaining.

It was dark outside, but the overhead lights hadn't been turned on, and the small bed lamps didn't penetrate the shadows around them. What incredible luck that Mrs. Caitlin had asked him to stay. And what better time than this lull before dinner, most of the attending doctors gone home for the day, the nurses busy at their station, the halls empty.

Queer to think he wouldn't be coming back here any more. He felt like a fixture.

He looked at Susannah, watched the still face. She must be asleep. She hadn't stirred since closing her eyes. A whiff of the anesthesia and she wouldn't feel a thing, would never know what had happened to her.

The medications nurse pushed his cart to the bed next to Susannah. The very same nurse who had given him the idea of what to do in case he had to.

Weeks ago he had sat here watching the nurse insert a needle in Susannah's wrist for the intravenous tube. Had noticed all the other needle marks on her hands and wrists, the bruises, the discoloration. Remembered injections at the clinic. Precautionary words.

One more needle mark on Susannah's still-discolored arm wouldn't be noticed. And the bubble of air injected into a vein would kill without incriminating.

They would think it had all been too much for her. That a blood vessel in her already injured head had ruptured.

Something.

Whatever they thought, it would have nothing to do with him.

He felt in one jacket pocket for the small syringe, in the other for the gauze pads and the vial of anesthesia that worked like chloroform but without the odor. Or so his friend at the clinic had said.

His hands were trembling. His body, too. The nausea had become a constant.

He looked around again.

The middle-aged woman had a headset on, watching TV. The two old ladies were asleep. Had their eyes closed, anyhow.

He had practiced doing it over and over. It would be a cinch.

The nurse pushed his cart to Susannah's bed.

Herb's heart started pounding. If the nurse gave Susannah a shot to knock her out, he wouldn't have to use the stuff he'd brought.

The nurse consulted a chart, picked up his key ring, selected a key.

Herb held his breath. The hospital wouldn't lock up

aspirin. And hadn't Dr. Aaronson told Susannah he
would give her something to calm her down?

The nurse unlocked a compartment, took out a syringe, filled it. Herb let his breath out. The hospital
was going to do half the job for him.

The nurse bent over Susannah, a hand on her arm.
"Susannah," he said gently. "Susannah?"

She didn't respond, didn't stir.

Straightening up, the nurse frowned down at her.
With a shake of his head he turned back to his cart and
consulted the chart again, frowning at it. "Typical," he
said to nobody in particular. "Typical." With another
shake of his head, syringe in hand, taking his key ring,
he left the room.

Herb stared after him. He must have gone to get a
doctor. No. Not *a* doctor. Dr. Aaronson. After what he
had told Susannah, Dr. Aaronson must have written
the order in her chart.

He had to act now. Use his drug after all.

He looked around the room again. Everything was
the same as before. He only had to pull the curtain a
little.

Left hand into left pocket to break the vial into the
gauze pads.

His friend was wrong. It did smell.

Maybe not enough to matter.

Hurry.

He had the soaked pads halfway to her face when he
stopped.

He couldn't do it.

Susannah. His beautiful, tantalizing, challenging
half-smiler with the silvery-blue eye shadow and the
jaunty man's cap.

Susannah.

He had to do it.

It had never been more than a dream to begin with.

He held the pads to her nose, trying not to look at
her or think about her.

Right hand into right pocket for the syringe. Find
a vein.

He found it, pinched it very gently, was ready to
inject the needle into it when he heard footsteps in the

hall outside, a voice saying, "She might be asleep, you know."

Cervantes.

A tremor shot through him like a jolt of electricity, the syringe clattering to the floor.

Cervantes and Jill came into the room. "Oh," Jill said, looking surprised. "Hi, Mr.—Hi, Herb. How's Mom?"

"Hello, Herb," Cervantes said.

Could they smell anything?

"She's asleep," he told them. "Mrs. Caitlin asked me to stay with her. Until the doctor came back."

"She okay?" Cervantes asked.

With his right foot Herb felt for the syringe. He couldn't find it. "Yeah. Except—uh—she's afraid of something."

Jill hunched over her mother, stroking the pillow by her head. "Do they know why yet?"

"No." Herb was sweating. He wiped his face with the sleeve of his jacket. "I—it's hot in here."

"I reckon," Cervantes said.

Cervantes had a stock of no-answer answers. I reckon. Yeah. No kidding. You don't mean it. Herb had never loathed Cervantes so much as now.

"I wanted to see if she remembered I'd been here," Jill said, disappointed. She looked to Cervantes. "Couldn't we wake her?"

How long would it take for the chloroform substitute to wear off? Would anybody be able to wake her?

"I don't know, kid," Cervantes was saying. "Maybe it's better to let her sleep." He turned to Herb. "She been asleep long?"

"No. But the nurse tried to wake her and couldn't."

He had that much going for him.

Jill looked scared. "Is anything wrong?"

It was all Herb could do to keep from screaming himself. Would they stop grilling him? And he still hadn't located the syringe. He shook his head. "I don't think so."

"From what I've heard," Cervantes said, "she's had one hell of a rough day. And in her condition. She must be exhausted."

Footsteps down the hall again, into the room. The male nurse. Dr. Aaronson with him.

Jill, stroking her mother's hair, stepped aside as the two men approached the bed, one on either side.

"Susannah," Dr. Aaronson said, jiggling her arm. She stirred but didn't open her eyes.

They couldn't have smelled anything. Herb hadn't taken his eyes from the doctor's face. He would have seen his nose twitch.

"You're probably right," Dr. Aaronson said to the nurse. He jiggled her arm again, harder. "Susannah?"

She opened her eyes, gave Dr. Aaronson a dazed look, turned from him toward the nurse, who still had the syringe in his hand. In one violent lurch she reared back in the bed screaming.

Jill stared at her mother, then burst into tears.

In the hubbub that followed—Dr. Aaronson and the nurse coping with Susannah, Cervantes coping with Jill—Herb took a pencil from his jacket pocket and dropped it, found the syringe, and pocketed it, his heart pounding again at what he had witnessed.

Susannah couldn't be acting, couldn't be putting on a performance for his benefit. She was too weak, too injured.

Dr. Aaronson had been half wrong.

She knew what, but she didn't know who.

"Mama," Jill said when they had both calmed down. "Do you remember I was here this afternoon? With Grandma?"

Susannah nodded. "Yes, bayside. Yes." She smiled at Jill, looked around to include others in her smile. Dr. Aaronson, Cervantes, the nurse, himself.

She didn't know he had attacked her.

Leaving the hospital a few minutes later with Jill and Cervantes, walking out with them into the bitter February night, Herb started trembling again.

"It's cold," Jill said, hunching her shoulders.

"You need to be refueled," Cervantes told her.

At the corner the three of them stopped.

"Well," Cervantes said, "see you, Herb."

He nodded.

Cervantes and Jill set off hand in hand toward Central Park West, then Jill turned back. "We're going for a hamburger. Want to come with us?"

Herb shook his head. "I can't. I'm having dinner with my mother."

"Your mother here in the city?" Jill asked. "Or your mother on Staten Island?"

"Here in the city. My real mother."

"Oh. Well, 'bye."

He watched them set off again.

Maybe she never would remember.

He didn't want to kill her. He'd never wanted that.

He turned and headed uptown. For once he was looking forward to having dinner with his mother. He hadn't told her the news yet about *Possessed*.

That would set the old bitch back on her heels.

It would also account for the exhilaration building up in him, the sense of knowing he could do what he had to. He doubted he could have hidden that. Not from her.

Fourteen

Dr. Aaronson perched on the side of her bed, his long white hospital coat spattered with dried blood, his stethoscope stuffed in one side pocket, papers bulging from the other. Aside from his position—chief resident in Neurosurgery—and his appearance—tall, dark-complected, dark-haired, a large man with gentle hands and a sweet, infectious smile—she knew nothing about him. She seldom saw him for more than a few minutes every day. She depended on him utterly.

"I have good news," he said, smiling. "You're going home tomorrow."

Ready to return the smile, expecting the good news to be—what? Miraculous instant return of language? Return of memory? Fleetness of foot? She clutched him. "No!"

His smile fading, he took her hands in his. "What are you afraid of, Susannah? What frightens you so?"

For the last week—more than a week—she had known she was right about what had happened to her, and Barbara Caitlin wrong. Not that she blamed the social worker. The fragment of information she had given her and the way she had given it would have raised anybody's eyebrows. She had to piece it out, explain it. Take a more rational approach. Not get so excited.

All week long, in and out of physical therapy, lifting weights (Session One), dressing, undressing, brushing hair, brushing teeth, tying shoes (Session Two), in and out of occupational therapy, sculpting a clay dog, in and out of every class except speech therapy, which demanded her brain as well as her body, she had tried desperately—though she knew it was no use—to remember more, had tried—of little more use—to coax out the right words for what little she did know.

Had tried to stay awake at the end of each long day to concentrate more. Had fought off sleep.

No use either.

Had taken what comfort she could in the belief she had plenty of time before she was physically ready to be discharged from the hospital.

Tomorrow?

A violent tremor shook her body.

He asked her again. "What frightens you so?"

She tried to shut everything else out of her mind. "Man."

Dr. Aaronson frowned. "What man? The man who attacked you?"

She nodded. "More."

"Attacked you and mugged you?"

"No." She pointed to his watch. "Comb. No. Thumb. No. Wait. Please." She rubbed the face of his watch, searching, searching. "Time. Yes. Time. Wait. Have. Have time?"

He looked from the watch to her. "Do I have time?"

"Yes." Sweat had formed on her forehead. It edged down her face.

"Let me make one phone call first. Okay?"

Nodding, she reached for a tissue and, while he made the call, concentrated on what to say next.

"Now," he said, cradling the phone. "You're frightened of the man who attacked you. Because you're afraid he'll attack you again?"

She could hardly believe she had heard him right. "Yes! Yes!"

"Susannah," he said, "I understand your fear. Believe me, if I were in your position, I'd probably feel the same way. But the chances of that happening are so small, they—"

"No! No! Wait. Please. Man—man— Call. No. Come. No. Wait. Please. Man—man—man— Kill. Yes! Kill! Man kill—man kill— You. No. You. No. Wait. Please. Wait." She thought as hard as she could. "Me. Yes! Me. Man—man kill—man kill me."

He was frowning again. "Are you saying the man who attacked you tried to kill you?"

"Yes! Yes! No mug. No. Kill. Yes."

"Are you saying he wasn't trying to mug you, he was trying to kill you?"

"Yes! Yes! Man—man—me—I—I know."

"You know who the man was?"

She shook her head. "No. Here. Wait. Please." She reached for pencil and paper. Laboriously she printed MAN I KNOW.

She handed him the paper, and he looked at it, frowning. "I thought you said you didn't know who the man is."

"I—yes. Right. Here." She took the paper from him and printed I KNOW MAN. NO. MAN I KNOW. YES. Once again she handed it to him.

"You mean it's some man you know, but you don't know who?"

She clapped her hands. "Yes! Yes!"

"Some man you know tried to kill you."

"Yes!"

"Why?"

She hadn't expected to be asked that, hadn't prepared for it. She reached for another tissue to wipe her face, streaming with sweat.

"Why, Susannah? Why would this man—some man you know—try to kill you? What for?"

She shook her head.

"You don't know why?"

She shook her head again. "No."

"Susannah..."

She stared at him, dismayed. He didn't believe her. "Wait. Please. Dark. Rain. Aban—aban— No." Why had she gone back to that? Why did she always go back to that? "Wait. Dark. Rain. Aban— No." She could have cried. Clutching his hand, she said, "Wait. Please."

He nodded. "Take your time, Susannah. Try to relax."

"Yes. All right. Yes. Man—man—slicker—yellow slicker."

"The man was wearing a yellow slicker?"

She hadn't known that until she said it. "Yes. Yellow slicker. Man—man yellow. No. Yell. Yes. Man yell, 'Die, die, die!'"

"The man in the yellow slicker yelled 'Die, die, die' at you?"

She could tell from the tone of his voice he didn't believe her. "Wait. Please. Man kill. Man kill. Afraid. Please. No go home. No. Man kill. Please. Please."

"Susannah..."

"Please." She clutched him again.

It was no use.

"Look," he said. "I know you're frightened, and I think I know why. Let me get somebody who can be more help to you than I can. Okay?"

The somebody was a psychiatrist. Dr. O'Neal. Except for his coloring—he was a redhead with a flowing red beard—he could have been Dr. Aaronson's twin. Same size, same age, same gentleness. And same conviction she was all mixed up inside.

They met in his office at the end of the day. Their first meeting, but he knew all about her.

"Do you remember asking your daughter why she hadn't come to see you—not even once—since you'd been in the hospital?"

"Yes."

"But she had in fact been here. Every day."

"Yes."

"You don't say that with much conviction."

Susannah had been looking at him. She looked away. "I—" She shook her head.

"It's still hard for you to accept that, Susannah, isn't it—that Jill could have been here all that time, day in and day out, and you not remember it."

Still not looking at him, she nodded. It was hard. Part of her still didn't believe it.

Any more than Dr. O'Neal believed her.

"I understand your anxiety," he said. "It's perfectly natural. Normal. You can't remember yet what happened to you, but it has frightened you terribly, and so you say to yourself it must have been something bad. Not just a street attack, a mugging, but something so horrible I've blocked it out of my mind. Maybe the man raped me. Maybe that was it."

If he expected her to react, she disappointed him. The word rape said nothing to her.

"Susannah," he said, "it's also possible—and more likely than not—that nothing at all happened to you beyond what we already know took place. Not that I'm discounting that. You were attacked, you were beaten and robbed—savagely beaten, Dr. Aaronson tells me. And left for dead. Now that's frightening enough. How much more frightening not to be able to remember it, not to be able to say this much happened and no more, this was how it happened, no other way. I was doing thus and such. I was on my way to."

"I—to—to find a telephone."

Surprised, she wanted time to think. He didn't give it to her. "You wanted to find a telephone to make a call to someone. Who?"

"Jill."

"Your daughter Jill. You wanted to call your—"

"No. Not wanted. Had—had—"

"Had to?"

"Yes."

"You had to call your daughter Jill. Why? For what reason?"

"Warn her— No. Not warn. Tell her—tell her not be afraid. Not be afraid. Grand—grandmother—grandmother not—not get custom. No. Custard. No. Cus—cus—"

Dr. O'Neal frowned. "Custody?"

"Yes. Grandmother not get custody."

His frown deepening, he looked at a sheaf of papers in the manila folder he held in his lap. "You're talking about Jill's paternal grandmother. Mrs. Whitney."

"Yes."

"According to my—before that night, the night you were attacked, had Mrs. Whitney given you any indication she was trying to get custody of Jill?"

Susannah frowned back at him. "No."

"What did she do that night?"

"She—she said—she said marriage my fault. Me pregnant. My fault." Susannah wiped her face again. "No. That not right. I don't know."

She was tired, too tired to go on. She wanted him to say that would be all, they would come back to this another time. "Susannah," he said, "are you afraid of losing custody of Jill?"

She started trembling. "Yes."

"To Mrs. Whitney?"

"Yes. No. Joe. Joe."

"Your ex-husband?"

"Yes."

"You're afraid he'll try to take Jill away from you?"

"Yes. Oh, yes." She was still trembling.

Dr. O'Neal consulted his papers again. "Susannah, how much time does your ex-husband spend with Jill?"

Susannah shook her head. "Not—not—".

"Not much, right?"

She nodded.

"He seldom comes to see her, he makes promises to her he doesn't keep, he doesn't consult with you about her, he almost never sends you child support. Yet you're afraid he'll try to take Jill away from you. Does that make sense?"

She ached with fatigue. "No."

"Susannah, bear with me a bit longer. My guess is that something happened the night you were attacked—or the day of the night you were attacked—maybe even a day or two before—that has to do with Jill. Something that frightens you. Maybe concerning your relationship with her. A quarrel, maybe."

Something flickered at the back of her mind.

"Something that fundamentally spells loss. Loss of affection. Loss of esteem. Loss of trust. Of harmony. Whatever. Now, unable to remember what that something is, but retaining the fear—indeed, maybe magnifying it all out of proportion because you can't remember what's causing it—you've substituted another kind of loss. Loss of custody. Now, why loss of custody? Consider. When Jill comes to see you, her grandmother is with her. More important, her grandmother is living with her, taking care of her. And because your ex-husband is close to his mother, because you're plagued with guilt feelings about your marriage, and—most important—because Jill, from everything I've been told, is very attached to her father, it's an easy step to go from the grandmother seeking custody to his seeking it."

Susannah wanted to say no, that wasn't right, he had missed the mark somewhere, it had something to do with Jill's grandmother but not what he said it did, but she said nothing. For one thing, she was too tired to make the effort, and for another, what he said sounded so right, so logical.

"Now," he went on, "I'm almost finished. I think that just as you've seized on loss of custody to explain your fear concerning Jill, so you've seized on the idea that somebody was trying to kill you to explain what happened to you the night you were attacked."

Tired or not, she had to speak. "No! No! You—you—no."

He smiled his gentle, compassionate smile. "Susannah, I know it upsets you that you can't remember the attack on you. You tell yourself you should be able to remember it. You ask yourself over and over what's the matter with you that you can't remember it. Isn't that so?"

She nodded.

"Everybody tells you you were mugged. That doesn't satisfy you. You come up with something—something pretty far out, I have to admit—that for some reason does. Somebody you know was trying to kill you."

"Yes! Please. Yes!"

It was no use.

"Susannah, I know it's hard for you, but try not to think about it. Give yourself time. Your brain still isn't fully healed, you know. And it isn't as if this is the only opportunity we'll have, you and I. We'll meet again, as often as you like, to work on the problem, to help you try to get your memory back. And you will get it back, I'm confident of that."

If she lived that long.

Barbara Caitlin stopped in the next morning to say goodbye.

"Not really goodbye, Susannah," she said, smiling, the gold-loop earrings she wore so often sparkling in the sunlight that streamed into the room. "I have your outpatient schedule. I'll look in on you when I can. And if there's anything I can do for you, be sure and let me know. I think I told you your friend Mr. Schlosser has volunteered to come back and forth to the hospital with you for as long as you need help getting around."

"Isn't that interesting!"

Despite her conditioning, Susannah jumped at the old lady's interjection.

Barbara smiled. "He knows where my office is. He can bring you there."

"Barbar." That was all she could manage of Barbara's name. "Barbar. No go. Please." Susannah made a face at herself. She sounded like a two-year-old. Maybe that was why they treated her like one.

The social worker, about to leave, turned back. "What is it, Susannah? What's the matter?"

"No go home. No. Please."

"I'm afraid you have to. Your physical condition warrants it. And—well—the cost, you know."

Medicaid was paying her hospital bill. How justify to Medicaid keeping a patient afraid to go home?

Barbara put a hand on her arm. "You'll be fine, Susannah. All the therapists say you're making excellent progress." A sound at the door made Barbara turn. She smiled again. "And here's your escort service. On the dot. Good morning, Mr. Schlosser."

Good morning, goodbye.

Herb pushed her to and from the elevator in the wheelchair required by hospital regulations to prevent some unforeseeable accident.

How prevent the unforeseeable accident once she was outside?

How make anybody understand there was going to be one.

Despite the sunshine, the March day was raw and windy. Susannah shivered at the foot of the hospital steps while Herb went to get the car he had come up with—borrowed, rented?—to take her home.

She felt exposed, vulnerable. The man who wanted her dead could be anywhere.

She looked in all directions. Nobody. Dr. Aaronson and Dr. O'Neal were right. It made no sense. Why would anybody want her dead?

Why was she trembling?

Why did she tremble at the thought of losing custody of Jill when that was patently absurd?

If only she could think why she was afraid of losing Jill, what it was about Jill that upset her.

Susannah looked around again, wishing Herb would hurry. If only she could remember what had happened to her that night.

There he came.

He was oversolicitous helping her into the car. There was something oppressive about Herb. The prospect of having to go back and forth with him to Oldenham Hospital every morning, five days a week, lay like a weight on her shoulders.

A good thing, maybe. The yearning to free herself from him would make her push herself harder in physical therapy.

He wasn't a good driver either. The kind of New Yorker who drove by sound and fury. Ride the horn and hit the brakes.

Glancing at him, seeing how tense he was, she felt ashamed. She was back to her old habit of label-and-condemn.

She owed this man her life. What did he have to be to merit her appreciation?

"Herb—I—I—grateful."

"It's all right." He looked flustered.

In any event, would she rather go back and forth alone to the hospital? Without any protection?

She wondered what Herb would say if she told him somebody had tried to kill her.

She didn't have to tell him. He already knew. He was there in her room when she told Barbara the man had yelled "die" at her.

Did Herb think she was mixed-up, too?

"Herb—I—I—Herb?"

"Yes?" Concentrating on the traffic, he didn't look at her.

Maybe she should wait until some other time.

"I—nothing."

The speech therapist was right. She was getting better every day at coming up with the word she wanted. Maybe it wasn't too much to hope that her language ability would eventually come back a hundred percent. Or almost. Enough that she could go on in the theater.

Oh, yes. By all means. Go on from where?

She shifted position, turning to look for signs of spring in Central Park, rolling by on her right. She was going to work herself into a severe depression if she didn't watch out.

If she didn't watch out, there wouldn't be anything left of her to be depressed about. The man who had tried to kill her would see to that.

She was trembling again.

"Susannah?" They had stopped for a red light, and Herb was looking at her.

She hadn't realized her trembling was visible. She tried to smile. "I scared, Herb. Scared. Man. Remember man yell 'Die, die, die'? I skoof—no. Skate. No." She clenched her hands to keep from swearing—something as automatic to her as the old lady's "Isn't that interesting!" She could no longer be sure of anything. Not even a word she had used moments ago. And after she'd just been telling herself— "Scared. Yes. Scared."

The light turned green. "Oh," he said, blasting his horn at the driver in front of him. "Yeah."

When she got home she would make a list of every man it could possibly be. Maybe writing the name would jog her memory.

When she got home she was too exhausted to do anything but lie down.

Her ex-mother-in-law was there to greet her, taking from Herb's outstretched hand the shopping bag that

had served as her suitcase, urging her to stretch out on
the sofa, asking Herb to stay for a cup of coffee.

To Susannah's relief Herb declined. He was still
tense. Parking the car had been an ordeal for him, re-
quiring almost half a dozen tries before he'd been able
to jockey it into the only available slot on the block.

Nor was the atmosphere inside the apartment con-
ducive to relaxation. The senior Mrs. Whitney, playing
hostess in the house of the enemy, having to welcome
the enemy home, was flushed and flustered.

At the same time he seemed reluctant to leave. "Will
you want me for speech therapy later today?"

Susannah shook her head. "No. I—I tired, Herb.
Need day off."

He nodded, yet stood where he was, making no move
to go. She thought she understood his reluctance. Apart
from her fear of being killed, she hadn't wanted to leave
the hospital, had stared, wordless, at Dr. Aaronson before reaching out to him for a quick, tight embrace. She
felt wrenched away, adrift, no longer part of something.
After coming to see her in the hospital day after day,
week after week, Herb must feel a bit that way, too.
She smiled encouragement at him. "Tomorrow." He was
to pick her up at ten in the morning to take her to the
hospital. By bus, she hoped.

He nodded again and, after another awkward silence, said goodbye and left.

She had hoped his departure would ease the tension.
A forlorn hope.

"Jill wanted to stay home from school today. To be
here when you came home. But she had an examination
in history, and I didn't think she should miss it."

The forced hospitality was gone. In its place was the
more familiar antagonism with its veneer of civility.

"I hope that was all right."

Even sometimes servility.

Susannah nodded.

"The principal of the school—the middle school, I
suppose I should say. In any event, she called to extend
her best wishes."

The middle school, I suppose I should say.

Jill's grandmother went to Shipley each Christmas

for the pageant, and she'd gone to an occasional Assembly at Jill's invitation, but her knowledge of the school was confined to her own preconceived notion of it as a pretentious and wasteful extravagance.

"I've tried to do things where Jill's schoolwork is concerned, the way I thought you would."

More servility—in a not-so-oblique reference to the hated trust fund, the blow Mrs. Whitney had received from her mother, when great-grandmother Fitzhugh set up the fund for Jill's education, its application left to the discretion of the custodian, the custodian not Joe but Susannah.

Mrs. Whitney was going home tonight, her bags packed and ready in a corner of the living room, but she had said she would commute into the city weekdays for as long as she was needed. Not certain she could manage without her, Susannah had agreed, but she wasn't any more certain she could manage with her.

She had never been on easy terms with her. Throughout her marriage to Joe, she couldn't bring herself to call her Mother and hadn't dared call her Eve. When she had to call her anything she called her Mrs. Whitney. She still did.

Her own parents had put the best possible face on the unexpected marriage, the too-soon baby. Mrs. Whitney had made no secret of her feeling it was all Susannah's doing, a position that hardened when Joe dropped out of college after Jill was born to take up the life he'd been leading ever since—an aimless drift from job to job and bar to bar.

Until they'd been able to afford an apartment of their own, they had lived for a time with Mrs. Whitney—the worst period of Susannah's life.

Until now.

Her ex-mother-in-law was asking her something.

"I—sorry. What?"

Mrs. Whitney raised her voice. "I said, would you rather go into your bedroom and lie down?"

"No. Have—stay up. Make—make—" Susannah sighed, her attention starting to wander. "I no—I don't know. Make something."

The older woman tried to help. "Make coffee. Was

that what you were trying to say?" She raised her voice again. "Would you like me to make you some coffee?"

"No. I—okay." She would have to tell people not to shout at her. Hearing wasn't her problem. Concentration was. Her attention span was sometimes so short it was almost nonexistent.

Mrs. Whitney went into the kitchen, and Susannah pulled herself into a sitting position on the sofa to look around. She had thought that at the sight of her apartment, her surroundings, her memory would come flooding back. It hadn't. It didn't now.

What was it she had meant to do when she got home? Something about a telephone?

As Mrs. Whitney came back with the coffee the doorbell rang. "I'll get it," the older woman said, setting the mugs down. She had made coffee for herself, too.

Tim Cervantes was at the door. "Sorry I couldn't pick you up at the hospital," he said, coming into the room after greeting her ex-mother-in-law, "but I was shooting in Central Park. That new film I told you about." He kissed her and sat down beside her, taking her hand in his. "How are you?"

"Okay." The list. That was what she had meant to do. Make a list of every— Surely it couldn't be Tim.

She was trembling again.

He gave her an anxious look. "What's the matter?"

Mrs. Whitney picked up one of the mugs and started back to the kitchen with it, her back rigid.

Susannah was getting too much input, more than she could handle. "No," she said. "No."

Not very descriptive, but Cervantes caught on. He knew all about Mrs. Superior Person. Scrambling to his feet, going after her, he said, "Susannah wants you to stay, Mrs. Whitney. Please. I only stopped by for a minute or two. I have to get back to the park. I'll tell you what. You and Susannah drink your coffee while I make myself some."

At the sight of her ex-mother-in-law's face, Susannah's trembling stopped, her fear forgotten. She wanted to whoop with laughter. In making himself at home that way, Cervantes couldn't have done anything more outrageous if he had tried. Knowing Tim, he probably had. He was a notorious jokester.

Nevertheless the older woman came back into the living room. Susannah patted the sofa cushion beside her, but Mrs. Whitney sat in the wreck of a chair Jill had found out on the sidewalk last summer.

She had other ways of getting back. "I've made an appointment for you at the welfare center. You're to go there Monday."

Susannah nodded. For what comfort there was in it, aphasia had one small advantage. If you could respond any other way, you weren't expected to speak.

The telephone rang.

It rang a second time before Cervantes picked it up. In that interval she remembered something.

The night of the attack on her she had left the apartment on her way to the callback for *The Glory Road.* For the Hollywood big shot. She had started down the stairs when she heard the phone ring, debated going back, decided not to, figuring Jill could take a message.

Whoever made that phone call had some connection with the man who tried to kill her. Maybe was the man. One or the other, it would establish his identity. She was certain of it.

"It's Dr. Dubinsky," Tim said, poking his head out of the kitchen. "Can you talk to him?"

She'd been wanting to talk to Dr. Dubinsky since she realized what had happened to her, but she was afraid if she let anything distract her now, the little shard of memory would slip away. She put up both hands, palms out, in a pushing motion. "Call back! Please. Call back!" She turned to her ex-mother-in-law. "Paper! Please. Paper!" She would write it down before she forgot it.

Mrs. Whitney stared at her as if she were possessed.

"Please. Now! Please." She must not forget.

"All right. Yes, Susannah." Coming out of her trance, moving with alacrity, the older woman hastened out of the room, returning with a lined yellow tablet and a fistful of ballpoint pens. "Here you are."

One of her speech therapists encouraged writing, the other printing. Wishing they'd get their act together,

Susannah usually ended up with a mélange of both.
Did now.

Still not confident that what she produced in writing
or speech was what she intended to produce, she handed
the tablet to Cervantes.

Something else she knew. Was sure of. It couldn't be
Cervantes. That wasn't possible.

He took the tablet. "You want me to read it to myself
or out loud?"

"Loud."

"Okay. It says, 'Night left hear. Call—'" He frowned.
"Call something. Your handwriting is atrocious."

"Back. Callback."

"Oh. Yeah. Okay. 'Night left hear. Callback. Stairs.
Fone ring. No go back. Jill take. Who call?'" He looked
at her. "That right?"

"Yes. Right. No forget. Right. Who call?"

He was still looking at her. "Does it matter?"

They were both looking at her.

Starting to tremble again, she reached out to Cervantes. "Not forget. Please?"

He sat down beside her, put an arm around her.
"What's the matter, Susannah? What's troubling you?"

She was sure she could trust Cervantes. Positive of
it. She concentrated. "Man. Man beat. Man kill."

"You're damn right," he said, tightening his grip on
her. "He damn near killed you."

"No," Susannah said. "No." She concentrated harder.
"Man try kill."

"I think," Mrs. Whitney said, "she's saying the man
tried to kill her."

Susannah nodded. "Yes! Yes!"

"It doesn't surprise me to hear it." Mrs. Superior
Person made a face. "This city is full of animals."

Cervantes gave her another squeeze. "Well, you're
safe now. And I've got to get back to work. I'll stop by
later. No. Sit still, Mrs. Whitney. I know the way out."

Beginning to feel like Alice in Wonderland, Susannah watched him go.

The effort required to produce the note about the
phone call, to try to explain what had happened to her,
had—as usual—exhausted her. She started to stretch

out again full length on the sofa when something else
occurred to her. She wondered why she hadn't thought
of it before. Tim had put the tablet down on the coffee
table. Picking it up, she half-printed, half-wrote, "Ask
Jill what wrong." If she and Jill had had a quarrel that
amounted to anything, Jill would surely remember it.

Jill did remember. But wouldn't say so.

She was late getting home that afternoon, and
though obviously pleased to see Susannah, her greeting
was restrained, self-conscious.

"I'm surprised at you," her grandmother said. "After
the fuss you put up this morning about going to school?
What kept you?"

"There was something I had to do."

"What was it?"

Jill tucked her long blond hair behind her ears, her
skin flushed. "Nothing."

"How can something be nothing?"

Jill's flush deepened. "Nothing much," she said. She
picked up her bag of schoolbooks and headed for her
bedroom.

"I declare," her grandmother said, but she said it
fondly, reaching out to ruffle Jill's hair in passing.

Watching the gesture, seeing Jill's shy smile in reaction to it, Susannah felt a stab of—of what? Lone-
liness? Jealousy? _Déjà vu?_

Again something flickered at the back of her mind.
Something to do with what had happened between
Jill and herself.

She had to know what it was.

"Bayside—bay—Jill?"

Jill turned back. "Yes?"

Susannah beckoned to her. "Night I—I beaten, we—
you—me—we fight?"

Jill hesitated, then shook her head. "No."

"We—something? What?"

Again the hesitation, the shake of the head. "No."

Susannah knew she wasn't telling the truth. "Jill.
Please. Need know. What?"

"Mom, it wasn't anything. I told you Herb said to
remind you about his reading, and you said you couldn't
make it because you had the callback, and you had to

go tell him so. And you said I shouldn't spend so much time in Horlick's."

Susannah listened intently, trying to remember, ready to seize on a word or phrase that would open up the encounter to her.

Nothing.

"Jill. Important. Important remember."

Jill shook her head again, the closed-in airport look on her face. Whatever it was, for whatever reason, she wasn't going to say.

Susannah lay back against the sofa pillows. Maybe it didn't matter. Maybe it wouldn't help to be told what had happened between them. She had been told over and over what had happened between her and her attacker, and it meant nothing to her.

Jill's grandmother was putting on her coat, ready to leave. "You wanted to ask Jill about the phone call, Susannah. Remember? There on the tablet."

Dear God.

The phone call.

How could she keep from being killed if she couldn't remember from one minute to the next something as vital to preventing it as that?

"Bayside—sorry. Jill. Here. Read." Susannah picked up the tablet and handed it to her.

Jill read the message, frowning.

"You—remember?"

She shook her head. "No."

"Bayside—important. Please. Think man call."

Jill frowned. "What man?"

"I—I no know. You say."

Jill's frown intensified. She wasn't feigning this time. She looked honestly perplexed. "Gee, Mom, I—how do you expect me to remember a phone call that far back? The phone rings all the time here."

Mrs. Whitney again to the rescue. "If the call was for your mother, Jill, wouldn't you have written the message down?"

"Well, yeah. I guess so."

"Then maybe you still have it. Can you think back to what you were doing that night? When your mother left the apartment to go to the theater?"

The closed-in airport look was back. With matching voice. "I don't have to think back. I know. I was in my room. Sitting at my desk." She glanced at Susannah. A fearful glance meant to tell her something. It told her nothing. Jill sighed. "Doing my homework."

"Well," her grandmother said, "maybe the message is still on your desk somewhere."

The way Jill took care of—didn't take care of—her room, it probably was.

And again something flickered at the back of her mind.

"In a notebook," Mrs. Whitney was saying. "Or in one of the desk drawers. If the phone call is that important to your mother, it's worth a little effort looking for it, isn't it?"

"Well, sure," Jill said. "I'll look." Once again she set off with her bag of books.

Susannah turned to her ex-mother-in-law. "I—I grateful."

"It's all right, Susannah," she said a bit stiffly, her face flushed. "I know this isn't an easy time for you."

Touched by the sincerity of the remark, wishing she and Mrs. Whitney had a friendlier relationship, Susannah searched for something to say that would communicate her feeling. The search was aborted by a squawk from Jill.

Coming back into the living room clutching a piece of paper, she said, "You were right, Grandma. I forgot all about it, but I remember now." She turned to Susannah. "You were right, too, Mom. It was a man."

Susannah's heart pounded. Protection, exoneration, retribution—all there on a piece of paper in her daughter's hands. "Who?" she said. "Who?"

Jill beamed. "Grandpa. Grandpa Burke."

Susannah stared at her. "My—my—my—father?"

Jill nodded. "He called to find out about *The Glory Road*—to see if you'd heard anything. I told him about the callback, and he said to tell you he wished you luck."

Fifteen

She couldn't tell whether Dr. Dubinsky believed her or not. He didn't say. A quiet, intense, wiry little man in his fifties, he had bushy gray hair that dwarfed his head, and he sat behind his desk in a high-backed chair that dwarfed his frame. After working with him twice a week for two years, Susannah still didn't know if the dwarfing was deliberate, but it made him seem at one and the same time less intimidating and more omnipotent.

She almost didn't care whether or not he believed her, almost hadn't told him, maybe wouldn't have if he hadn't probed so insistently into why she was so depressed, why she had first put off returning his call, then coming to see him.

"Don't know who," she said before he could ask her. "Don't know why. Know sounds crazy. Doctors at hospital no believe. Nobody believe."

"But you do," he said.

She didn't have to answer that. She was, as usual, trembling.

"You say you don't know who," he said, "but you

must have given it thought. A great deal of thought,
I would imagine."

Susannah nodded. In the nearly three weeks since
she had left the hospital her speech had improved mark-
edly, but she still relied heavily on nonverbal responses.

"Do you have any idea who?"

About to shake her head, she hesitated. Eyeing him
she said, "Seem crazy."

"Susannah, let me be the judge of that."

"All right. I— No. Crazy. No." The revelation that
it had been her father calling her had devastated her.

Susannah had always thought of herself as a survivor. Tough-minded, independent of spirit, tenacious.
It wasn't only what she thought. She had bucked both
parents to become an actress. She had resisted Joe's
pleas, withstood his demands that she submit to a back-
room abortion. She had stood up to her mother-in-law.
Until she'd been disabled she had supported herself and
her child.

A survivor with style. More important than looks,
though she had those, too. Style. Panache. On her way
to getting where she wanted to go. Not looking for foot-
draggers. Impatient, neurotic, a little paranoid, a little
arrogant.

Her man's cap set at a jaunty angle, she went out
each day to meet the world.

No longer.

She no longer had a sense of self. She felt fragmented,
schizoid. Part of her was missing, lost in a void of not
remembering, not knowing, not being able to piece herself together.

She had no confidence. Time after time she had been
sure of this, certain of that, only to find out she was
wrong. Had it demonstrated. Proved.

She was more than a little paranoid. Several sessions
with Dr. O'Neal had shown her that. Despite hard evi-
dence of mugging—the missing billfold, the stolen
credit card—she kept insisting somebody had tried to
kill her. Agreeing with Dr. O'Neal that her fears re-
garding custody of Jill made no sense, she nursed them
still. Although she had never encountered him before,
she continued to be terrified of the nurse's aide who

dragged his feet. And she could give no reason, no explanation for anything.

No wonder nobody believed her.

She had begun to disbelieve herself.

"Susannah, whether or not somebody tried to kill you, that somebody is locked away inside your head. Whether or not your notion of who he is is crazy, it's there. I can't help you, you can't help yourself if we don't pursue whatever thoughts you have. Now. Tell me what you think about this man."

"I think—think—not know man well."

"Why? What gives you that impression?"

She had to struggle for the words, search for them. "Nobody—can't imagine—anybody else—kill. Not Joe. Not Tim. Not other—other men love." She swallowed. "Men here—group—group—please?"

"The men here in group therapy?"

"Yes. Men here—group—therapy. Men—men—rest—rest—restaurant—I work."

"You're saying you think the man who attacked you is either one of those here in group therapy—I take it you mean the two groups you work with on Thursday evenings. Worked with."

She nodded. There were sixteen persons in the two groups, nine of them men. On Tuesday evenings she had worked with three patients in private session, but all of them were women.

"All right. Either one of those men or one of the men patronizing the restaurant where you worked."

She nodded again. "Only—only else make sense."

It wasn't what she had wanted to say, but he understood. "You're saying otherwise it doesn't make sense. Is that right?"

"Yes."

He nodded his bushy head. "I'm inclined to agree with you. Unless—no jealous ex-lover?"

She hesitated, then shook her head. "No think so."

"No potential—and potentially violent—lover whom you've rejected?"

She shook her head again. "No lover—while. Tim yes. But—but—Tim off-on lover. On friend. Okay?"

"Yes. I understand." He reached into a desk drawer,

took out a black notebook, opened it, studied it, turned a page, studied that, turned another page, studied that. "I don't know," he said at last. "Has any of the men in therapy ever approached you, asked you for a date, walked home with you, talked to you about your role playing—anything like that?"

Tears filled her eyes and rolled down her face.

Dr. Dubinsky frowned. "What is it, Susannah?"

The tears kept coming. "Nobody—you—first—ask questions—like me no crazy. Me right. Help find. Down business. I—oh. Sorry, sorry."

He held out the box of tissues always at hand. "Take your time," he said. "Take all the time you need."

She spent the rest of the fifty-minute session with him going over names, recalling contacts, while he made notes. None of the names stirred any part of her memory that was missing, but she hadn't dared hope they would. She had been disappointed too many times before.

When she came out of the doctor's office Herb was waiting for her. She knew he would be. When he had left her here an hour ago he had said he'd be back to pick her up. If he hadn't come she would have been surprised. Yet, as much as she depended on him, as terrified as she would be to have to go out in the streets alone, a part of her always hoped he wouldn't show.

She didn't know why she felt that way about him, why there seemed something oppressive about him, but it made her feel weighed down, as if she were tied to him for all time to come.

She shook her head at herself.

She *was* tied to him—though, with any luck, not for all time to come. He arrived every weekday morning at ten to take her to the hospital—by bus. When she was ready to go home at one o'clock he was there. More evenings than not he was back at her apartment at eight to help with her speech therapy. Plus various extras at odd times of day, such as this visit to Dr. Dubinsky.

He spent so much time with her she didn't see how he managed his job at Horlick's or the rewrites the woman who was directing his play at the Manhattan Theater Club had asked for.

The Manhattan Theater Club.

As happy as she was for Herb, the thought of his play made her heart ache. Even discounting what had happened to her, she knew that the chances of her being cast in the role of Sabrina were almost nonexistent, but still, the role had been so right for her that if they had let her read for the part, maybe...

She shook her head at herself again.

Possessed didn't bear thinking on.

She had tried asking Herb what kind of arrangement he had worked out with Mr. Zekiel, how he was able to squeeze in the writing time he needed, but between his natural reticence about himself and her language difficulty, she hadn't learned much.

She had learned next to nothing about him as a person. From what she remembered of *Possessed*, she had tried casting him in each of its major roles, the foolish, stubborn, idealistic young priest, the tyrannical, destructive—and ultimately destroyed—mother superior, the innocent, frail-seeming Sabrina, for and in whose soul the battle raged, the fierce, shrewd, awesome Satan, and the lesser roles—the government official, the doctor, the paralyzed polio victim.

In order to create those characters, or any others, he had to have drawn upon and from himself. He had to be sensitive, imaginative, a complex person whose emotions ranged from tenderness to fury, from trust to blasphemy. Some part of the genius that had gone into the writing of *Possessed* had to be visible to her.

It wasn't.

Satan had a corrosive wit, the doctor a gentler one. Herb never said anything remotely humorous. The priest had a weakness for chocolate éclairs. Herb shrugged off all offers of sweets, saying he didn't care for them. If the mother superior was anything like Herb's mother, he must despise her, yet if he spoke of her at all, it was without emotion one way or the other.

After almost three weeks of continuous exposure, he had never once opened himself up to her, never laid himself bare. For whatever reason—or no reason at all—he kept himself as locked away from her as the man inside her head.

Maybe there was a reason. Although he had never said or done anything specific to indicate it, he seemed desperately unhappy to her. Desperately something. As if he wanted to reach out and couldn't. Couldn't tolerate anybody reaching out to him.

She both pitied and hated him for that. A part of her didn't want to reach out to anybody either, but she had no choice. She had to.

And mostly to him.

Cervantes was still making the film. What time he found for her had to be sandwiched in around the shooting schedule. Most of her other friends were actors. When they weren't making rounds or auditioning, they were in acting class or dance class—or waitressing or driving a cab. As eager as they were to help her, they had to put themselves and their dog-eat-dog profession first, one or another phoning to say sorry about this evening, something's come up—an audition, a job, an interview, an appointment with a new voice teacher.

What she would do without him she didn't know, and she didn't like that either. She didn't like having to be grateful to him, to owe him so much.

Not that he asked for her gratitude. He asked for nothing. He never accepted an invitation to stay after the therapy or the escorting for a cup of coffee or a glass of wine. He brushed her stammering thanks aside.

Worst of all, he cared about her. He had to, to make such a continuing sacrifice. At least he cared about her recovery. He was always asking how she felt, was her memory improving, did she have any idea who had attacked her.

Maybe that was it.

Maybe, in a way she didn't fully understand, helping her recover from her aphasia was its own reward. Barbara Caitlin said he had a proprietary feeling toward her because of finding her, and that was natural enough. Maybe he felt a responsibility as well, a need to see through to the finish what he had in a sense begun.

Except for Cervantes, Herb was the best as well as

the most faithful of her amateur therapists. In the hospital Cervantes had been uncomfortable around her. Now that he could help her, he was at ease again, dependable, rock-steady, with enduring patience and—alone among all her friends—a readiness to laugh at her mistakes.

Herb was never at ease with her. He wasn't at ease with himself. He was tense, irritable. His patience often seemed on the verge of snapping, though so far it never had. But despite his tension and the strain on his nerves, and unlike her other friends, who were too tenderhearted to push her past her capacity, he worked them both to exhaustion, exhorting her when her spirits flagged, refusing to let her attention wander, drumming into her head with one exercise after another that it was concentration they were after. Concentration and recall.

And never any letup.

Such as now.

Returning from Dr. Dubinsky's office up near Columbia University, they got off the bus not at Eighty-eighth Street and Columbus Avenue but at Eighty-sixth Street. Susannah felt jittery, anxious to get home. He steered her past Horlick's to the bakery next door and pointed to the window display. "I spy."

I Spy was one of the problem-solving games recommended by the Oldenham Hospital therapists to improve concentration. Susannah nodded. "What spy?"

"C.F.B."

She searched the window. "Choco—chocolate—C.C.B.?"

"C.F.B."

C.F.B. She searched again. C.F.B. "Ah. Chocolate—chocolate—frappe—no. No. Frosted. Chocolate frosted brown boys."

"Almost," he said. "Brownies. Brownies."

"Brown boys," she said again. She put a hand out. "I know. I think what you say. Comes out wrong. Try again. Brown—brown—ease. Ease. There. Brown boys." She shook her head. "No use, Herb. Go on something else."

The other night she had repeatedly said shoemaker

for umbrella and taffy for hairbrush. No connection she
could think of between either set of words. She had
finally said to Herb what she believed was true. "Wires
crossed."

Next to the bakery was a produce stall. They walked
to that. "I spy," he said.

"What say?" No. Wrong.

She was retrogressing—one of the most depressing
aspects of this business. She would master a word, a
phrase, a sentence one day or one moment and be unable to come up with it the next.

She was tired as well as jittery. She was always tired,
but the session with Dr. Dubinsky had drained her
physically and emotionally. She wanted to tell Herb to
stop playing this game and take her home, but she
knew as well as he did that she had to push herself,
had to struggle constantly not to give in to inertia,
boredom, frustration, depression.

At the hospital an elderly man, a stroke victim, had
said to her, "Stay awake on your feet if you can."

He hadn't been exaggerating.

Sighing, she tried again. "What spy?"

"E."

Radishes, cucumbers, carrots—ah. "Eggplant." Her
turn now. "I spy."

"What do you spy?"

"Also E."

He looked at the fruits and vegetables for some time,
frowning. Finally he shook his head. "I give up."

She beamed at him. "Esplanade."

He stared at her.

She frowned. "I—what wrong, Herb?"

He said nothing but went on staring at her.

She didn't know what to make of it. "Here." She
tugged him into the store. "Here." Various kinds of
lettuce were bunched together. She picked up a head
of curly escarole. "See? Esplanade. Oh." Only then did
she hear her mistake. No wonder he had stared at her,
though he ought to be used to her mistakes by this
time. "No. Not Esplanade. Crazy. Esplanade hotel. This
es—es—es—please?"

"Escarole."

"Right." She put the lettuce back. "Escarole. Herb, you okay?"

He nodded, his mouth working the way it did when he sometimes had difficulty speaking. "What made you—why did you—what made you think of the Esplanade?"

She shrugged. "Who know?" They had left the produce stall and—blessedly—were headed back toward Horlick's on the corner. With the cane she always carried when she went out, she pointed to a display of umbrellas in the newsstand's window. "What make me call them shoemaker? Who know? I tell you other night. Wires crossed."

He nodded.

They turned up Columbus toward her apartment on Eighty-seventh Street. She didn't need the cane. By the time the doctors removed the leg brace she had worn after recovering from her right-side paralysis, her muscles had been strengthened by swimming and other exercises to the point where she could limp along unaided. But she was fearful of being jostled on the street and falling. People respected the cane, giving her a wide berth.

The cane also served as a potential weapon, something she could use to strike back at the man she was sure lurked somewhere near, waiting to strike at her again.

Even with Herb along to protect her, she didn't like being on the street. Walking was a prescribed exercise. She would never be fully recovered physically, able to resume her acting career, until she could walk, run, dance, as freely as before. Yet she shrank from going out and, once out, was anxious to get back in again.

The first morning Herb had come to pick her up, leaving the apartment building had required more courage than she possessed. She stood in the vestibule downstairs for several minutes swallowing against the nausea roiling up in her, trying to control the tremors in her legs, saying to him, "Wait. Please. Wait. Please. Soon. Try. Wait. Please."

"What's the matter?" he asked.

"I scared, Herb. Scared. Man out there kill me."

"What man?"

"You know. You hear—you hear—tell Barbar. Man yell 'Die, die, die.' Try kill me."

"Do you know who he is? The man?"

"No. No know. Try think. No use."

"Do you know anything about him?"

"No. Yes." The tremors in her legs became more violent. "He near."

He frowned at her. "Near?"

"Yes."

"How do you—how do you know that?"

She shook her head. "Don't know how. Feel. Man near. Somewhere near. Look. Look. Man in slicker. Yellow slicker. Please look. Please."

She knew as she said it it made no sense. The man wouldn't be wearing his yellow slicker on a bright, sunny day. Nor would he stand around out in the open waiting for Herb to catch sight of him. But she couldn't help herself. Through chattering teeth she said, "Man in slicker. Yellow slicker. Dark. Rain. Aban—aban—Dark. Rain. Aban—aban—" She was babbling. She clenched her fists.

If Herb thought she was losing what few undamaged brain cells she had left, he didn't say so. He said nothing, did nothing. He just hovered over her in that oppressive way he had.

That was what finally drove her outside. His hovering. What drove her outside after that was her fear of repeating that draining, half-mad performance.

Today there was no sun. A storm was brewing; gray clouds massing in the west, a raw, wet wind whipping down Columbus Avenue, scattering debris, rattling the tinned-up windows of the clump of abandoned tenements across the street.

A long, thin piece of slate skirled up out of an empty lot and sailed into the side of the northernmost building, shattering. At the noise Susannah stopped.

Herb looked at her. "What's the matter?"

"Hotel Esplanade. You rent room. Read play. Right?"

He nodded.

"I no—no can take part." She frowned down at the sidewalk, trying to remember. Ghosts at the back of her mind reached out to her, then slipped away. She turned back to Herb. "I—I—I telephone?"

"To me, you mean?"

She shook her head. "I don't know. I telephone somebody. Everything all mixed up inside. I—I come tell you Horlick's?"

He nodded again. "You came to Horlick's. To tell me. About the callback. *The Glory Road.* Remember?"

She shook her head again. "Try. Can't. People say what I do. I don't know."

A gust of wind blew the hat off a man walking in front of them. Whipping around to chase after it, he almost charged into them.

Susannah gasped and lurched to one side, making wild stabs with the cane in the air and at the sidewalk to keep from falling.

"What is it?" Herb said, reaching out to steady her. "What's the matter?"

She shrank from his touch. She didn't like anybody touching her, not even Cervantes, unless she first reached out to him. "I—sorry, Herb. I—it nothing. Thought man after me." She turned to stare after him. He was still chasing his hat. "Something about—about—"

Herb turned to look, too. "About what? What about him?"

Susannah shook her head. "I don't know. Gone. Things come, go. I tired, Herb. Go home."

Her ex-mother-in-law was a hoverer, too. At the door to greet them, helping Susannah out of her coat, she said, "Well. How did it go?"

She always said that, no matter what the reason for going out, said it with that same cheery, forced hospitality. Maybe to make up in advance for the answer forthcoming. Never more than a tired "Okay." Sometimes only a nod and a shrug.

Herb hovered at the edge of the living room while her ex-mother-in-law shepherded her to the sofa. "Then I'll see you tonight," he said.

Susannah nodded. "Okay. I—thanks, Herb."

"It's nothing. I'll see you."

Maybe, Susannah thought, as Mrs. Whitney showed

him out, then returned to the sofa to ask if she wanted
a cup of tea, maybe everybody hovered, and she only
noticed it in people she was uncomfortable around.

Maybe part of Mrs. Whitney's hovering was her way
of saying hurry up and get well enough so you won't
need me any more. I want to get back to my own home,
my own life, my own way of doing things.

She had to be thinking that, and Susannah didn't
blame her. In spite of counseling from Barbara Caitlin,
her ex-mother-in-law never seemed to know whether
to offer physical assistance or withhold it, supply the
missing word or let her go on searching, encourage her
to try something new or discourage her for fear failure
to succeed at it might further depress her.

Susannah herself didn't know. Most things in life
had come easily to her. Nothing came easily any more.
The simple act of peeling a potato was beyond her. Her
inclination was to let people wait on her, do the things
for her she either couldn't do at all or could manage to
do only with the most intensive, exhausting effort. But
she knew that each time she gave in to her inclination,
full recovery receded from her grasp.

At war with herself, she was at war with others. Not
only with her ex-mother-in-law, who couldn't do anything right, who drove her up the wall one day by being
too helpful, only to let her flounder the next until she
cursed or cried or both.

Susannah was at war with Jill as well. She didn't
know what was the matter with Jill. The constraint
with which her child had greeted her on her return
from the hospital hadn't lessened. It had increased. She
seemed to prefer her grandmother's company. True, the
interval between Jill's coming home from school and
Mrs. Whitney's going home to Syosset was spent largely
in the kitchen, with Jill's grandmother explaining how
to finish the dinner she had started. But it was obvious
the two had a good rapport. Listening to them from her
customary spot on the sofa, Susannah felt left out,
abandoned, jealous—and more convinced than ever
that the Whitneys, mother and son, were not only
trying to take Jill away from her, they were succeeding.

There was more to it than that. Aware how badly

the attack on her had frightened Jill, Susannah didn't
want to exacerbate her fear by telling her some man
had tried to kill her—with its logical corollary that,
having failed, he would try again.

Trying to protect her, she had alienated her. Jill
couldn't understand why, when it was supposed to be
so good for her, her mother didn't want to go out walking with her, why she resisted going with her on er-
rands to the store. Nor could she understand why her
mother was forever going to the French doors in the
living room to look out onto the fire escape at the back
of the building when there was nothing there except
the flimsy-looking metal stairway with its narrow platform and its dizzying view of the mostly concrete garden
four stories down.

The alienation extended to Cervantes. Jill had always liked Cervantes, had always been at ease with
him, reveling in the attention he paid her, making it
plain she wished he lived with them.

No more.

The last few days she would have nothing to do with
him, barely responding to his greeting before finding
an excuse to leave the room, denying after he left that
she felt any different toward him. She had homework
to do, that was all. Susannah was convinced the change
in Jill's attitude had something to do with Joe, but what
she couldn't imagine.

And there was something funny going on there, too.

The Saturday after Susannah's homecoming, with
Mrs. Whitney out in Syosset for the weekend, Joe had
stopped by to take Jill out for the afternoon. It was the
first time Susannah had seen him or spoken to him in
months—since Christmas maybe—and Jill took advantage of that and her mother's condition as a semi-
invalid to try, as she had tried so many futile times
before, to effect a reconciliation.

She was aided in her attempt by a phone call from
Polly Berkmyer saying she'd be a few minutes late getting there—Polly was coming to spend the afternoon—
and by Susannah's obvious distress, though she tried
to hide it, at being left alone in the apartment.

Jill, who believed Susannah's fear of being left alone

was part of the aftermath of the attack on her, said,
"We're not in any hurry, are we, Daddy? We can wait
till Polly gets here."

The question answered for him, Joe sat down.

Something in his face as he turned to her brought
to Susannah's mind the shadowy recall she had of her
father sitting in her hospital room, kindly, remote, patient, a man long accustomed as a minister to calling
on the sick, and now, because of her mother's arthritis,
conditioned to it as a way of life.

The two men didn't look alike—her father tall, pa-
trician, prematurely gray, Joe not as tall as she, round-
faced, blond—but Joe had always reminded her a little
of her father. Underneath her father's piety, his mien
of sober responsibility, lay a flair for the theatrical that
Susannah suspected had turned him to the ministry,
where he had channeled the flair, put it to use. Joe had
the same flair, but as the only child of a strong, determined, widowed mother, he had had to concentrate his
energy so intently on escape that it had dissipated itself
before it could take him anywhere.

Overloaded with a sense of responsibility when she
met Joe, Susannah had found his disregard for it en-
chanting. The enchantment had survived, more or less
intact, until the pregnancy.

Even without aphasia, talking to Joe wasn't easy.
Nor was it necessarily productive. Fact and fancy in-
terwove, sometimes seamlessly, more often of late with
a desperation underlying the smooth façade.

Jill's eagerness to reunite them added pain to difficulty. Wanting neither to hurt her nor stir false hope,
they retreated to shells of politeness, the most ready-
to-hand topic of conversation the attack on Susannah
and her recovery from it.

Jill eyed them with increasing anxiety, looking for
signs where none existed, trying to create something
out of nothing. "Will Dr. Dubinsky invite Daddy to take
part in your psychodrama?" she asked Susannah.

Susannah shrugged. "I don't know."

Jill frowned. "Well, shouldn't he?"

Joe looked interested. "You're going to have your
own psychodrama?" On one occasion a year or more ago

he had talked at some length about going into psycho-therapy. Like so many things he talked about, nothing came of it.

Susannah nodded and turned to Jill. "You tell." It was easier for Jill to explain it to him.

When Jill had finished, Joe said, "Well, if he wants me to take part in it, let me know, and I'll be there."

"Okay," Susannah said, suspecting that if Dr. Dubinsky did want Joe, Joe would find some excuse for not being able to make it.

A psychodrama was potentially explosive, the participants in a scene often switching roles to play each other, or one person playing another's alter ego. Before the attack on her, Susannah customarily came home after the three Tuesday sessions and the two Thursday ones too exhausted—at eight o'clock in the evening—to do anything but sit and stare at the TV, and those were psychodramas in which she worked as a paid professional, an actress, with no personal involvement in the conflicts that were dramatized or in the patients' private lives.

As much as she appreciated Dr. Dubinsky's desire to help her, as much as she felt she needed the psychodrama to restore balance to her life, to put it back in focus, as certain as she was that if all else failed, the psychodrama would trigger the restoration of her memory, the prospect of what she might have to go through filled her with dread.

Especially where Jill was concerned. She was convinced she couldn't remember her encounter with Jill because subconsciously she didn't want to face up to it. She was also convinced that the substance of that encounter lay behind Jill's increasing constraint, maybe even explained her bizarre behavior where Joe was concerned.

After the chatty Saturday, Joe hadn't reappeared until the day before yesterday, when he had stopped by to take his mother to the train station, and his mother, saying she would take a later train, had manufactured an errand to send him on with Jill.

Under ordinary circumstances Jill would have seen through her grandmother's machinations, but she was as anxious to get Joe out of the apartment as her grandmother was to get the two of them together.

Queried by Susannah afterward, she denied anything except pleasure at going somewhere with her father and, without waiting for the speech therapist to arrive—it happened to be Herb that evening—shut herself away in her room, headset clamped to her ears, although she knew that wearing the headset isolated her mother almost as effectively as leaving her alone in the apartment.

And nothing had happened since to ease the tension.

Sixteen

Turning down Mrs. Whitney's offer to make her a cup of tea, wanting nothing so much as rest after her session with Dr. Dubinsky, Susannah stretched out on the sofa to take a nap. She was just drifting off to sleep when the older woman jarred her awake by coming back into the living room from the kitchen to say, "I forgot to tell you. I don't see how it could be anything important, but your answering service called."

While Susannah was in the hospital her ex-mother-in-law had wanted to give up the service, arguing that it had become a waste of money. Jill had refused to let her do it. Understanding Mrs. Whitney's point of view, agreeing with it, Susannah was nevertheless grateful to Jill. Having the service gave her a psychological boost, something she was extremely short of these days.

Mrs. Whitney thrust a piece of paper at her. "There are two messages for you. I had the girl repeat them so I'd be sure to get them right."

Her ex-mother-in-law's continuing vacillation from antagonism to servility grated on Susannah's nerves as much as her vacillation from being overly helpful to being no help at all. Susannah wished she could be cast in a scene as Mrs. Whitney's alter ego. *Not that they're going to do you the least bit of good, my girl. Eighteen dollars a month to pamper yourself. And not your money to waste either. Now that you're on welfare, it's the taxpayers' money you're throwing around.*

The first message told her to be at an address on West Fifty-third Street tomorrow morning at ten to audition for an airline commercial. Call Sam Sheridan to confirm.

Back in the hospital, when she had regained enough of her wits to understand what had happened to her—and enough language ability to communicate—she had given Cervantes a list of agents and other theater people to call to say she had been injured, but Sam Sheridan hadn't sent her out on a call in more than six months. When Jill came home from school she would have her call him. Susannah still shied away from using the phone, especially for business. It made her nervous, and nervousness aggravated her disability.

The second message asked her to call Lucy Cummings. Susannah frowned at the slip of paper. A casting director at an advertising agency, Lucy Cummings was a friend of sorts. Enough of a friend to give Susannah bit parts from time to time on the two soaps Lucy cast. Not enough of a friend to let her audition for a running part for the producer and client or to cast her in a TV commercial, where the residuals could run anywhere from two or three thousand dollars to twelve or thirteen or more.

A success in her own field, Lucy begrudged other people success in theirs. Nor was she known for her generosity of spirit. It would never occur to Lucy to leave a message with the service as encouragement, a way of saying I know you'll be back at work soon; meanwhile give me a call to tell me how you're getting along.

Susannah couldn't imagine what she wanted. Lucy knew she was unable to work. She was on the list Susannah had given Cervantes. She had sent flowers.

Maybe she needed an extra to sit in the background of a scene and thought Susannah could handle that. Or maybe—more likely—she was casting a flat-fee public-

service spot for victims of aphasia and wanted somebody who wasn't old and doddering as well.

Susannah frowned at the slip of paper for some time,
trying to make up her mind what to do. Letting Jill
return the call for her might antagonize Lucy. Lucy
didn't like dealing with in-betweens. Returning the call
herself might jeopardize future jobs, giving Lucy the
impression she'd never be fit to work again. Talking
with Lucy would be worse than talking to Joe. Lucy
gushed, her voice skipping up and down the scale the
way Susannah vocalized when she was horsing around.
It would be hard to keep up with her, let alone absorb
what she said.

At length Susannah got up from the sofa and went
back to her bedroom and closed the door. If she was
going to be humiliated it would be done in private. Her
hands trembling, she picked up the phone and dialed.

Lucy was seldom available when called, even when
a call from her was being returned, but she came on
the line at once.

"Well," she said brightly, "congratulations!" Every
syllable hit a different note.

Expecting Lucy to ask how she was, concentrating
on answering that, Susannah went blank.

"Susannah?" Lucy said. "Are you there?"

"Y-y-yes. I—I here. I—I—I—" She swallowed and
tried again, concentrating as hard as she could. "I—I—
no—talk well. I—no—no—yet."

"So I can hear." Lucy's voice pulsated with sympathy. "Darling, I was really sorry to hear about you. I
mean, what a tough break."

"I—yes. I—take—no—think—no—thank. Yes.
Thank. Fowl—no—flow—flowers." Susannah was
trembling all over.

"Oh, darling, don't mention it. I'm just glad to know
you got them all right. I hope they cheered you up a
little."

"I—I—no—write well, too."

"That's perfectly all right, darling. Don't apologize.
Please. I should apologize for not coming to see you. I
really wanted to. Really. But I've been so desperately
busy. You know how it is."

"Y-y-yes. I—I know."

"I only called to see how you were. Oh. And yes. To congratulate you. I think it's wonderful news." Wonderful cascaded down three notes of the scale.

It had to be obvious to Lucy Susannah didn't know what she was talking about, but Lucy was going to make her ask. Susannah wished she had the guts not to, to pretend she knew, to thank her and let it go at that. She would never have credited Lucy with being this mean.

"I—I—no—what talk about."

"Oh, really?" Three notes up the scale. "You know nothing about it—nothing at all?" Lucy couldn't hide the satisfaction in her voice.

"N-no."

"I can't imagine. Oh. I suppose it was meant as a surprise, and now I've ruined it. Oh, darling. Tell her I'm sorry."

Sweating, exhausted, wanting to yank the phone out of the wall, Susannah understood abruptly what had never before occurred to her, that Lucy wanted to be an actress herself. It explained a lot of things about her. She swallowed again. "T-t-tell who?"

"Why, that darling child of yours, of course. Why is it I never can remember her name?"

"J-J-Jill?"

"Yes. Jill. Right. And how about that? A room full of professionals. Every kid in the business. And Jill walks in and takes it away from them. Just like that. Of course, I suppose it didn't hurt any being brought to the audition in Dick Holliday's chauffeur-driven limousine. I couldn't imagine how Jill had an edge with Dick Holliday, but somebody mentioned he has a daughter at Shipley—Patsy, I think her name is—and then I remembered Jill went there, too, and then of course it all clicked." A long sigh. "You have no idea how lucky you are, darling. Or—" A little giggle. "—maybe I should say Jill. She stands to make a minimum of twenty thou. Minimum. The Child's Play campaign is one of the year's biggest. Oops. Somebody's on my other line. Hurry up and get well, darling. 'Bye." The phone clicked.

Susannah sat on the side of the bed staring at the phone in her hands, then, with a shake of her head, she put it back in its cradle. She wasn't sure what Jill had done, but she was sure Lucy would never give her another job. In Lucy's place she wouldn't either.

Feeling lower than she had in days—lower than a snake's belly, her Irish grandmother would have said—she went back into the living room and turned on the TV to watch *Sesame Street*. The program served as a visual aid in language reconstruction. It was also the only program she had no trouble following.

She was still watching it when Jill came home. Turning to her, Susannah said, "Turn off, please."

Jill, who thought watching *Sesame Street* was gross, turned the set off, dropping her bag of books to the floor as she did so, shedding the blue sausage-casing on top of them.

"Jill! No!" Susannah spoke more sharply than she intended. "Pick—pick up, please." Sloppiness had always bothered her. These days it irritated her to the breaking point. "Pick up. Put away. Have talk. Have have talk." The elusiveness of the little words, the connectives—*to, and, but, for*—also irritated her. She hated the way she sounded and was sure everybody imitated her behind her back.

More paranoia. More self-pity.

Jill picked up her coat and her bag of books and disappeared with them, taking her time, stopping to glance at a magazine, going into the kitchen to greet her grandmother, staying to get her dinner instructions.

Susannah tried not to get more irritated, but she was convinced Jill's time-taking was deliberate, and finally she could bear it no longer. "Jill! Now! Here! Now!"

Jill reappeared, looking put upon. "I had to hear what Grandma had to tell me."

"Hear—hear what I say." Susannah gritted her teeth. She couldn't even manage an intelligible quarrel. "Want know—want know what do."

Jill frowned. "I'm not doing anything. I'm standing here listening to you."

Susannah could have hit her. She knew her speech difficulty made Jill uneasy. She knew Jill was frightened it might be permanent, but Jill wasn't above taking advantage of it—and her—when there was something she didn't want to talk about. "Not talk now. Not talk about now. Talk about what—what you do school. Oh, God. God damn it."

Jill went on frowning at her, saying nothing, offering no help. There wasn't a sound in the apartment except a hiss and thunk from the living-room radiator. Out in the kitchen Mrs. Whitney had stopped whatever she was doing to listen.

Her ex-mother-in-law made a great show of not coming between Jill and herself, but she came between them just by being there, by having taken care of Jill, and Jill wasn't above taking advantage of that either. *Grandma let me go to the park with Marybeth. Grandma said I could stay up late on Friday.*

Gritting her teeth again, trying to ignore the Presence in the kitchen, Susannah made another stab at it. "Want know what do—Patsy—what do Patsy Holliday father."

Red suffused Jill's face. "Who said I did anything?"

Susannah yearned for something she could pick up and hurl across the room. "What difference make who. Know hard me talk. You not do anything?"

The airport was beginning to close in. "I didn't say that."

"Jill." With the greatest of effort Susannah managed an entire sentence. "Don't—pull—that—on—me. What do?"

Jill spoke so softly she could hardly hear her. "I made a commercial. For Patsy Holliday's father."

"A commercial?"

Something—Susannah didn't know what—maybe the expression on her face, maybe the way she repeated the two words, maybe simply the weight on Jill of carrying this thing around unspoken, unacknowledged—whatever it was, the airport opened in a flash.

Looking angry, looking scared, her face redder than before, speaking so fast Susannah could hardly keep up with her, Jill said, "Patsy Holliday's been going around school for weeks now saying her father was going to put on this big advertising campaign, and he might let her do a spot for it—the main spot, according to her—and then Grandma told me you were going to have to go on welfare, so I went to see Mr. Holliday to ask if I could try out for it, and I did, and I got it."

Susannah stared at her, bewildered, trying to absorb what she had said, trying to figure out why Jill was angry. Why she was scared, for that matter. She was still trying to absorb, to figure out, when Jill stunned her by bursting into tears.

"And you can think what you want of me," she said. Not said. Shouted. "I don't care. But it isn't true my father tried to kill you. He didn't! He didn't!" She spun around and raced out of the room, into the kitchen, into her grandmother's no-doubt waiting arms.

For the next few minutes Susannah sat listening to the sounds from the kitchen—Jill sobbing, her grandmother soothing. When the sobbing eased to hiccups, she got up from the sofa, started toward her bedroom, then went instead into the kitchen to use the phone there.

She dialed Dr. Dubinsky's number. When he answered she said, "Doctor, Susannah. Need come see. Few—few minutes. Now. Emergency."

When he agreed to see her she hung up the phone and turned to Jill and her grandmother. "Come, too. Please. Both. Later train?"

Mrs. Whitney nodded. She looked almost as distraught as Jill.

Outside a cab approached. Susannah hailed it. If she and Jill were going to be affluent, why not? Her ex-mother-in-law, maybe thinking the same thing, said nothing.

In Dr. Dubinsky's office, everybody greeted and seated, Susannah said to him, "Want you tell Jill, tell grandmother what I tell you today. Tell all."

Dr. Dubinsky frowned. "You mean about the man who tried to kill you?"

Susannah nodded. "Yes."

"I can do better than that," he said. "I taped our session."

Susannah was so accustomed to Dr. Dubinsky's frequent use of the tape recorder, she hadn't paid any attention, but she was glad Jill and her grandmother could hear in her own words what she thought about the man who had tried to kill her. Glad, too, she had explained to Dr. Dubinsky during the session why she hadn't told Jill the threat was there.

When the tape reached the spot where she and Dr. Dubinsky had started checking out those men in the Thursday groups who had had any outside contact with her, Dr. Dubinsky switched off the machine, explaining that that had occupied the remainder of the session. Unless either Jill or her grandmother believed that Susannah was trying in some way to trick them, he didn't see any need for listening further.

There was no objection.

Susannah turned to Jill. "How know about man?"

Jill's face was streaked, but she seemed calmer now. "Herb told me. Well, no," she corrected herself, "he didn't tell me. But when I was in Horlick's the other day he asked me if you had any idea yet who had tried to kill you."

Susannah sighed. Such was the state of her thinking, it had never occurred to her to warn Herb or any of the others not to say anything to Jill.

On the way home she decided to call Herb to cancel tonight's speech therapy. She was too drained for his exhorting, his nervous energy. It was a bad night anyhow. The storm that had threatened that afternoon was already breaking, the wind high, the rain hard.

The decision made, she forgot about it until he rang the bell at eight.

"Oh, Herb," she said, dismayed. "I forget call you. Say no come tonight."

Stooping to take off his galoshes, he straightened up. "What's happened?"

She shook her head. "Too long, too hard explain. All right if no come in, no do?"

"Well—sure. I—sure." He wore a black raincoat hanging open. Buttoning the raincoat, he said, "Tomorrow okay? Tomorrow morning at ten?"

Susannah nodded. "Yes. Tomorrow."

She intended to remain in the doorway until he walked to the elevator and stepped into it. She was always so anxious to be rid of him she was afraid he sensed it. But before he turned to go, the phone rang, and she hadn't the strength not to seize on the excuse it offered her to wave good night and shut the door.

The call was for Jill. From Patsy Holliday.

Susannah had made up with Jill as best she could. She was touched by Jill's concern for her on the matter of welfare. She was poignantly aware of the conflict that raged in Jill between her love and loyalty for her father, who so often disappointed her, and her love for Cervantes, who did not, and who thus had to bear the brunt of Jill's guilt and anger and resentment.

But Jill still shied away from talking about the commercial, even with Patsy, obviously calling for information. Her face turned red again, her throat tightened up, and the answers she gave were as oblique as she could make them, all the while casting uneasy glances at Susannah.

Susannah knew why Jill had been angry. To cover up being scared.

Why scared? She didn't know.

On the way out of his office this evening Dr. Dubinsky had urged her not to put off the psychodrama too long, not to insist on waiting until she was fully recovered from her aphasia. "It will do more than anything I can think of," he said, "to provoke memory. Whole spurts of it. I'm sure of it."

Susannah was no longer so certain. She had been certain Jill's constraint with her was an outgrowth of their encounter the night of the attack on her. She saw now it had nothing to do with their encounter. It was because of the commercial.

To enable Jill to speak freely with Patsy, Susannah got up from the sofa and walked out of the living room, back to her bedroom. She wished she knew why—even after making up with Jill—she continued to feel so low.

Sitting down on the side of her bed, she saw the slip of paper her ex-mother-in-law had written the messages on from the answering service. Confirm with Sam Sheridan. Call Lucy Cummings.

And suddenly she knew.

Lucy had not been mean enough to say it, though she had hinted at it. Jill was sensitive enough to see it, making her scared when she should have been triumphant.

In getting the commercial, something Susannah had yet to do, Jill was beating her at her own game.

Seventeen

Leaving Susannah's apartment building, heading out into the downpour, trying to figure out what could have happened to make her cancel tonight's therapy, Herb saw somebody slip into an entryway across the street.

Raising his umbrella, he walked to the foot of the sidewalk and stood watching the entryway, expecting to see one of the neighborhood toughs, waiting for the inevitable catcall, the obscenity.

Or maybe it was a cop. An undercover man.

He stood motionless, watching, waiting, the rain going *pop, pop, pop* over his head.

A man and woman came out of the building, raised an umbrella, and, huddling together, set off down the street.

There was nobody in the entryway.

With a shake of his head he turned west toward Columbus.

Scrape, scrape.

Scrape, scrape.

He could feel the pressure building up in him. From having to contend with too many things.

To do the rewrites the director wanted, he had cut

back on his medication again. The new medication was
worse than the old when it came to inhibiting his writing. The feeling of dissociation, of part of him being one
place and part somewhere else, had intensified. So had
the attacks of vertigo. There were times he could hardly
hold himself together enough to concentrate on and
comprehend a think piece in the *New York Times*. He
had had to cut back on the drug.

But he had to be careful. Watch for the signs.

Doubly careful now, the situation he was in.

The surest sign was the paranoia, the conviction
somebody was out to get him. And the hallucinating.
Like a few minutes ago.

The trick was to stay this side of believing either
was real.

From off in the distance he heard a siren. New York
was full of sirens. Police, fire, ambulance. Nothing to
do with him.

The siren was getting louder. Coming his way. Despite himself he tensed up.

Louder still.

Reaching Columbus, he stopped, stood listening,
looking. A blue police car roaring toward him down the
avenue.

*When he comes tonight for speech therapy, I'll tell
him I'm too tired, does he mind not coming in? That
means he'll be at the corner of Columbus and Eighty-
seventh Street at—*

The police car roared past.

He stood where he was through several light changes.
Fool.

His mother thought he was losing weight on purpose.

The next time the light turned green he crossed the
avenue and headed for Broadway. He ought to go to
Horlick's, put in some time. He owed Zekiel so much
time he'd never get out from under. But he couldn't face
going there tonight. He was too nerved up.

He had worked out a way to test her memory, see
whether she knew more than she admitted. He had
planned to spring it on her tonight. Could she have
suspected? Was that why she canceled?

No. Fool. How could she know?

Two adolescent black boys coming toward him, passing him, taking no notice, one saying to the other, "Shit, man, you gotta lighten up. Y'know what I'm saying?"

Chocolate frosted brown boys.

Maybe it wasn't anything more than her being too tired. She tired so easily, had so little strength.

Other times he had thought she'd remembered, he'd been wrong. And he was wrong tonight. If Susannah had set up a trap with the cops it would have shown in her face, her manner. He had seen her in soap operas and in off-off-Broadway shows. She was a good actress. But not when she wasn't working, when she was just being herself.

And she had no intention of going to the police. Mrs. Caitlin had tried to get her to go, but she said, what was the point of reporting a mugging when she hadn't been mugged, and what was the point of reporting an attempted murder when nobody would back her up on that? And anyhow, what good would it do when she didn't know anything more about it than that and doubted she ever would?

When he got to Broadway there was some kind of commotion going on. The rain had subsided to a drizzle, a crowd gathering in the middle of the block. He walked down to investigate.

Somebody was shooting a movie. A production assistant stood at the curb trying to keep the crowd moving, calling out, "Please keep going. Don't stay to watch. Please. Sir? Ma'am? Please keep going." Nobody paid any attention to him.

Three actors—two men and a woman—came out of a clothing store, stopped, had an animated exchange, then went back inside. The sequence was repeated several times.

The camera shooting the scene was mounted on a small flatbed truck standing at the curb. Cervantes manned the camera. Another man, the director probably, went inside the store to huddle with the actors, and Cervantes relaxed back in his chair, looking around.

Herb tensed up again. He didn't want Cervantes to see him.

If it weren't for Cervantes it would all be behind him. The worry, the fear, the sickness of knowing it had to be done. The growing anxiety that if the time came, when the time came, he might not be able to get to her before she got to him.

How he hated the photographer.

Things hadn't worked out the way he'd expected after she left the hospital. For all the time he spent with Susannah, he wasn't alone with her all that much. Not where he could take advantage of it if he had to. To the bus, from the bus. Never in her apartment.

He sat up nights wondering how he could manage it.

Herb waited until Cervantes looked off in another direction, then he turned and headed north on Broadway. To the Hotel Esplanade.

She remembered that.

A piece of slate shattered against a tenement, and she remembered he had rented a room at the Hotel Esplanade to hold the reading of his play. Remembered she had to tell him she couldn't take part in it.

The man chasing his hat had stirred more memory. Something about him, something about what he was doing. *Something about* was as far as it went. Or so she said. She claimed it had come and gone.

Maybe it had, but if it had come once, it would come again, wouldn't it?

He walked into the Esplanade and looked around the dingy, cavernous lobby.

Last Thursday on the way back from Oldenham Hospital, Susannah had asked to stop in Horlick's. It was the first time she'd been there since the accident. Herb thought she wanted to say hello to the Zekiels or buy the trade papers so she could keep up with what was going on.

She said hello and bought the trades, but there was more to it than that. Walking around the store, she ran her hand over a counter top, fingered the newspaper rack, touched the cash register, frowned at the soda vending machine.

If he had looked puzzled, he wasn't the only one. The Zekiels didn't know what to make of it until she explained. "Somebody hedgerow—no—sorry, sorry. No hedgerow. Hum—ho—hos—somebody hospital—say—say—maybe help get memory back going place—places—where part memory gone." She frowned again and shook her head. "No work. No here."

Mrs. Zekiel said, "Dearie, I wouldn't fret about it. Maybe the next time you come in it will."

Several people, most of them old, sat in the lobby of the Esplanade. Some read newspapers. Some just sat. Herb walked around, trying to see what Susannah would see when she asked Cervantes to bring her here.

He knew she would ask Cervantes to bring her here, because after that business this afternoon she hadn't asked him, and where he didn't take her Cervantes did.

What would she see that might trigger her memory?

Dark wood and graying plaster, sagging, peeling fake-leather furniture, worn marble floor, chrome ashtrays, dim paintings, dim lamps.

Nothing. Not that he could see.

He walked around a sofa, *scrape, scrape,* and an old woman gave him an exasperated look. Just like his mother.

Mrs. Zekiel had said something more to Susannah. Herb shook his head. Like she knew he was thinking it. But then he thought about it, worried about it all the time.

"Maybe it'll come to you without you being here. Of its own accord." Mrs. Zekiel snapped finger and thumb. "Just like that. The way a name you're trying to remember will pop into your head."

That was an even bigger problem than finding the right opportunity. What if sometime when he wasn't with her it popped into Susannah's head that he was the man in the yellow slicker? When Cervantes brought her to the Esplanade, and they were standing here looking around, what if somebody dropped something that shattered on the marble floor, and Susannah turned to Cervantes and said, "Herb—Herb man in yellow slicker." What then?

With another shake of his head, Herb crossed the lobby and went out the side entrance on Ninety-third Street, then headed home. Maybe Susannah would never know who the man in the yellow slicker was. Wasn't there as much chance of that as the other?

More.

Almost never would the person remember the accident itself.

The next morning the skies had cleared. Going to pick Susannah up he felt tense, edgy. He had been up past midnight revising and polishing *Possessed*. He didn't know whether he liked what he had done or not.

He didn't know what to expect from Susannah. If a policeman opened her door he wouldn't be surprised.

There was no policeman. Only Mrs. Whitney senior. Same greeting, same smile. Same helping Susannah into her dark-blue coat.

Susannah wasn't the same. She was always anxious about going outside. Not today. Today she didn't seem to care.

He was instantly alarmed. More so when she wouldn't tell him what was wrong, when she shrugged him off with, "Too hard explain."

She must have remembered something.

What?

What it was about the man chasing his hat?

That he reminded her of him?

But if that were it, if man-chasing-hat/Herb brought her only a step away from man-chasing-hat/Herb/man-in-yellow-slicker, would she be going out with him today as though nothing had changed? When she was far too weak to put up any kind of struggle against him?

No.

Fool.

He had to stop imagining things.

Finish the revisions. Get back on his medication. Feeling dissociated and sometimes dizzy was easier to cope with than seeing something where nothing was.

Coming back from the hospital that afternoon, Susannah shrugged him off again when he asked her what was wrong, what had happened. He had to bite his tongue to keep from pressing her. He worried about asking too many questions, probing too much. He would have to wait for his next turn at speech therapy and the memory test he had devised.

He didn't have to wait. When they got off the bus she asked him to take her to Eighty-eighth Street between Columbus and Amsterdam.

He had wanted to take her there more times than he could count, had pictured doing it, holding his breath while she looked around, his heart straining against his chest. Would she remember?

He had never had the guts.

Now she was asking for it.

He fingered the new vial of drug in his left pocket and thought he was going to be sick.

They turned off Columbus at Eighty-eighth Street and started toward Amsterdam. First the vacant lot where he had thrown away her billfold. Then the row of boarded-up brownstones.

"Herb?"

"Yes?"

"Where—where find?"

He made a show of having to remember. Why not? One house looked like the next. Anyhow he wasn't certain. He hadn't been himself that night. He pointed to the sidewalk. "Here."

She looked and looked. Like she was searching for a contact lens. What did she expect to find?

He had to keep swallowing not to throw up.

She shook her head. "Nothing. Tell me nothing." On her beautiful face defeat, everything given up. "Go home now."

He could feel himself start to relax.

He might be home free after all.

And if he was safe, she was safe.

They were both safe.

As they headed back toward Columbus Avenue she said, "Nothing any good. Put that in diary."

He turned to stare at her. "Diary? What diary?"

"Diary been keeping. Since come home. You no know diary?"

"No."

"Hospital—Dr. O'Neal say help remember. Maybe. Put anything in. Make sense. No make sense. Who know what—what—what damn word? Trigger." She shrugged. "Nothing trigger."

"Who do you—who sees the diary?"

"Nobody."

Maybe it didn't matter, then.

"Nobody yet. Dr. O'Neal sometime."

He sucked in his breath. He would have to get hold of it, see what was in it. "Maybe—when you put something in your diary—maybe when the doctor reads it, it'll mean something to him."

Susannah frowned at him. "What good that do? Has mean something me. No good else."

He nodded. He had already said too much. How could he get her to show him the diary? Maybe he could work something out with Jill. Come up with some pretext.

"Dr. O'Neal try hypnosis. Get memory back that way."

He had to steel himself not to turn and stare at her again. She was full of surprises today. "Did it—has it—"

She answered before he finished asking. "No work either. No yet."

What else was she up to? What more did she know that she hadn't told him?

"Dr. O'Neal try re—re—oh, God—regress. Go back before happen. First tryout *Glory Road*. Sing part. Read part. Remember that. Remember callback. First callback. Second callback. Biggest thing ever happen—" Susannah shook her head. "Biggest thing almost ever happen. Not happen again. All over. Done. No care. No matter. All done."

On her face again the look of defeat. And something else. Apology. She put out a hand to him. "I know how hard you work. Help. I—I grateful, Herb. No help theater though. Theater need all back one piece. Head. What say. How move. Not going happen. Afraid not. No."

The rest of the way to her apartment building they walked in silence.

"Well," Mrs. Whitney said, helping Susannah out of her coat, "how did it go?"

Susannah only nodded.

The older woman looked from Susannah to him, as if she wanted to help but didn't know how. He had to say something.

"Susannah's down today. Discouraged."

Mrs. Whitney shook her head and sighed. A long sigh. "I don't wonder." She nodded to him. "Well, at least we've had one piece of good news. Wonderful news. Did Susannah tell you about Jill?"

Nobody told him anything. He had to ferret everything out. He shook his head.

"You tell," Susannah said to Mrs. Whitney. "I rest." She settled herself on the sofa.

Mrs. Whitney reminded him of his mother. Formidable. The kind of person used to taking charge. She even looked a little like her. Today especially. He frowned and blinked, wanting to get away, unable to now that he'd started the conversation.

"Jill moneymaker," Susannah said. "You ask what happen. That what happen." She nodded to Mrs. Whitney. "She tell you."

"Indeed I will."

He sat down to listen, but he only half heard what his mother said about Jill, part of him wondering where Susannah kept her diary, maybe in her tote bag, where she kept everything else, part of him wondering how his mother knew Jill.

Fool. Not his mother. Mrs. Whitney. Susannah's former mother-in-law.

He was hallucinating.

He had to stop.

He also had to get hold of that diary.

Back outside again, he headed for Central Park West. He would go to the clinic, talk to one of the doctors, explain about the play and the revisions he was making on it, see if there wasn't something they could give him, if only for a while, so he'd be able to write without being pulled toward the brink of madness.

Halfway down the block he stopped, hesitated, retraced his steps. He didn't dare see one of the doctors. He was afraid of what else he might tell him. He would have to work things out alone.

When he got to Horlick's, Zekiel had a message for him. Call Dr. Dubinsky.

The doctor Susannah worked for. The one he'd taken

her to see yesterday afternoon. What had she told him? What did he want?

He was shaking when he picked up the phone. He was shaking harder when he put it down. Take part in a psychodrama Dr. Dubinsky was putting on for Susannah.

Why him?

How could he help restore balance to her life?

He was nothing to her.

A neighborhood tough stood at the soda vending machine. He took a can out, shook it, snapped the tab, laughed at the onrush of fizz, put the can to his mouth, and drank the soda down chugalug.

Restore balance.

Restore memory.

The last thing he wanted.

No. No way.

The tough crushed the empty soda can and flipped it toward the vending machine's waste receptacle. It hit the machine as he hit the street.

Herb stared after him.

He would have to figure a way out.

He had already figured out how to get hold of the diary. When they got on the bus going to the hospital he would sit on the side she carried her tote on. He would start a game of *I Spy*, using the advertising placards over the windows. While she concentrated on the placards he would slip the diary out of the tote.

If that was where she kept it.

It had to be.

It was.

It took him almost a week to bring it off, but once he had everything set up, getting the diary out of her tote was like the campaign Jill was going to make all that money on. Child's play.

Usually after taking Susannah to the outpatient department, he went back uptown to Horlick's to work until it was time to pick her up again. Today he headed for a bench in Central Park.

She wrote the way she talked. And words were misspelled.

"Ten a.m. go hospital Herb. Mat exercises. Speech

therapy. Help make egg salid lunch. Peal eggs no easy.
Drop knife. Twice. Lunnch. Wash dishes. All therapy.
Go home with!!!!!! Herb. With, with, with."

Some of the entries were dated. Some weren't.

"March 8. Wensday. No therapy hospital today. Jill
come take Assemmbly. Middle School do calissthenix.
Teachers, Jill frends come up, say how be, glad see you
up, around. Not easy talk. Them. Me. Nobody like talking me. Make them uneasy."

The longest entry was half a page, her handwriting
becoming almost illegible toward the end. Some entries
were only a couple of lines. Sometimes she broke off in
midsentence, the writing wobbling across the page as
if she had fallen asleep. She probably had.

"Tired, tired. Hard stay awake sometimes when
should. Doctor say "

One was about her parents.

"March 10. Mom, Dad call last night. Want come
see. Mom most housebound. Dad try get away Aperl.
May have go church meeing Filadelfia. Come New
York. Explain can't go Indiana while do therapy. Maybe
later. Remind me Tom girthday next week. Send card.
Wish not remind. Me do, not do on own. When Jill get
my age member leave alone. Nice talking them, harder
talk fone than face face. Damn. No trouble swearing.
Little words hide. TO. TO. TO. That word want. Face
to face. There. Tired. Good night, diary.

"March 11. No have say good night, dairy last night.
Cervantes spend night. First time long time. Very good.
Better than very good. Damn near perfect. Glad some
sistems still go."

Damn Cervantes. Herb wished the photographer had
never moved into the neighborhood, never met Susannah. He still couldn't get it out of his head that Cervantes had some connection with what had happened
that night on the street. Either he knew something or
he had done something or—

Herb shook his head. Something.

There was more to the entry.

"Cervantes spend weekend. Move in. Ask—I ask Jill
go Siosset grandmother. Jill seem prefer gr me, but she
not like idea Syosset. Not want go. Not say anything,

but not want go. Seem—? Afraid. Why? No make cents.
Ask Jill you afraid what? She say no, look yes."

Another entry about Cervantes.

"March 12. Cervantes and I long talk last night after
make love. Easier talk in dark. Don't know why. Easier
talk Tim. He not like uthers. Not strain, uneasy. He
laff, make fun, hold tight in arms. Last night try talk
what going happen. Long run. Will get well? Don't
know. Fear not. Fear lot else. Where man in yellow
slicker? What waiting for? When try again? Where?
How? Who? Try so hard remember. Can't. Not talk
Cervantes that. He like uthers on man in yellow slicker.
Think I mixed up inside. I know not. Man in yellow
slicker know not, too."

Frowning, Herb read the entry again. If Cervantes
didn't think there was a man in a yellow slicker, if he
didn't believe somebody had tried to kill Susannah,
then how could he have any connection of any kind
with what had happened that night?

Herb shook his head. He didn't know. But he couldn't
shake the conviction either.

On the following page there was an undated entry.

"Here one thing no make sense. Last night speech
therapy Herb rite out sentence like do many before, cut
up sentence, give me pieces put back again. No can do.
Words: trash, the, out, pleeze, take. I no find noun. He
finally do for me. Pleeze take out the trash. I start say
trash verb, not noun. No say. Sumthing scare. No know
what. No know why think trash verb. Ghosts at back
of mind reach out, go away."

Herb stared at the entry, not understanding it, not
knowing any more than Susannah why she should
think trash was a verb, or why it should stir her memory. What bothered him more was "Sumthing scare."
When the shrink saw that he'd probe. What frightened
you? Think. Maybe not a what. Who. Who frightened
you? Who was in the room with you? Nobody but Herb?
Does Herb frighten you? Think. Could Herb be the man
in the yellow slicker?

Shit, man, why you jiving yourself like that?

With a start Herb looked up. Across the walk a young
punk sat on a bench grinning at him.

Was he real?

Had he said that?

Trembling, Herb stood up and walked to another bench about fifty yards away. He forced himself to turn and look back. The punk was gone.

If he had been there to begin with.

Still trembling, he sat down again with the diary.

"March 27. Early March spent five plus hours welfare office get on welfare. Today spent five plus hours welfare office getting off.

"March 28. Grandma Burke right—what word? Mettaphor? Simile. Feel lower than snake belly. That how I feel. Plus feel bad Jill. She want help. Do help. I try be grateful. Be bitter, too. She know that. I try hide. Can't. Make feel worse.

"March 29. Speech therapist today say now beginning master aposs—apostrophe. Be 31 August 8. Maybe by then can say Happy Birthday TO You. Shit.

"March 30. Thursday. Day trades come out. On way from hospital Herb ask stop in Horlick's by—buy them. Say no. What use?

"How ever pay back Herb? Why he work so hard? Why he care? Why man in yellow slik—slicker try kill me? I try not feel sorry self. Can't help. What I ever do man in yellow—do to man in yellow slicker make him lash out—why I say lash out? Why ghosts move around back there? Hey, ghosts, come closer.

"Ghosts no come."

Herb stared at the last few entries. He had meant to slip the diary back into her tote the way he had slipped it out. Now he couldn't. She was getting too close.

She might not see that, might not see who she was getting close to, but the shrink would. He couldn't miss it.

Herb walked over to the pond in the southeast corner of the park and threw the diary into it.

Eighteen

Dr. Aaronson wore his long white hospital coat. Probably, Susannah thought, because he would seem strange to her without it, and the psychodrama aimed to invoke the familiar, not dispel it. Yet he seemed out of place.

Everybody seemed out of place. Barbara Caitlin, who had come with Dr. Aaronson and Dr. O'Neal and sat in a corner of the room with them, looked incomplete without her clipboard and her folders and her own white coat.

Everybody had an air about them of waiting for something to happen. Dr. Aaronson looked interested, attentive. Barbara looked expectant. Dr. O'Neal, whose own methods for retrieving memory had so far failed, had an air of professional well-wishing about him.

Jill looked scared, her fingers pleating and unpleating the hem of the light-green jumper that was the middle school's spring uniform.

The room they waited in was a large, high-ceilinged studio apartment with wall-to-wall dark-red carpeting, a Pullman kitchen along one side, and access to Dr. Dubinsky's office cut through an old-fashioned bathroom off another. Except for two dozen folding chairs

and an assortment of pillows, the room was sparsely
furnished. Two card tables, a large round cocktail table,
an ancient sofa, some easy chairs, lamps. The furniture
was ringed around the room, the carpeted center bare.

On Thursday evenings, when the two therapy groups
met, one of Susannah's jobs had been to summon Dr.
Dubinsky through the passageway after everybody had
assembled. Tonight he functioned as host, greeting people as they came in, thanking them for coming, asking
them to sit anywhere.

The first surprise of the evening was Joe. Even Jill,
vehement that her father be included, looked astonished when he came in with his mother. Mrs. Whitney
had not wanted to come, had left the apartment that
afternoon saying she didn't understand how psychodrama worked, didn't see how she could be a factor in the
restoration of Susannah's memory or of balance in her
life, certainly had no intention of getting up in front of
all those people and making a fool of herself. Maybe
the only way Joe could be certain his mother would
show was to bring her. Susannah flashed him a look of
gratitude, mouthing a "Thank you."

Susannah wasn't certain herself how or if Mrs. Whitney fit into whatever situation might be constructed
here—any more than she was certain that the psychodrama that evolved tonight would restore her memory. Or that she would recognize it if it did. Maybe her
passionate conviction that somebody had tried to kill
her was like so many of her other passionate convic-
tions. Set against reality, it would peter out to nothing.

She might be able to trigger the memory of what had
happened between Jill and herself before the attack.
But that would mean confronting Jill before all these
people, reversing roles with her, playing her alter ego
to tempt, tease, trick, force out of her something she
was determined to keep to herself.

To play a role, to pretend to be the protagonist's
spouse or boss or mother or child, to stage a pseudo-
conflict in order to explore real problems and emotions—that was one thing. To create real conflict with
real people was something else. No matter how impor-

tant the restoration of her memory was to her, Susannah didn't know if she could be that brutal to her child.

Jill had some idea of how psychodrama worked. No wonder she looked scared.

The second surprise was Cervantes, who hadn't expected to be able to make it.

"What happened?" Susannah asked as he came over to sit beside her. The speech therapist at Oldenham was right. Her grammar was beginning to improve.

Cervantes bent to kiss her. "I told the producer what was happening, and he adjusted the schedule." He frowned. "What's the matter, babe?"

Tears filled her eyes. She blinked them away. "Just—just more of same." Susannah thought she had hit bottom when Jill got the commercial, succeeding where Susannah had failed, but since the loss of her diary any stray kindness reduced her to tears.

Cervantes poked her in the ribs. "You've got a big night ahead of you. Don't go to pieces before it starts. And don't waste your tears on Shacker. When I said he adjusted the schedule, I meant it literally. This evening's shooting we're doing tomorrow evening. Tomorrow night's we're doing tonight—after this breaks."

The last to arrive was Herb. He looked moody and withdrawn, scarcely glancing at Dr. Dubinsky, his handshake brief and jerky. Herb hadn't wanted to come either, had said he wasn't coming. Susannah didn't know what had changed his mind. Maybe the dramatist in him. Or curiosity. Or the same feeling of responsibility that compelled him to give so much of himself to her therapy.

He sat by himself in a far corner of the room, as if to say he wished only to observe. Susannah shook her head. Some of Dr. Dubinsky's patients came here with that same idea. It never worked.

Occasionally, as part of a training program, Dr. Dubinsky permitted a therapist to observe a psychodrama. A man was here tonight in that capacity. Not a young man. Maybe an established psychiatrist investigating a new technique.

Glancing at the list of names he'd drawn up, tucking the piece of paper in his vest pocket, Dr. Dubinsky

walked to the bare center and cleared his throat. The
silence pervading the room became absolute.

"Once again I want to thank all of you for coming
here this evening to give us your time—and what may
turn out to be an emotional expenditure as well."

He held a hand out to Susannah. With Cervantes'
help she stood up and walked slowly out to join him.
She still had difficulty getting to her feet, but her walking had improved. She no longer used the cane to keep
pedestrians at bay. She no longer carried it. It made
her feel foolish, paranoid.

Dr. Dubinsky smiled and put an arm around her,
making her start blinking again. Cervantes was right.
It was going to be a long, hard evening. She had to get
a grip on herself.

With a sweep of his other arm Dr. Dubinsky said,
"We all know why we're here. To help Susannah. Help
her confront and explore the problems facing her as a
result of the attack on her."

He smiled again. Dr. Dubinsky had an engaging
smile and a soft way of talking that went with his small
frame and put people at ease. "One way to explore problems," he continued, "is to talk about them. The method
we're going to use is called psychodrama. Instead of
talking about her problems, Susannah—with your
help—will dramatize them, act them out. Now. Some
of you already know how psychodrama works. Those of
you who don't will learn as we go along."

Dr. Dubinsky walked over to a stack of folding chairs
and brought two chairs back with him. Settling Susannah in one of them, setting up the other one beside her,
he turned once again to his audience. "First let me say
that the gentleman in the dark blue suit over there"—
all heads turned to look—"is a colleague of mine who
is here to observe. Pay no attention to him. I'm going
to ask each of the rest of you to pick up a folding chair
and bring it here so we can form a nice big semicircle
around Susannah."

Asking the participants to set the chairs up instead
of having them set up in advance was part of Dr. Dubinsky's warm-up technique. Susannah wondered what
exercise he would choose next and what the response

would be. It didn't surprise her to see that the Whitneys had chosen to sit at one end of the semicircle and Herb at the other, as far away from her—and the action— as they could get.

"Now," Dr. Dubinsky said, smiling again, coming back to stand beside her, "I think we first ought to get acquainted. As most of you—maybe all of you—know, Susannah has worked for me on a part-time basis for the last two years as a professional alternate ego, drawing on her ability—her considerable ability, I might say—as an actress to help me put on psychodramas for my patients, both in private consultation and in group therapy."

He turned to the Whitney end of the semicircle. "Suppose we go next to you, Mr. Whitney."

So much for seeking obscurity.

Light glinting on the glasses he had recently started wearing, Joe looked nonplussed. "Do you want me to stand?"

"I want all of you to do whatever is most comfortable for you—short of crawling under your chair and hoping this whole business will go away."

A ripple of laughter.

Joe stood up. "I'm Joe Whitney, Susannah's hus— Susannah's former husband." He glanced at Jill, seated at her grandmother's other side. "And Jill's father." He sat down.

Mrs. Whitney did not get up. "My name is Eve Whitney," she said. "I'm Joe's mother and Jill's grandmother." Susannah expected her to stop there, but to her surprise she went on to say, "I've been helping Susannah in her apartment until she and Jill can manage on their own." Maybe Mrs. Whitney felt she had to explain her present involvement with a former daughter-in-law. Probably.

Jill stood. "I'm Jill," she said. "I'm—" She stood thinking, then shrugged, flushed and self-conscious. "She's my mother."

Barbara Caitlin, Dr. Aaronson, Dr. O'Neal, Polly Berkmyer, Cervantes, Eugenia Eckardt—all said something about themselves. It was Herb's turn.

After a glance at the observer sitting in the shadows,

Herb stood up. What he had to say came out as if he had rehearsed it. Maybe he had. He had had time.

"My name is Herb Schlosser. I work at Horlick's. I write plays. I—I found Susannah and brought her to the hospital. I help with her therapy." He sat down.

During the introductions Dr. Dubinsky had sat beside Susannah. Now he stood up again. "As you all know, much of Susannah's imbalance, much of her depression and anxiety, stem from her inability to remember—not only the attack itself—and she may never remember that—but events leading up to the attack." He looked from one end of the semicircle to the other. "Now, those events I'm confident she can and will remember. Are you ready to help her try?"

Heads nodded. Somebody said "Yes." Somebody else—Eugenia, probably—said "Right on." Joe continued to look nonplussed behind his glasses.

For the last few days, in spite of every effort not to, Susannah had thought about this evening almost without letup. She was afraid she wouldn't remember anything. She was afraid she would remember everything. She hoped everybody Dr. Dubinsky had invited would come. She hoped nobody would.

Until its unaccountable loss—she had searched everywhere, gone to every possible Lost and Found—she had labored over her diary. A single sentence could take as long as five minutes to write. Find the words, pull them out, put them down. She kept at it when fatigue and frustration screamed at her to give up. She pored over it, reading each entry time and again, feeling the ghosts stirring, reaching out to her, the conviction growing within her that sooner or later she would make contact.

She could no longer bear to think about the diary. Or this evening. She could not bear another loss, another disappointment of that magnitude.

"Now," Dr. Dubinsky said, "some of you—again, maybe all of you—know that Susannah doesn't believe she was the victim of a random mugging. She thinks somebody—some man she knows—was trying to kill her."

Gasps from Polly and Eugenia, who hadn't known.

An exchange of glances between Barbara Caitlin and
Dr. Aaronson. Impossible to tell what they were thinking.

As Herb had done earlier, Susannah glanced at the
observer sitting in the shadows, wondering for the first
time if he really was a therapist interested in a new
technique or if he was something more than that. If so,
who? And why?

She shivered.

"You may not agree with Susannah," Dr. Dubinsky
continued, "but I'm going to ask you to pretend you do.
For a little while. As I explained to her when she first
talked to me about it, whether or not somebody tried
to kill her, that somebody and that idea of him are
locked away inside her head. What matters—if only to
her peace of mind—is getting that information out."

He walked over to the Pullman kitchen and picked
up a folder lying on a counter top. Coming back to stand
beside her, he said, "Susannah and I have drawn up
profiles of some possible suspects. To protect her, to
protect them, we have given them false names. I'm
going to ask some of you to take a profile, study it, then
act out a scene with Susannah or with somebody playing Susannah. A scene that provokes an argument. An
argument that becomes violent enough to lead to an
attack on her."

Dr. Dubinsky held up a hand. "I don't of course mean
for anybody to hit anybody. You see some pillows over
there. We'll provide an empty chair and a couple of
pillows for that purpose. Now." He opened the folder
and took out a sheet of paper. "Our first suspect is called
Frank. Frank is a tall, thin, boyish-looking fellow who
had a brief relationship with Susannah some time ago.
He wanted the relationship to continue, but she broke
off with him because he was extremely jealous and proprietary. He became so abusive to her on the telephone
she had it changed to an unlisted number. She could
not prevent him from coming into the café where she
worked Friday and Sunday nights and Monday during
the day, and he continued to come in there from time
to time."

Dr. Dubinsky held the sheet of paper out to Cervantes. "I'm told everybody calls you Cervantes. Is that right? Will you play Frank?"

Nodding, Cervantes took the sheet of paper and came to the center of the semicircle. Dr. Dubinsky set up a third chair and put two pillows on it. "Oh, yes," he said, turning to his audience. "The night Susannah was attacked there was a thunderstorm with thunder and lightning and a heavy downpour. Now. Susannah recalls that the man who attacked her wore a yellow slicker and screamed 'Die, die, die!' at her." Turning back to Cervantes, he said, "Any time you're ready." He walked around behind the semicircle, standing not far from where the observer sat, but not, so far as Susannah could see, exchanging glances with him.

When Dr. Dubinsky had first queried her about possible suspects, Susannah hadn't thought of Phil Zerita, now called Frank. He hadn't been in the café for several months, and she assumed he had left town. As Cervantes sat down beside her she wondered if Dr. Dubinsky had asked him to play Phil because Cervantes was also tall and thin and boyish-looking.

"Hello, Sue," he said.

She turned away from him.

"Where you off to?"

"No—none your business."

"Pretty dark street for you to be walking along. And a miserable night out. You meeting somebody?"

"No."

"I bet not."

"No—none your business I am." She was still turned away from him.

"There was a time, Sue, when you wouldn't have turned away from me like that."

"Go away."

"Damn you." He reached for her wrist and jerked her around to him.

Susannah gasped.

Somebody else gasped. Maybe Polly or Eugenia. Susannah hadn't seen, only heard. Her eyes were locked on Cervantes' face.

"What is it?" he said, frowning, puzzled, speaking as himself.

Dr. Dubinsky stepped forward. "What is it, Susannah?"

She rubbed a hand across her forehead. "I—I—man—man in yellow slicker pull that way. Face close—close mine. See face."

A loud crash, making them jump.

Everybody turned to see.

One of the folded card tables had been leaning against a radiator near Herb's end of the semicircle. He must have made some movement, had shifted somehow in his chair, causing it to fall. Red-faced, frowning, he stood up to retrieve it. "Sorry,". he said. "I didn't—"

Dr. Dubinsky waved a hand. "That's all right, Herb. It's all right if I call you Herb? Good. Don't worry about it. Now, Susannah. You saw the man's face. Can you describe it?"

She frowned. The face was blurred, out of focus, a subject moving as she snapped the picture. She tried to make the face come clear. "Like—like—all twisted. Con—con—con—please?"

"Contorted?"

"Yes. Much—many teeth."

"Can you identify the face? Do you know who it belongs to?"

Not a sound in the room. Not a stir.

After a moment she shook her head. "No. No recognize."

"Do you want to go on with the scene?"

She shook her head again. "No. I no—I don't—I no think Phil. Sorry. Frank. No think him." She looked from Cervantes to Dr. Dubinsky. "Rest, please?" She was beginning to tire, and the evening had hardly begun.

"Of course." Dr. Dubinsky turned to Barbara Caitlin. "Will you play Susannah in our next scene? And Dr. Aaronson, will you play the next suspect for us?"

As the four of them changed places, Susannah going to sit in Barbara's chair, Dr. Dubinsky took a second sheet out of the folder. "This man's name is Mike. He lives with his girl friend Gloria. Mike and Gloria are unstable personalities—hotheads who fight a lot—physically as well as verbally. The fights usually grow

out of arguments about Mike's love-hate relationship
with his mother, and his emotional dependence on her."

Dr. Dubinsky handed Mike's profile to Dr. Aaronson.
While he and Barbara looked at it together, Susannah
turned to Jill in the chair at her left. Susannah had
thought that hearing the tape recording of her session
with Dr. Dubinsky had convinced Jill Joe was not and
never had been suspected of being the man in the yellow
slicker. Now she wasn't sure. Even to her, who knew
better, Mike sounded like a thin disguise of Joe. Touching Jill's arm, leaning close to her, she whispered,
"Mike man in group therapy."

Jill nodded, her face a mask.

Susannah sighed. She didn't know what was bugging
Jill now. Not the commercial. They had had that out,
gotten it straight, all of it. Pride, fear, jealousy—the
works.

Something about Cervantes again. Not simply resentment that Cervantes measured up where her father
didn't. There was more to it than that.

Something about that weekend in Syosset with her
grandmother. Not the making love. Jill was old enough
and quick enough to know what was going on between
her mother and Cervantes, what had gone on between
them off and on for the last year or more.

That was what had led Jill to hope Cervantes would
move in with them.

Jill also knew her mother was too much the minister's daughter for that to happen easily or, until and
unless it did, for Cervantes to show up at the breakfast
table now and again. Susannah and Cervantes had always gone to his place to make love. But his place was
a walk-up, the stairs too hard for her to navigate. More
than that Susannah had wanted, had needed something
beyond sexual satisfaction. She had needed comfort,
male companionship, love.

She had known it wouldn't be easy asking Mrs. Superior Person to take Jill for the weekend. What had
surprised her, puzzled her, was Jill's opposition. Un-
voiced, unacknowledged, but there.

It still puzzled her.

Susannah sighed again and turned her attention back to Dr. Dubinsky, who had resumed speaking.

"One more point. Mike is a member of one of the therapy groups Susannah works with. She has often played the role of Gloria. On at least two occasions Susannah has been approached by Mike after an enactment here. On one of those occasions what began as a discussion of a disturbing encounter turned into encounter itself as Mike began to confuse Susannah with Gloria."

Dr. Dubinsky started to his place behind the semicircle, then stopped. "One further point. Susannah asked for a rest, and I gave it to her. But that wasn't my only reason for asking Mrs. Caitlin to stand in. Observing the scene from the sidelines may give Susannah insight she couldn't get as a participant." He nodded to Barbara and Dr. Aaronson. "Whenever you're ready."

Dr. Aaronson and Barbara whispered together, then, a little awkward, a little stiff, began the scene.

"Mind if I walk along with you, Susannah?"

"No."

"This is a dark, dangerous street for you to be on."

"Well, I don't intend to be on it long."

A ghost stirred, reached out, receded.

Dr. Aaronson looked at Barbara as if he were taking a plunge. "How often do you see Gloria?"

She frowned at him. "How often? Gloria? I've never once seen her. I wouldn't know Gloria if she walked right by me."

"I find that hard to believe."

"Why?"

He shrugged. "You read her so well."

"I'm an actress playing a part."

"You could be playing a part with me."

She looked at him. "Mike, why are you so suspicious of people?"

"Now you sound like my mother."

"And you sound like a kid. Do you realize a person can't have a conversation with you for five minutes without you bringing your mother into it? What is it with you and her?"

He glared at her. "I resent that, Gloria."

"I'm not Gloria."

"My mother's been very decent to you."

"Mike, I'm not Gloria. I'm Susannah. I don't even know your mother, but I'm sure she's a—"

"How dare you talk about her like that? What has she ever done to you?"

"Nothing. Mike, listen to me. I'm not—"

Dr. Aaronson jumped up from his chair, grabbed a pillow and slammed it against the chair he'd jumped up from. "I'll teach you to have some respect. Take that!" He started to slam the pillow down again, then stopped, frowning toward the semicircle, the mock rage draining out of him, looking embarrassed. "Oh. I forgot. I was supposed to say, 'Die, die, die!'" He shrugged. "It doesn't sound right, somehow."

Dr. Dubinsky stepped forward. "No," he agreed, "it doesn't. But no matter." He turned to Susannah. "How about it, Susannah? Anything?"

She looked at the faces turned to hers. Again that feeling of motion suspended, of somebody waiting.

Susannah frowned. What had made her think that? Somebody waiting.

She glanced at the observer sitting in the shadows. Was it likely Dr. Dubinsky would invite an observer, no matter how distinguished a therapist he might be, to this particular psychodrama?

Again she shivered.

"Well?" Dr. Dubinsky prompted her.

"I—I—not sure. Something. Can't say what."

Dr. Dubinsky smiled and nodded. "It's coming. I'm sure of it. Now. Let me see who's next." He took a third sheet out of the folder.

She and Dr. Dubinsky had drawn up profiles of four men. They were all she could come up with, and none of them seemed right to her. Now, as she played opposite Dr. O'Neal, then watched Joe play the fourth man with Polly as herself, they seemed even less right. And no ghosts stirred.

The only thing to come out of it was a backstage romance. As Joe and Polly acted out their scene it became obvious they were turning each other on.

Undaunted by his failure to trigger more than a blurry, unrecognizable face and a vague something she couldn't identify, Dr. Dubinsky said they would try another approach. Dismissing Polly, he asked Joe to stay and beckoned to Jill.

Giving Polly her seat back, Susannah went to sit beside her ex-mother-in-law. She was very tired now.

Dr. Dubinsky conferred with his two players, then turned to the semicircle. "The day before the attack on Susannah, Jill had a conversation with her father. They're going to try to repeat it for us." He nodded to them, then walked back to his customary place.

Flushed, self-conscious, Jill sat down in one of the chairs and pantomimed picking up a telephone and dialing.

Joe followed suit, picking up an imaginary receiver. "Hello."

"Hello, Daddy?"

Susannah was trying to think what the conversation could have been about when she felt Mrs. Whitney tense up beside her, and suddenly she knew. Jill had called Joe to ask him to come to Assembly the next day, and he had said he would, though he had no intention of doing so.

"You will come?" Jill was saying, voice and face anxious.

"Yes. I'll be there." Joe, also remembering, had the grace to look chagrined.

"Okay, Daddy. G'bye."

"Goodbye, sweetheart."

Jill replaced her imaginary phone, tucked her long blond hair behind her ears, and turned a questioning face to Dr. Dubinsky.

He came around the end of the semicircle where Susannah was seated, helping her to her feet. "Do you remember that conversation?" he asked.

She shook her head. "I no— Wait. Please." Tired or not, hard to do or not, if she did not start concentrating, correcting herself, she would be talking like a two-year-old the rest of her life.

Dr. Dubinsky nodded. "Take all the time you need, Susannah."

"I did—I did not hear call. I know—knew afterward—next day—Jill made. Made it. I forgot. Now
remember."

Somebody sighed.

In the shadows the man stirred, crossing his feet.

Dr. Dubinsky looked encouraged. "You had forgotten
there had been a phone call, but now you remember?"

She nodded.

He beamed. "Good. Great. All right. Now. Joe, you
may return to your seat. Jill will stay, please." He
turned to the semicircle. "Let me say here something
I should have said earlier. In recreating events and
situations prior to the attack on Susannah, we're going
to expose some feelings. Susannah's feelings, other people's feelings. In trying to make Susannah remember,
we're going to make others remember. Maybe things
we'd sooner forget." He spread his hands. "I beg your
understanding and your tolerance. Now. We move
ahead to the day of the attack. Late in the afternoon
Susannah came home." He turned to her. "Where had
you been?"

"Make—making rounds."

He nodded. "All right. You came home. You received
a phone call. From whom?"

"Service. Phone ring—ringing I get off elevator."

Dr. Dubinsky held a hand up. "Just a moment. Eugenia, will you come take the role of the answering
service?"

Eugenia, who subscribed to the same service, went
into the Carlton-the-Doorman routine with gusto. "Susannah? This is your service calling."

People laughed.

Eugenia knew about the callback. All her friends
knew about it by this time. "The Weingarten office
called." She was still talking in Carlton's lugubrious
monotone. "You're to be at the Regency Theater tonight
at—um—seven-thirty for a callback. For one of the
Hollywood—um—backers, I think. Anyhow, you're to
be there. Okay?"

"Okay."

Eugenia put a hand over the imaginary mouthpiece.
"Did I say anything else?"

"You wish luck. In—in regular voice." Remembering how touched she had been, thinking how luck had failed her, Susannah swallowed. She glanced at Cervantes, who frowned and shook his head at her.

"Good luck, Susannah," Eugenia said.

She nodded.

"Now," Dr. Dubinsky said, "what happened next?"

Susannah turned to him in dismay. It was like shutting a book. She couldn't even remember hanging up the phone. She shook her head. "I no—I don't know."

"Was Jill at home?"

She frowned, trying to think. "I no—I don't think so."

He turned to Jill. "Were you at home that day when your mother came in?"

Jill shook her head. "No." Out of the corner of her eye she looked at Susannah. The airport was getting ready to close.

"When you came home what was your mother doing?"

Jill shrugged. "I don't know." After a moment and another look out of the corner of her eye she said, "She was in the kitchen."

"Maybe," Dr. Dubinsky suggested, "she had just finished getting her phone call."

"Maybe," Jill agreed.

He studied her a moment. "Try to recreate the scene. All right, Jill?"

She shrugged again.

"And I'm going to ask Polly to play your alter ego. To say some of the things you might be feeling but don't want to say."

Of course, Susannah thought. She should have known Dr. Dubinsky wouldn't ask her to play Jill's alter ego. Nor, for all his cautionary words a few moments ago, would he let Jill suffer unnecessarily or too much. One of his functions as the director was to keep any scene, any conflict from getting out of hand.

Polly joined the two of them in the center of the semicircle, and Dr. Dubinsky took up his position behind it. For the next few moments nobody moved, nobody spoke. Jill had played her scene with Joe without hesitation. This time she didn't seem to know what to do.

Out in the semicircle throats were cleared, weight shifted. Herb picked at a thread on the sleeve of his turtleneck. The man in the shadows uncrossed his feet.

Finally, without looking at her, Jill said, "You opened the door for me."

She had no memory of doing it. She pantomimed opening the door. "Hello, bay— Sorry. Hello, Jill."

"Hello." Jill stood where she was.

Not knowing what else to say, Susannah said, "Come in."

As Jill took a couple of steps toward her, Polly spoke up. "All right," she said. "I'll come in. But I wish I didn't have to."

Startled, Jill turned to stare at her.

Dr. Dubinsky stepped forward. "Jill, if your alter ego says something wrong, something you weren't thinking at all, you must stop and correct Polly. It isn't her role to put thoughts into your head. She's simply trying to take thoughts out of your head and give voice to them. Do you understand?"

Jill nodded. She looked again at Polly but said nothing.

Susannah still had no inkling of this homecoming, but she remembered others. "Take—take off coat, Jill. Hang—hang up, please."

Jill pantomimed doing that.

"Always leaning on my case," her alter ego said. "It wouldn't hurt to leave my things where I put them."

"You always—almost always home time," Susannah said, wondering what had put that thought in her head, wishing she could have expressed it more coherently. She tried not to sound reproachful. "Where been?"

"Nowhere."

"Nowhere you'd approve of," her alter ego said.

Jill turned to Polly. "No. That's not so." She bit her lip. "Well, I did say I'd been to Horlick's, and Mom said she didn't want me to hang around there, so I guess..." Her voice trailed off.

After a few moments of silence Dr. Dubinsky said, "Can we go on with the scene?"

Susannah tried desperately to remember something of that homecoming—anything—though she knew from past experience trying didn't help. Since Jill obviously hadn't volunteered the information about Horlick's, she must have brought the subject up by telling Jill she couldn't take part in the reading of Herb's play. "I have callback for *Road,* Jill. No. Sorry. *Glory Road.* Callback tonight. Have—have go tell Herb no—tell Herb can't read play." She ached with fatigue. "Herb play. His play."

"Oh," Jill said.

Nothing.

Nothing from Polly either.

The audience stirred again. Dr. Aaronson whispered something to Dr. O'Neal, who was looking skeptical now. Mrs. Whitney looked at her watch. Cervantes must have to leave soon for tonight's filming.

Susannah glanced at Joe, who was glancing at Polly, and something clicked. Of course. Whatever Jill was hiding from her about that afternoon's encounter had to have something to do with Joe. Jill always came home upset when he disappointed her.

Turning to Jill, she said, "Father. Wait. Please. Your father. Did come Assembly today?"

"No."

"Did—did say—did he say would come?"

"Yes."

Susannah frowned. That couldn't have been the way it went. She hadn't overheard the phone call, hadn't known ahead of time Joe was supposed to have come to Assembly. And Jill wouldn't have volunteered that information either. Her frown deepened. How had she found out?

What made her think that wasn't all she'd found out?

She turned to Jill. "What else happen?"

"Nothing."

Polly spoke up again. "I don't want to talk about it."

"Why not?" Susannah asked.

Jill only looked at her.

They weren't getting anywhere, and they would have to stop soon. She was getting too tired to think straight.

Dr. Dubinsky stepped forward again. "Jill, I want you to change places with your mother. Change places and reverse roles with her. Do you understand what I mean? You play your mother. She'll play you. Polly, you continue to play Jill's alter ego. That's right. Stand behind Susannah, because she's Jill now. Now let me see." He turned to the semicircle.

Herb's chair creaked as he shifted position, drawing Dr. Dubinsky's attention. "Herb. Yes. Excellent. Herb, will you come here, please, and play Susannah's alter ego?"

The chair creaked more as Herb stood up. He hesitated, looking at them, then moved to join them.

"Good," Dr. Dubinsky said. "Right. Stand behind Jill, who's playing Susannah. All right. Now. Let's talk about Jill's father. Susannah, you begin. As Jill."

Dr. Dubinsky stepped back.

Susannah tried to think. "Maybe Daddy say no sure come."

"Maybe," Jill, as Susannah, agreed.

"Oh, sure," Herb said, startling them all by his readiness to speak up. He hadn't looked eager to take part. "That's—that's what you'd like to think, isn't it, Jill?"

Susannah was even more startled by Herb's accurate reading of her thoughts.

She remembered something.

Jill had told her Herb's father had died recently. Why had she told her that? In what connection?

Pursue it. Find out. "Mom," Susannah said, as Jill, "Herb father die. You know that?"

Jill looked suspicious, fearful. "No. I don't know anything about Herb."

Herb nodded. "And I don't—I don't want to know anything about him."

Jill's eyes went wide.

As her alter ego, Polly said, "I don't like any of this. It scares me. What would Herb say, Mom, if he knew you put him down like that?"

"What do I—what do I care what Herb thinks?" Herb said.

Beginning to share Jill's suspicions and fears, not sure where the scene was taking them, aware of the now rapt attention of the semicircle of listeners, of the man in the shadows, of her own throbbing fatigue, Susannah said, "Mom, Herb upset father die."

Jill crossed her arms, impatience flashing across her face. "I don't have much time to talk, and what little time I do have I don't want to spend talking about your friend Herb."

The ghosts reached out.

Without thinking Susannah said, "Well, who we talk about then?"

Jill's eyes widened again.

Polly spoke up. "I don't want to talk about anybody or anything. Leave me alone."

Susannah shook her head. "Can't leave alone. Have talk about—oh. Sorry." She turned to look at Dr. Dubinsky. "Sorry. Forget am Jill. Think me."

Dr. Dubinsky stepped forward. "All right. Go back to being yourselves. Everybody change places. Good. All right. Now, Susannah. Repeat what you said to Jill. As yourself."

Susannah nodded. "Can't leave—leave you alone, Jill. Have talk about—about—" About what? Some aspect of Jill's relationship with Joe, surely, but which one?

Pick anything. Pick something you've talked with her about before.

"Joe not mean disappoint you. Joe love you." From the corner of her eye Susannah could see both of the Whitney observers. Joe looked discomfited. Mrs. Whitney senior looked angry, affronted.

Jill looked ready to cry, and again Susannah remembered.

Remembered being in the kitchen, hearing Jill's key in the lock, opening the door, seeing Jill standing there in the blue sausage-casing, her face streaked with dirt. From crying.

"You cry," she said to Jill. "That day you come home. Been crying. Face—face—" She couldn't come up with the word. Could think it, couldn't say it. She rubbed at her face with the tips of her fingers. "Face—face—" She gave up. "Why you cry?"

Jill didn't answer.

Polly said what she'd said earlier. "I don't want to talk about it."

Herb said nothing.

They were back to getting nowhere.

Susannah turned to Dr. Dubinsky. She couldn't go on. "I tired. I no—I can't—" She thought of the old man at the hospital. *Stay awake on your feet if you can.* She didn't know whether she could or not.

Dr. Dubinsky stepped forward and turned to address the semicircle. "All right. Let's stop for now. We've made some progress. Not as much as I'd hoped for, but—" He smiled his engaging smile. "Like Susannah, I'm overanxious. Now. I want to thank all of you for coming and helping. I'll be in touch with you about getting together to try again."

Chairs pushed back. People got to their feet, milled about, getting their gear. Joe and Polly huddled. Susannah silently wished Polly luck. She was going to need it. Mrs. Whitney stood apart from them, still looking angry and affronted. She also looked impatient to be gone.

Dr. Dubinsky came up to Susannah, clasping her hands in his. "Don't be discouraged, Susannah. You really did make progress."

She nodded, wishing she could believe him. She had been wrong about the psychodrama the same as she'd been wrong about everything else. It hadn't been all or nothing. Only little pieces of something.

To go with the other little pieces she had.

Add a blurry, unidentifiable face to the death of Herb's father to Jill crying about something. Add all that to the need to call Jill to reassure her, to the telephone that was one place one time and somewhere else another, to the fear that the Whitneys were trying to take Jill away from her, to the dark, the rain, the abandoned houses. To the man in the yellow slicker.

It didn't add up to anything. She was still a collection of fragments. Still schizoid.

And paranoid.

"You'll make more progress," Dr. Dubinsky said. "I know you will."

She nodded again.

Cervantes hovered in the background.

He offered to take her home, but she knew he was anxious to get to his filming, to oversee the setting up. "Joe—somebody—drop us off," she said. "You go."

He took off, and Dr. Dubinsky squeezed her hand. "Ending the psychodrama doesn't necessarily end the progress of recall, you know. A number of things were triggered here tonight. They may have started a chain reaction that will keep on working, first in your subconscious, then up into your conscious." He squeezed her hand again. "If not, we'll have another go at it in a few days."

The observer came up to them. Dr. Dubinsky introduced him. He was a noted psychiatrist who had recently become interested in psychodrama.

It figured.

By the time she extricated herself, Joe had gone. Almost everybody had gone. Jill was waiting for her, her secrets safe, her manner prickly, wound up tight.

Susannah didn't know why Jill was hiding what she was hiding, whether it was something she was ashamed to have known or afraid to have known, or whether, having made such a thing of it, she was now too embarrassed to admit it wasn't anything of much importance.

Whatever it was, Jill's secrets were the key to everything. Or seemed to be.

Herb was waiting, too. Her alter ego. Her astonishingly perceptive alter ego.

They set off for the bus stop.

Maybe Dr. Dubinsky was right about the psychodrama starting a chain reaction. Before tonight the ghosts reaching out to her were pale, wispy creatures, ribbons of smoke. Tonight they thrashed about like a nest of snakes.

Nineteen

Hardly anybody on the bus.

He had to clamp his hand around the steel support pole to keep from hurling himself out the window.

He didn't understand.

He had gone back on his medication night before last. He had finished the revisions sometime after midnight, desperate, almost over the edge. He had taken the drug at once. A full day's dosage. The same yesterday morning. At regular intervals since.

He should have calmed down by now. Instead he was all churned up inside.

She was saying something to him. He had to strain to hear her.

"No have—you no have—you don't have come all way home. With us. Herb."

Windows rattled and shook—bones rattled and shook—as the bus bounced through potholes.

Was she trying to get rid of him?

Before he could answer her, Jill answered for him. "I know I don't have to go all the way home with you. I'm sure you'd rather I wouldn't. I expect you get tired of seeing me day after day, but you're stuck with me, duckie."

He stared from Jill to Susannah and back again. Had she actually said that, or had he imagined it?

Was he starting to hallucinate again? He tightened his grip on the pole.

Jill looked at him, her face flushing. "I can be an alter ego, too."

She had said it. He was okay.

"Jill," Susannah said. "Not nice."

Okay? Fool. He was far from okay.

Jill shrugged. "Polly wasn't nice to me when she was my alter ego."

"That psychodrama. This different." Susannah looked at him. "Sorry, Herb. Jill not—Jill does not mean say that."

Maybe the churning-up inside was a delayed reaction to the psychodrama. He had sat transfixed through most of it, sure he was finished. More than once.

Especially when Cervantes grabbed her by the wrist, and she gasped.

He couldn't believe the look Cervantes gave him afterward.

He couldn't have imagined that.

He was right about Cervantes having some connection.

Had he been there on the street that night? Did he know what happened?

If he did, why hadn't he said anything about it?

"I was only telling you what he's thinking, Mom. You don't think he thinks that?"

"Jill."

He wanted them to stop. He put a hand up, the one not clamped around the pole. "It doesn't matter, Susannah."

What mattered was how much she knew.

More than she claimed?

How could she have seen his face and not know it was his?

Maybe she only imagined she saw a face. It was her business to imagine things, wasn't it?

And his business to find out.

If the doctor was right, if what had been triggered tonight was starting a chain reaction, better she remember now, while he was with her and could do something about it.

He gripped the pole harder. "Susannah?"

Her eyes were closed. She opened them, blinking at him. "Yes?"

Adrenaline surged through him like somebody had opened a dam. "The face. The man's face you saw."

She frowned at him. Was she putting that face against his? Matching them? Recognizing him? Wondering why she hadn't before?

"What about—about face?"

It was like hurling himself out the window. "You can't—you didn't recognize it?"

In speech therapy he was always devising sentences, springing words on her designed to test how much she knew, what she might be hiding, but he had never put himself in this kind of jeopardy before.

More adrenaline surged through him.

Nausea, too.

He swallowed against the nausea. He could handle it.

He could handle anything.

She must recognize him. She must, she must.

She shook her head. "No. Don't know who. Know man. Don't know face. Sound crazy, but true." She shook her head again. "Lot of things don't know. Don't remember. Maybe sometime. Maybe never. Think never."

He should have been relieved. He was chagrined.

Rehearsals on his play were starting next week. It was set to open the eighteenth of May. He wanted this behind him. He had to have it behind him. He couldn't go on sacrificing his life to hers, caught in a timeless, endless game of cat and mouse.

Cat and mouse.

Was she putting him on?

No. She couldn't look that low and be putting him on. She was telling the truth.

Her head drooped, then jerked up as the bus ground

to a stop. She smiled a wan smile. "Psychodrama take all everything out. Out of me."

He nodded.

With a grinding lurch the bus took off again.

"You—you must tired, too. You get off your stop when come. Jill enough company home."

Jill pleated and unpleated the hem of her skirt. "You don't have to keep telling me you don't want me to come home with you. I heard you the first time."

"Jill."

Herb turned to look at Jill. What was she getting at?

"I know what you think of me."

She knew nothing.

"Jill. Stop."

"You think I care, but I don't. I stopped caring a long time ago. You want to know something funny? Just to show you how long it's been since I cared. One year my father gave me something for Christmas. It was a sweater. A dark blue sweater. Only it wasn't from him. My—the people I lived with except on weekends, they bought it for me and put my father's name on the tag. So I'd think it was from him. So I wouldn't know he thought so little of me he forgot to give me anything for Christmas."

He didn't think about his father any more. It no longer bothered him. The shit.

"Jill. Bayside. Don't."

Nothing bothered him since the Manhattan Theater Club had taken his play. That was all that mattered now.

"But what can you expect when your father's a shit-heel?"

"Jill!"

Jill lurched to a seat across the aisle. "I'll tell you what you can expect, duckie. You can expect to turn out just like him. Why not? You look just like him, don't you?"

"Jill. Please."

He had never seen the kid worked up like this. The psychodrama must have gotten to her, too.

Why not Susannah, the one it was meant to get to?

He had told the director he would sit in on rehearsals,

to see if more changes were needed. He had to get this business behind him. What could he do to make her remember?

Nothing.

Nobody could do anything. Not even Susannah.

It had to come on its own.

"Oh. Herb. You miss—missed your stop."

He nodded. "It doesn't matter. I'll see you home."

She always asked him in for a cup of coffee. This time he'd accept. He'd get rid of Jill. Ask her if she'd listened to the record she'd bought the other day. Jill never needed any persuasion to put that headset on. He'd get rid of her one way or another, then tell Susannah he was the man in the yellow slicker.

She would be totally isolated, totally helpless.

And it wouldn't matter whether she remembered he was the man or not. He was sorry, but he had given her all the time he could. He didn't have any more time to give her.

Jill crossed back to the seat she had left, the beads she wore slapping against a support pole as the bus slammed to a stop for a red light. "I told you you were stuck with me, duckie."

Susannah sighed. "Jill, why you do—" Her eyes went wide. She gasped and pointed.

Herb sucked in his breath. She had remembered something. He could see it in her face.

Remembered what?

"Beads," Susannah said. "Pink glass beads."

Jill frowned and fingered them. "What about them?"

Herb looked from one to the other of them. Was it possible she would remember too soon?

"Pink glass beads," Susannah said again. "On bed. Jill. Your bed." She frowned. "Why on bed?" She shook her head, the animation fading from her face. "I no— I don't know. Things run—running around inside. In head. Maybe wake up tomorrow everything come clear." She shook her head again, the corners of her mouth turned down. "Yeah. Sure."

He sighed.

Eighty-eighth Street coming up.

She wouldn't be waking up tomorrow.

The bus stopped. They got off. He had to help Susannah down the steps. She still couldn't do it by herself.

A pity, all that wasted effort at rehabilitation.

Nobody much around. Two punks walking uptown on the other side of the street.

Not much reason for foot traffic here. A block of abandoned tenements. Dim street lights. Shadowed entryways.

Susannah stopped at the new-style pay phone on the corner of Eighty-seventh Street. She never passed this way without stopping there. She said it had something to do with something. She couldn't remember what.

New-style or not, the phone was always out of order.

Not tonight.

Tonight, while she stood there frowning in at the phone, it rang.

She jumped, then her body went rigid.

In the dim light he saw the color drain from her face. She turned around to him, stared at him, drew in her breath.

She knew.

Twenty

She couldn't think.

She had to, but she couldn't.

A scream was already welling up in her.

Think.

She didn't have to think about the danger she was in. She knew that without thinking.

The scream ripped through her throat.

Jill and Herb staring at her.

Think.

A moment indelibly stamped on her brain flashed through her head. The old Irish woman. Her grandmother's friend. At her grandson's wake. The terrible moment when she had started keening.

Why that?

Don't question. Do it.

She pitched the scream upward, outward, into the harsh, high lament for the dead.

The look on Herb's face changed. He didn't know what she was up to.

She didn't either.

Jill was white-faced. "Mom," she said, grabbing at

her, clinging to her. "Mama, what is it? What's the matter?"

Think.

How was it possible? How could it be? Herb the man in the—why would he—

No!

Don't think about that. Think what to do.

"Mom," Jill begged. "What is it? What's happened?"

It was no use. How could she think? She was too tired, too weak, too—she had to have help. She couldn't do it alone.

She was no longer keening. She was sobbing.

The thing she did best.

"Jill," Herb said.

Fresh terror assailed her. What did he intend to do to Jill? She put out a hand to him. "No. Herb have—must help." She hadn't known what she intended to say.

A cry for the dead?

Help?

Who would he believe was dead?

No. Not who. What.

Think.

Something Cervantes had told her. What?

"Herb. Must—must help. Please say—say will?"

He still looked puzzled.

She wiped her face with her arm, the tears running down her face. Could she do it? Did she have the strength?

She had no strength. She didn't even know what she was doing. Let him kill her. It would all be over in a minute.

"Cervantes," she said, her voice breaking on his name. "Cervantes man in yellow slicker."

Herb stared at her.

Jill gasped.

She started sobbing again. Her knees trembled so she could hardly stand. "I thought Cervantes love. Say love. Act love." She was hiccupping through her sobs. So much out of control. So little in. "Act love. Make love."

She couldn't stand any longer. She sank to her knees,

the urge to give up, give in, beg for mercy running through her like blood.

"Cervantes kind. Cervantes help. Cervantes pay—pay—" How could she possibly hope to divert him when the words wouldn't come? "Cer—Cervantes pay—patient. He say no worry. Say no strain. No try so hard. No matter no remember." She dared not look up. "Past past. No—can't bring back. What count future." She was still hiccupping. "Cervantes make think every—everything okay. Cervantes strong. Man lean on."

She swallowed and started keening once again.

Jill stood like a stone statue of herself.

Why didn't somebody hear? Come help? She had to have help. She couldn't go on.

She had to go on.

She stopped keening and clenched her fists, made herself sound angry. "Cervantes make fool me. Think believe him. Think no find out what do. Cervantes wrong. He find out he wrong. Herb help."

She couldn't bear to look at him.

She had to.

She put a plea on her face, stretched her arms up to him.

He helped her to her feet.

She lay like a dead weight against him.

The man in the yellow slicker.

Shuddering, she lurched away, grabbed the corner of the phone booth to steady herself. Reaching for Jill's hand, taking tight hold of it, she turned to him. "Herb help? Please. Herb care me. Care what happen me. All time show. Day—day in, day—day out. Is no—is not so?"

He nodded.

She gripped Jill's hand more tightly. Was there a chance she—

Don't think about that either.

Concentrate. You have so little to concentrate with.

"Can't do alone, Herb. Have have help. You help?"

He nodded again.

"No even have cane. That Cervantes' doing, too. He laugh at me. Poke fun. Say crazy lady beat—beat off

crazy man. No carry cane more. Feel fool." She beckoned to him. "Come. We go home. Think what do."

"Yes," he said. "Home." The first words he had spoken. He took her by the arm and started across Columbus Avenue.

Something must be wrong with that suggestion.

What was she doing wrong?

Think.

Oh, my God.

Not home. The last place to go with him. Alone.
Isolated. No way to get help.

She had to have help.

They were almost across the avenue.

How get him to stop? How make him believe? Why
couldn't she think?

Stepping to the curb, she gasped and stopped, giving
him a frightened look.

That had to be the easiest thing she'd done yet.

Don't! You must not. Concentrate.

"No, Herb. No. Can't go home. Not safe. Cervantes
have—has kite—no—coke—no. No." Oh, God. Keys.
Keys. Her oldest stumbling block. The word she always
had such trouble coming up with. Concentrate. Think.
Help me, God. You have to help me. You have to.

She clenched her free hand into a fist. "Please.
Please. Cervantes has—has—has—keys. Keys! Can
get in. Might be there waiting." She shook with exhaustion. Swayed with it.

"Mom." Jill spoke in a tight, congested voice. "Cervantes said he had to shoot that movie."

Jill. Baby. Don't say something that will ruin everything. If it isn't already ruined. Please.

She nodded. "Know what say. Maybe trick. No go
home. Go police."

Oh, God, he would never buy that. Wasn't buying it,
his hand tightening on her arm.

Why couldn't she think?

"No. Can't go police. Police no believe. Can't let Cervantes know I—I'm on him—onto him—oh, God—
can't—can't let happen till safe. What do? Oh, God,
what do?"

Herb said nothing, offered no suggestion, the expression on his face unreadable. Jill looked from one to the other of them, her eyes wide and frightened.

Think.

She sighed. "I know what do. Cervantes either home—my home—either, either? Or. Or shoot movie. Can't go home. Go movie. Cervan—if Cervantes there, pretend all okay. Tell him lost kite—no—coke—no— God, please—lost—lost keys—lost my keys. Please give his me. Take—take—take keys. Keys. Go home. Herb come—come with. Safe. Cervantes no can get in. I think—Herb and I think what do next. Okay?" She beckoned. "Come. Show where. Down Columbus. Be- low—below—come. I show."

He must be buying what she said. He made no move to stop her as she limped down the avenue, but walked along beside her, keeping tight hold of her, whether to support her or keep her prisoner, she didn't know.

Couldn't think.

Didn't care.

If he didn't keep hold of her she would collapse.

Jill was frowning. "Mom," she said, tugging at her, "how could Cervantes—"

"Hush. I explain. Remember psychodrama? Remem- ber man called—called—forget what called. Can't think. Too tired." She sighed again. "No matter. Jealous man. That man. Cervantes play him. Remember I no want finish scene? Feel—felt funny Cervantes then. No know why. No understand. Do now. Cervantes like man he play. Jealous. Cervantes think—thought I find somebody else. He no—he not—he don't like that. I no have time Cervantes any more. He follow me that night. We fight. He hit me. Near kill. Leave me. Herb find. Herb save my life. I—I grateful, Herb."

"But, Mom—"

"Hush. Hurry. Come. Faster."

They crossed Eighty-sixth Street. She stumbled and staggered, hardly able to hold her head up, Herb keep- ing his tight grip on her.

So many blocks away. So far down Columbus. How could she manage it? Where could she find the strength? Every bone in her body ached. Even with Herb sup- porting her, she was ready to drop.

And Jill.

How could she save Jill when Jill didn't believe her? What could she say to make her think Cervantes—?

No.

Not that.

Hadn't Jill suffered enough?

She would never get over it. Never.

"But, Mom," Jill said. "If Cervantes—"

Dear God. She had to. There was no other way.

"Hush. Explain more. You think Cervantes friend. Spend time you. Take you movies, hamburger. Like you. Yes?"

Jill nodded.

Susannah shook her head, hardly able to look at her. "All put on. All fake. Cervantes use you get me." Her voice was ragged, drained. She strained to make it harsh. "Give example. You think I want you go live Grandma. Live with Grandma. Out—out in Syosset. Yes?"

Jill stared at her, wide-eyed.

"Not me. Cervantes. His idea. He want you out, him in. Get rid. Like weekend. Remember weekend not long back?"

Jill nodded, a glazed look on her face.

"Cervantes. His doing. He want you out of—out of way."

She might as well have struck her.

"But, Mom," Jill said like a broken record, her face pasty white, a catch in her voice.

"Hush, bayside. Explain later all. Know seem no make sense, but—"

She had been so intent on silencing Jill, so sickened by how she was having to do it, she had almost forgotten Herb.

A little sound escaped from him. An indrawn breath. A sigh. Something.

"No," he said, tightening his already tight grip on her, pulling her to a stop. "No. Wait."

She almost collapsed in a heap at his feet. A heap of bones and clothes. There was nothing more to her than that.

Something else had gone wrong.

What?

Think.

She couldn't.

"What—what matter, Herb?"

"Your diary," he said. "What you wrote in your diary."

Her diary? How did he know what she had— He must have taken it. Oh, God. The diary. What had she written in it?

Jill.

She had to save Jill quickly, quickly. Before he said anything more, and Jill was as lost as she was.

He surely couldn't want to harm Jill, but then she never would have thought—

"Bayside," she said, bending down to her, hardly able to keep herself from falling, "I no— I can't go on. Too tired. You—you go. Tell Cervantes—no. Ask Cervantes—" She swallowed, trying to think. "Ask Cervantes—oh, God." Damn her traitor brain. It had given out completely. "What ask Cervantes?"

Jill looked at her, white-faced, frowning. "You said you were going to say you lost your keys. And ask for his."

"Oh. Right. You say, you ask for me. Okay?"

Jill's frown deepened. "But, Mom, it's only a few blocks more. You can make it. Herb and I will help you, won't we, Herb?"

Susannah shook her head. "No." From the concentrated effort she put into the single word, it should have come out a shout. It came out a whisper. She strained harder. "No. Please, bayside. Go. I—I—" She couldn't think what more to say.

Herb said it for her. "Yes, Jill. Go. Do what your mother says. I'll take her home. We'll wait for you there."

Yes. Why not? Home.

She ached for it, yearned for it. She would be safe there. It was her haven, her refuge.

Only—

Wasn't there some reason she shouldn't be going there?

She shook her tired head. If there was, she'd forgotten it.

"But, Mom," Jill said, "you're not supposed to be able to get in. Remember? You're supposed to have lost your keys." ·

"I no—I can't think, bayside. Go. Please." Please, baby. Save yourself. Go. Go.

Herb again. "Tell him we're waiting outside. We can't get in, so we're waiting outside."

"Yes. Tell—tell that."

"Okay." Reluctant, unwilling, turning to look back, Jill set off, while they stood there watching her.

At the corner of Eighty-fourth Street she turned to look back again, crossed the intersection, looked back, kept going.

Jill.

Bayside.

No. Don't think about it.

Think how to save yourself. You still have to do that.

"Come on," Herb said, turning her around, heading her back toward Eighty-fifth Street. "We'll go to your place and wait for her there."

He was half dragging her. She could barely walk.

He hadn't half dragged her before. He wanted to take her home. He liked that idea. Think. Try to remember. There must be some reason she shouldn't go with him.

If she couldn't think, how could she save herself?

Traffic moved down Columbus in surges timed with the lights, yellow taxis zooming in and out of lanes, jockeying for position, horns blaring, tires screeching, drivers cursing. Any one of them could save her. If only they knew. If only they saw.

They hurtled by, paying no attention.

Pedestrians on the street could save her.

Nobody much in the neighborhood. Mom-and-pop stores. Closed for the night. Dark. Deserted. Only a few people walking by.

Some looked and looked away. Some didn't look at all. Weren't interested. Wrapped up in their own concerns.

They were approaching Eighty-sixth Street, a cross-town-bus street. More lights, more people here. She could reach out, grab somebody, beg for help. They might believe her.

Only, what if they didn't?

Whatever she had written in her diary, whatever Herb might think, he couldn't be certain she didn't believe Cervantes was the man in the yellow slicker. But if she grabbed out to somebody to beg for help, and they thought she was just freaked out...

She couldn't risk it.

"Come on," he said again, more than half dragging her now. Half carrying her.

They crossed Eighty-sixth Street.

Hadn't she suggested earlier he take her home? Hadn't he liked the idea then, too? Hadn't that made her think it was a bad suggestion? Hadn't she realized why?

She put a hand to her head. Where it ached. Throbbed.

It was no use. She couldn't think. Couldn't remember.

They turned the corner at Eighty-seventh Street.

Almost home.

She couldn't do it alone. She hadn't the strength. There was nothing left to her but bones and water and a bursting head.

She had to have help.

They had reached her building.

Nobody around.

It came to her then. The reason she shouldn't have let him bring her here. Not to her apartment. The last place. In her apartment she would be alone with him. Isolated. Helpless.

. When he opened the outside door she hung back. "You—you said—we—we—we wait—here. Outside. Please, Herb. Not safe go in. He—Cervantes—he might not—not give kite—no—coke—no—no—keys—keys Jill. Might—might come her. Come with her."

He held his free hand out for her keys. "You can tell

him you found your keys, after all. You had just mis-
placed them."

She gave them to him. She had to. There was still
a chance he didn't—

Wasn't there?

Twenty-One

Jill could see the floodlights up ahead. She stopped and turned around to look for her mother and Herb, but she couldn't see them. She supposed they were too far away by now.

A stationery store at her left had the Safe Haven decal pasted on its glass door. That meant the storekeeper would let her come inside and use his phone to call for help if she needed to, whether she had a dime or not.

She wanted to go in and tell the storekeeper she needed more than to use his phone, but there wasn't anybody in the store. It was closed for the night.

She ought not to stand here staring in the window. She ought to keep walking. Do it the way the Parents League Child Safety Campaign handbook said to do it on your way to and from school. *Do not stroll. Walk purposefully, as if you are meeting someone at a specific time.*

Walk in the middle of the sidewalk, neither too close to the buildings, nor too close to the curb.

If you have the feeling that something might go

wrong, and no store is available, wave or call, "Hi, Mom," and start to run in that direction.

Only her mother was in the wrong direction.

With a last look at the stationery-store window, Jill set off again toward the floodlights up ahead.

If you are in trouble, call as loudly as you can, "Police, Help!" This loud and repeated call is important because it summons help, and no wrongdoer wants to be caught.

It wasn't possible Cervantes—

She swallowed. Swallowed a second time and a third.

It wasn't possible.

The world had gone crazy.

He couldn't have—

No. She wouldn't think about it. Couldn't think about it. She would do what her mother had asked her to do. That and only that. Tell him her mother had lost the keys to their apartment, and would he give her his set?

She could see more than the floodlights now. Police cars were parked along the curb, their blue lights spinning, there to block off the side street where the scene was being filmed, to keep the traffic moving down the avenue, keep a crowd from getting in the way.

The sound truck.

The big blue-and-ivory vans with curtained windows that were the actors' dressing rooms. A small flatbed truck with a camera mounted on it.

Cervantes.

Jill stopped, shivering, then ducked behind a tree so he couldn't see her.

They were filming.

A man held out a scene marker, shouted what take it was, and snapped the two halves of the marker together.

A man and a woman came out of a brownstone, laughing about something, walked down the steps, stopped, stopped laughing, looked at each other, kissed.

"Cut!" the director yelled, and went to speak to them.

They had to do it three more times before he was satisfied with it. Before Cervantes was free for her to speak to him. If she could bring herself to do it.

He climbed down from the flatbed truck to supervise the electricians setting up the lights for the next scene.

She couldn't believe he had used her to get to her mother. That he wanted to farm her out to her grandmother Whitney so he and her mother would be rid of her.

She wanted to call as loudly as she could, "Police, Help! Police, Help! Police, Help!" And when they came running, she would point to him and let them surround him and handcuff him and take him away, and then she wouldn't have to speak to him or let him see what he had done to her.

Why couldn't her mother have asked her to do that?

Why did she have to make up that story about losing her keys?

If Cervantes had wanted to get rid of her so he could be with her mother, then why had he tried to kill her mother?

Nothing made any sense.

He'd never acted jealous any time he was around her. But then, if he was only around her so he could be around her mother, he wouldn't have anything to be jealous about when he was around her, would he?

Two policemen stood by a patrol car listening to the squawk-box inside it.

Police, Help! Police, Help! Police, Help!

The two policemen blurred.

"All set!" one of the electricians called out.

Cervantes and a man stood talking together. In a minute or two they'd start filming again. Maybe a dozen takes this time. Her mother hadn't said anything about hurrying, but if she was going to wait outside with Herb, there wouldn't be any place for her to sit down.

She might as well tell him now.

She turned her back against the tree and pressed against it to stiffen her spine. The thing was, not to let him see it mattered to her. Pretend it was only a scene in a movie. Or a Child's Play commercial.

She'd done three or four of them already, the director telling her how good she was, what a natural she was.

She could do this as well.

Take a deep breath and go.

She stepped out from behind the tree. "Cervantes?"

He turned from the man to her, his eyebrows shooting up. "Jill! What is it? What are you doing here? What's the matter?" He was at her side before he'd finished asking all his questions. Before he started in again. "Jill? What's the matter?"

She burst into tears.

Twenty-Two

The elevator was stuck between the second and third floors. They would have to walk.

A little thrill of hope shot through her. "Herb. No. Please. Wait—wait here. No can—I can't—no climb stairs. Too many. Too—I too tired. Please."

He shook his head. "We can't wait here. I'll help you up the stairs."

He had become a stranger to her. Somebody she didn't know, had never met. Somebody she didn't want to know. Was terrified of.

If only she could think how to save herself from him.

On the landing she stopped to gasp for breath. He stood watching her, impatient, hard-looking, no sign of recognition on his face, she as much a stranger to him as he to her.

Then on to the next flight of stairs, half dragged, half carried.

She couldn't understand why he was so determined to get her into her apartment. They would be alone there, yes. But how could he kill her there and get away with it? And didn't he have to get away with it for it to do him any good?

She didn't know, couldn't think. What was water in her bones was fire and brimstone in her head.

If only somebody from one of the other apartments would come along.

Second floor.

Third floor.

Gasping, panting, thinking she would keel over and die from exhaustion before he had a chance to kill her, she wanted to ask him why. Why. Why. She wanted to say, Never mind why, please stop, please don't do anything to me. She wanted to beg him for mercy. In spite of the way he looked at her now, he had once cared for her. How could he do whatever it was he was planning to do to her?

She hadn't the strength to speak to him.

Or the nerve.

As long as the truth lay unspoken between them, she had a chance.

Didn't she?

As long as he thought she believed Cervantes was the man in the yellow—

Cervantes.

Even if Jill got to Cervantes—and would she be in any hurry to get to him after all the hurtful things that had been said?

Even if Jill got to Cervantes, would he understand?

Fourth floor.

Dear God, send somebody.

Anybody.

Fifth floor.

Nobody.

Even if Cervantes understood, time was running out.

And still she didn't understand what Herb intended doing.

Until he went to the French doors in the living room and flung them open, went out on the fire escape and kicked at the metal railing at one end of the narrow platform until it split away from the side of the building.

Dear God.

She knew then.

He was going to throw her over the side, down into

the concrete garden below. Palm it off as an accident. An accident she herself had set up for him by saying she couldn't go home, the man in the yellow slicker had keys to her apartment and might be waiting there for her.

It wouldn't even be hard for him to do.

She was mixed up, confused. She had this notion in her head I couldn't shake her of that Cervantes was waiting there, hiding on the fire escape. She insisted on going out to look, stumbled—she wasn't steady on her feet to begin with, and she was exhausted from the psychodrama. Anyhow, she stumbled, lost her balance, fell against that railing there, and it gave.

Dear God in heaven.

No!

No! She couldn't let him do it. She had no strength, but she would find it somewhere. She had to.

Hang onto the sofa. Don't let him pull you. Grab on to the table. Cling to the door.

Don't let him do it. Don't let him. Don't let him.

Help me, God. Help me.

Outside on the fire escape, he loosened his grip a little. Why? What was he doing?

He fumbled in his jacket pocket, took something out of it. Gauze. Why gauze? What was it for?

A slight tinkle. An odd smell. Harsh, unpleasant. She had smelled it before.

Oh, my God, he was going to anesthetize her. That was what the gauze was for. Anesthetize her and then throw her over the side.

No.

A *bleep-blare* from somewhere. *Bleep-blare, bleep-blare.* Coming closer.

She struggled against him, shook her head away from the gauze soaked with the smell.

Brakes screeched. A crack like gunfire.

Thunder on the stairs.

And still she struggled.

No.

No.

She twisted away from him, found voice to scream.

A roar like doomsday out in the hall.

Herb gasped, lurched away from her, then flung himself out over the fire escape, bounced off a tree, screamed, and fell onto the concrete below.

Cervantes at her side, putting his hand over her face, holding her tight.

Thank God for Cervantes. He had understood.

Thank God for being a minister's daughter. Cervantes had no keys to her apartment.

Twenty-Three

Cervantes had to pry her hands loose from the metal bar finger by finger, then carry her inside. She could neither walk nor stand.

Inside the apartment a haze of dust and the acrid smell of gunfire. The front door hanging from one hinge.

Voices outside in the hall. Jill glassy-eyed, ghostly.

Policemen coming and going.

Sounds drifted up from the garden below. More sirens. Ambulance. Another ring of the doorbell.

Herb was dead.

Somebody brought her something to drink. She drank it, not knowing before or afterward what it was.

There was something she—

Jill.

She had to explain to her, apologize, get everything straight.

Before she could finish the thought she had fallen asleep.

Cervantes spent the night in the living room waiting for the homicide detectives. When Susannah woke up the next morning they had come and gone. In an en-

velope among Herb's things they had found her Master
Charge and twenty-two dollars.

They had no explanation. Not yet. They hoped they
would find one. Maybe after talking to his mother. They
would get back to her.

Jill and Cervantes were eating breakfast.

Stiff, sore, Susannah sat down with them, drinking
some coffee to clear her head, concentrating on what
to say to Jill.

"When I—that night January. When I say how you
like live in suburbs, I no—I don't—I didn't mean you
go live with Grandma. I mean—I meant you I both go
suburbs. I think maybe quit acting, work all time—full
time Dr. Dubinsky. Okay?"

Jill nodded. She was grave, subdued.

"Last night all I say Cervantes—about Cervantes
and you. Not true. Cervantes want you out, him in. Not
true. Cervantes use you get me. Not true. I—I'm sorry
I have—had do that. I not—I didn't know what Herb
think, what do. Might do. Might do anything. Have
think fast. Make up story make—try to make Herb
believe. Had—had to keep you not—from—from asking questions, make him wonder I fool—fooling him.
Okay?"

Jill nodded again.

"Think—I think—I thought Herb care me. Care for
me. Knew he not like Cervantes. Knew jealous Cervan—jealous of Cervantes. Try play on—on both those.
They work. Worked. For while."

Cervantes patted her hand. "Let me fix you something to eat."

She started to say she could fix it herself, then let
him go. The effort to make Jill understand had exhausted her. She was still tired from the night before,
still in shock, trying to absorb what had happened.
What had been happening all those weeks.

Too much to take in.

She would talk to Dr. Dubinsky about Jill, as she
had been thinking of doing the night she was attacked.
Get him to help Jill work out her problems about aban-
donment.

Talk to him, too, about herself.

At least she had herself back.

After breakfast she yearned to go back to bed, crawl under the covers, take refuge.

She got dressed.

Cervantes offered to take her to the hospital, but she said she had nothing to be afraid of any more. It was time to start doing things on her own again.

Taking her coat out of the foyer closet, she spied the gray wool man's cap she used to wear. She put it on, setting it at a jaunty angle, grinning into the mirror on the closet door before setting out to meet the world.

It was a bright, clear, balmy April day outside.

Spring.

The time of hope, of growth, renewal.

She was going to get well.

She was going to stick with acting.

That was for sure.

Whatever else she had done last night, against almost insurmountable odds, with no time whatever for preparation, she had given one hell of an improvisation.